Dream Weaver

Book 3
Spellbound in Sedona

Anna Lowe

Contents

Other books in this series

Spellbound in Sedona

Wind Whisperer (Book 1)

Fire Dancer (Book 2)

Dream Weaver (Book 3)

www.annalowebooks.com

Free Books

Get your free e-books now!

Sign up for my newsletter at *annalowebooks.com* to get three free books!

- *Desert Wolf*: Friend or Foe (Book 1.1 in the Twin Moon Ranch series)

- *Off the Charts* (the prequel to the Serendipity Adventure series)

- *Perfection* (the prequel to the Blue Moon Saloon series)

Chapter One

COOPER

Nothing beat the drive home after a successful fight with a wildfire. Soot-smeared, sweaty, exhausted, but proud and happy, everyone would joke and laugh, even if they weren't entirely coherent. Nothing bonded a group of near-strangers faster, forging them into a brotherhood for life, even if some of those "brothers" were women. Age, race, sex, pay grade — none of that mattered, because you were a team, working together.

The drive home after an operation gone wrong, on the other hand...

That was soot-smeared, sweaty, exhausted, and very, very quiet. Everyone had their eyes shut or on their boots, and the only sound was the creak of equipment and the rumble of tires over asphalt.

On my right, Joe checked his watch, then showed it to me. I knew exactly what he was thinking. The helicopter that had airlifted Sam out had probably just arrived at the hospital. It wasn't life-or-death, but a leg broken that badly could be career-ending, in as much as this crazy job could be called a career.

Passion was more like it, even if most people didn't understand — like that California congressman who'd called wildland firefighters "unskilled labor."

Unskilled, my ass. We'd worked three days straight with only about three hours of fitful sleep.

I fingered my ax, wondering how well that congressman could heft it and for how long. How many acres of pristine wilderness he would be able to save, or how many homes. Or how pitifully he would beg if his home were surrounded by flames.

The truck hit a bump, making everyone jostle.

"If my helmet could talk, it would cough," Vic grumbled, tracing a line through the soot.

"If only we'd had our lucky ax..." Joe sighed.

All the veterans nodded. Some of the newbies too.

I was somewhere in between — new to this fire crew as of a week ago, but on the cusp of my eleventh season of firefighting.

"You really think it was the ax?" Mark, one of the rookies, asked.

The veterans stared, like he'd suggested Jesus wasn't Mary's baby.

"We've had it for three years," Alice, eight-year veteran of the Yavapai Hotshots, finally answered. "Three years without an accident. Nothing worth mentioning anyway."

Ha. Knowing what firefighters considered *worth mentioning*, that left a lot of scope for pain and suffering.

"No accidents, and not a single fire that caught us as off guard as this one," Alice finished grimly.

Another understatement. The fire had jumped a road and come roaring at us on an out-of-nowhere wind shift. We'd been lucky to escape with just one serious injury and most of our equipment.

My secret, animal side mourned for all the forest dwellers that hadn't escaped the inferno.

It had taken us and three other crews days to get the blaze under control. And this was just the preseason.

"Ever had a call that close?" Chuck, another rookie, whispered.

Much, much closer, actually. A fire that still figured in my nightmares.

I nodded quietly.

"You really think the ax would have made a difference?" Mark asked.

No one actually came out and said, *Of course, you idiot,* but their looks did. I half expected them to cross themselves and murmur *Amen* at such heresy.

Baseball players were famous for being superstitious, but firefighters were even worse. Every squad had a lucky token of some kind, and every crew member had their own personal totems. Lucky underwear, lucky bandannas, lucky socks... My sister even carried a lucky straw.

I'd never felt the need for a lucky anything, but now, I was reconsidering.

"I don't get it. Who would steal an ax?" Joe muttered. "From a fire crew, no less."

"And not just any ax, but our lucky ax," Alice said bitterly.

I'd arrived a day after it had disappeared, but apparently, it was a beauty, commanding a place of honor in our lead truck on every single operation since it had joined the department three years ago.

Yes, *joined* really was the term the crew used, like the ax had marched in of its own volition one day.

You'd think that ax was a holy relic, the way the crew spoke of it.

"We should never have told that reporter about it," Vic muttered.

That was another thing about this crew — all the conspiracy theories about who'd stolen the lucky ax and why. Most started with the magazine article that had brought the lucky ax to the attention of budding thieves across the country.

And, hey. Who wouldn't want a tool that was rumored to control fire?

Personally, I found the whole thing a little nutty.

"What made it so special, again?" Mark asked.

Vic snorted. "Where do I start?" He let a beat go by, then ticked off an entire list on ash-smeared fingers. "Custom-made. Perfectly balanced. Never needed sharpening..."

"Gorgeous lines. A real beauty," Joe added.

Chuck gave me a look that asked, *Is he talking about an ax or a thoroughbred?*

"Where did you get it?" Mark asked.

"A local blacksmith made it for us," Alice said.

"Can we get him to make a new one?"

"Get *her* to make a new one, you mean." Alice looked at the cab of the truck, considering. "Maybe we can. I'll ask the captain when we get in." Then she sighed. "I just hope she can work her magic again."

I shifted in my seat. Magic?

Rumor had it, you couldn't swing a black cat in Sedona without hitting some kind of supernatural, be that a witch, warlock, shifter — like me — or even the occasional vampire. Enough that a secret government agency tasked with monitoring such things maintained an office in town. I even knew the agent staffing it — Ingo, a wolf shifter I'd worked with a few times before he'd left firefighting. I'd given Ingo a call when I'd arrived in Sedona, but we hadn't had a chance to meet up yet.

I made a mental note to ask him, though I hoped the rumors were exaggerated, especially when it came to magic. My clan didn't exactly pal around with witches and warlocks — not since a series of deadly clashes in my home range. That bloody interlude happened two centuries ago, but old grudges still ran deep.

Parched scenery blurred past the truck window. I stared off into the distance, thinking. Had it been a mistake to leave Wyoming for a season in Arizona? I hoped not. But things weren't exactly off to a great start, and we were technically still in the preseason.

I closed my eyes, trying to reserve judgment. If this crew turned out to be as weird as I feared, I could always head back to Wyoming. But I would see the season through first — and hopefully quench the inexplicable urge to come to Sedona that had been eating at me ever since I'd passed through for a fire a few years earlier.

It's our destiny, my inner beast rumbled.

I snorted, thinking of the arid landscape and this superstitious crew. This was my destiny?

God, I hoped not.

I folded my arms, tucked my chin against my chest, and let myself drift off to sleep.

Chapter Two

ABBY

Dreams visited my sleep the way tourists visited Sedona — lots of them and all too often. I rarely remembered them, though, other than the overall feeling.

Some were scary dreams, where I rushed to a critical destination without ever arriving. Other were happy dreams, just as vague but much more welcome. Still others were sensual dreams. Those were also a little fuzzy in terms of details, but scorching and satisfying.

Or not so satisfying, because I always woke up alone. So, like a lot of things in life, I'd learned to enjoy them while I could.

And that Tuesday morning, I was in the middle of a doozy of a sex dream, and boy, was it good. A very large man and I were going at it on a flat, hard surface in a large, industrial building... or was it under the stars? My partner — whoever he was — had gentle hands and a soft voice that contrasted with the firmness of his muscles and — er, other parts. Parts he put to very good use. So good that when I came, the earth moved. Once... twice...

I snapped out of the dream because, whoa. Had the earth really moved?

I closed my eyes and sank back down to the mattress, willing to risk an earthquake for one more taste of that dream.

And for a few blissful moments, I did just that, replaying the part where my mystery man hammered home and rocked my world.

But instead of howling in ecstasy, I jerked out of the dream. Eyes wide, I sat up, every sense piqued.

Something was happening. Something real, not a dream.

The earth moved again, and I tensed. The bed didn't shake, nor did the walls, but the air — or something in the air — rumbled. Something powerful and mysterious.

Not thunder. Not a plane. Something else.

Magic.

My heart raced.

Sedona was full of it — especially around Painted Rock Ranch, where my sisters and I lived. The most powerful outlets for that magic were Sedona's famous vortexes — and the couple of secret vortexes right here on our land — but magic was sprinkled all over the spectacular landscape.

I stared out the window, studying the dark, jagged outline of the surrounding mesas. Over on the rug at the foot of the bed, my dog, Roscoe, raised his furry head and looked too. But a moment later, he sighed and settled back to sleep.

For the next few minutes, I strained for any sound or motion, but none came. Had I been imagining things, or had that been real?

Real, instinct told me. Or a real warning, at least.

My hands tightened in the sheets. Warning of what? When? Where?

∞∞∞∞

The sense of foreboding stayed with me through the long hours of morning and during my commute to work. But once I settled into my latest project, that uneasy feeling dissolved. Strange and unexpected were par for the course in Sedona. Meanwhile, work was work, so I had to concentrate.

Flipping my welder's mask down, I leaned over the classic Volkswagen and let the plasma torch rip. Sparks flew as I cut a paisley shape into the hood, moving more confidently than I felt. A 1972 VW Beetle might not be worth much, but if I messed up, my client would be furious. And Lord knew my lifetime ratio of successes to mess-ups tilted heavily in the wrong direction.

But, hey. The minor thrill was worth it.

Over on the other side of the shop, my hammers and anvil called to me jealously. I was a blacksmith at heart, but I dabbled in all kinds of metalwork.

Soon, I promised them.

I cut the right side of the teardrop shape, then the left, and finally, across the top. Then, *ding! Ding!* A few taps of the butt end of the torch freed the cut-out from the surrounding metal, and it clattered to the floor.

I leaned back, checking my work. Five paisleys done. Many, many more to go. But the effect was exactly what I'd hoped for. The car looked as if it were made of lace, not metal.

I gave myself a mental high five, then flipped my mask down and started on the next section.

Behind me, the other three employees of Heavy Metal Sedona were banging away on their projects. Some were functional, others more artistic — a ranch gate here, a custom trellis there, along with whimsical wine racks, all done in metal.

When I stopped for a sip of water, I spotted Rich, chief of the Sedona-based wildfire crew, entering my boss's office with a guy who could have been a body double for Paul Bunyan, the legendary lumberjack — big, bulky, and clad in the same red-and-black flannel shirt associated with the folk hero.

I whirled, drawn to him instinctively, then — oops. I forced myself to focus on my work.

Well, I tried. But when his scent wafted over, I caught a smoky odor.

Firefighter, my nose said.

A heightened sense of smell was one of the few supernatural traits my mother had passed down to me. And as far as I was concerned, the fewer, the better.

Unfortunately, picking out a person's scent from half a workshop away was normal for me — and not particularly practical in a shop filled with sweaty men.

But underneath that smoky aroma was something nice. Different. I found myself sniffing delicately, picking apart a dreamy scent that swept me away to the banks of a mossy creek somewhere high in the Rockies.

I closed my eyes. The scent was that soothing.

Then someone started banging at metal, and the feeling evaporated. I blinked and went back to work.

Several paisleys later, something bumped my legs, and I turned to find Louie, my boss's floppy-eared mutt.

I petted him, then tensed, spotting his master approaching.

"Hi, Abby," Walt said, smiling broadly.

Uh-oh. Something was up.

Walt gave me The Look — the one that said *Remember who's boss here* — then shooed Louie away and indicated one of the two men beside him.

"You know Rich, right?"

I forced a tight smile. "Hi."

Not that I didn't like Rich. As the leader of the elite fire-fighting crew based in Sedona, he was one of a handful of men on my green list. The remainder of his crew were on my equally short list of neutral yellow, while every other man in the world fell into the red list. Maybe they didn't all deserve to be there, but it was safer to assume that.

Like the flannel-clad, dark-haired Paul Bunyan crowding the space next to Rich. Definitely red-list material. No matter how good he smelled or how well he faked a friendly smile.

"This is Cooper, who's joined our squad for this season. Cooper, meet Abby," Rich said. "She used to work on a hot-shot crew back in Colorado."

You could judge a man by his facial hair, and this Cooper guy had long, slicing sideburns that angled toward his chin, like Hugo Jackman in one of Wolverine's more endearing moments. A man to lust after, maybe, but definitely, *definitely* not to be trusted.

"Hi," Cooper rumbled.

The voice went with the scent — all deep, earthy, and grainy.

"I guess you're here about the ax, huh?" I asked, knowing Rich had called Walt yesterday.

Rich nodded. "Axes, actually."

I tilted my head. The ax I'd made three years ago might have been laced with a little low-grade magic, but it certainly wasn't capable of asexual reproduction.

Well, I hoped not. But, yikes. Anything was possible, given the hit-or-miss nature of my magic. The little bit I had inherited from my father, at least.

"You know the theft of our ax made the Phoenix newspapers, right?" Rich asked, and I nodded for him to go on. "One lady was so touched by the ax and...well, you know, Kevin's story..." His voice went a little gritty, and he cleared his throat. "She wants to sponsor a new set of lucky custom axes — twenty, enough for the whole squad."

My jaw swung open and stayed there. So many reasons, such mixed emotions.

Three years ago, I'd made the ax in honor of a local firefighter killed in a horrific blaze. His family had gifted it back to the squad, saying that was where his spirit would live on. Over the years, the ax had gained a reputation as a lucky charm.

And now, I was supposed to make twenty of them? Not just twenty axes, but *lucky* axes for men and women in one of the world's most dangerous professions?

Pressure, anyone?

"Um... Uh..." I hemmed and hawed, trying to figure out how to talk my way out of this.

Yes, the original ax had a little magic forged into the metal. But only a tiny dose, and very amateurish, in hopes of keeping it sharp and shiny. Otherwise, all I'd poured into that project were heart, soul, and sorrow. I hadn't known Kevin, but I'd been a firefighter too, and every tragedy struck deep into my soul.

"I know it's a lot," Rich added. "But if anyone can do it, you can. I know it."

That mound of *no pressure* grew into Everest, towering so high, clouds covered the peak.

My hold on my welding mask turned into a death grip as I did the math.

"Twenty axes...for this season? Which starts in...three weeks?"

"Officially," Rich said quickly.

Ha. We both knew how meaningless *officially* was when it came to Mother Nature and climate change. The number of wildfires had skyrocketed over the years, and we'd endured longer fire seasons with record blazes.

Case in point: Rich's crew had already returned from their first preseason fire. I'd read about it in the newspaper, but it showed just as clearly in the dark rings around his eyes.

Walt gave me a significant look.

I waved at the Volkswagen. "I'd love to make them, but the client who commissioned this project—"

"Has kindly agreed to put it on hold for a good cause," Walt cut in.

I blinked. Oh.

Walt's eyes twinkled. All in all, he was a fair boss who respected my skills and my desire to be left alone. He was also a good businessman and a keen supporter of firefighters, partly because it was the right thing to do, partly due to tax benefits. This project ticked both those boxes.

Still, twenty axes in three weeks would be tight. Really tight.

I rubbed my chin. "From scratch or refurbishments?"

Rich didn't hesitate. "From scratch. Like last time."

Oh. My. A man who believed in miracles.

"You know the *lucky* part was just…well, luck, right?" I tried.

Rich chuckled. "Sure. But we know we can count on you."

My stomach twisted, and I could already see the headlines. *Crew wielding "lucky" axes meets tragic end in unforeseen circumstances…*

I'd come a long way since my younger, wilder days and prided myself on being a responsible person. But, hell. *That* kind of responsibility?

I did a quick calculation. "I can make an ax a day at best, and only a basic one. Kevin's was much more intricate."

Rich nodded, and I was sure his mind, like mine, was recalling every swirl I'd etched into the gleaming surface. Each of those artistic elements had taken hours.

"We want these to be just like Kevin's," he insisted.

I turned to Walt, praying for the voice of reason to speak.

But, ha. *Prayers answered* versus *ignored* was another ratio that tilted the wrong way in my life.

Walt thumped my shoulder. "I told Rich I'm confident you can do it."

The subtext jumped out at me in neon subtitles.

"This is important, Abby," Walt added gravely. "Our top priority."

I stuck up my hands. "I can make twenty axes by... mid-May, maybe. You can phase them in gradually."

Rich shook his head. "Our sponsor wants to present them in a ceremony in Kevin's honor at the end of the month."

"*This* month?" I yelped.

Rich nodded. "Kevin's family has agreed to be there and everything. And although we're not in this for the publicity... Well, you know as well as I that we could use all the recognition we can get."

We meant the firefighting profession, and I couldn't agree more. That and funding were always at the top of a firefighter's wish list.

But, shit. What about the fallout if — when? — the axes didn't prove all that lucky?

Walt patted the air with his hands. "I have it all figured out."

Ha. He'd said the same thing about employee 401(k) plans, and those still hadn't materialized.

"You can get it done with a little help," he continued.

My heart sank as I glanced around the shop. Walt was going to make this a group project, wasn't he? Even as far back as first grade, I'd hated group projects. I still hated them.

"I work alone." I glared.

"Call it an opportunity to develop your leadership skills," Walt shot back.

Dammit, I hated when he anticipated my arguments.

"What about your other clients?" I tried. "You haven't talked them all into postponing their deadlines, have you?"

Walt shook his head. "The other guys will stay on their projects. We've found you a different assistant."

I frowned. We, who?

Walt and Rich grinned at each other, then turned to Paul Bunyan — er, Cooper.

He blinked at them, then did a double take.

"Me?"

Rich clapped him on his boulder of a shoulder. "Yes, you. Didn't you say you do some metalwork in the off-season?"

Cooper's eyes just about bugged out of his head. Very nice, warm brown eyes, I couldn't help noticing. Warm and deep, like there was a whole world to discover beneath the surface.

Red list, I reminded myself. Nothing to get all hot and bothered by.

"I do a lot of *woodwork* in the off-season. I've helped my uncle with a few metal projects, but nothing like this." His stiff posture and clipped tone made it clear he wanted no part of this.

Good. That made two of us.

"Don't worry," Walt said. "Abby will get the job done. All you have to do is assist."

My eyes met Cooper's by angling way, way up. I came to about the height of his shoulders, and if I'd wanted to peek behind him, I would have had to lean way out to one side. He was that broad, and all that bulk was muscle. But once we locked eyes, I knew we were absolutely, totally, completely on the same page about one thing: not wanting this job. Otherwise, I could already tell we had nothing in common. He looked like a nice, polite, grounded guy who'd been raised in a normal nuclear family.

I'd had flames tattooed on my arms when I was fifteen.

His mother, I was sure, would flip out at such a thing. My mother hadn't noticed the artwork until about a year in.

There was no way this was going to work, and I opened my mouth to say so.

But a funny thing happened as our eyes remained locked. My inner alarms faded, replaced by a flush of warmth, along with a sense of soul-deep connection. And for that split second, my soul did what it rarely did.

It felt at peace. Absolute, calm, complete peace. A little like some evenings after I tucked my daughter into bed and stayed there, listening to her steady breaths after she fell asleep.

Then I snapped back to my senses. "I don't want or need an assistant."

And, ouch. My own tone made me mourn. Was I that jaded? That isolated?

But the walls of my inner fortress were already flying up, the drawbridge drawn, the moat filled.

Walt sighed, then turned to Rich. "Can you give us a second, please?"

Without waiting for a response, he pulled me gently aside. "Now, Abby..."

As a kid, I'd dreamed of a father figure who spoke in exactly that calm, steady tone. Someone to explain how the world worked and how I could fit in. Instead, I'd had to figure things out for myself — and always, always, the hard way.

I crossed my arms and glared.

"This is an important contract, and there's no one who can do it better than you."

Making me feel good was stage one of Walt's argument. Stage two would be the business side, I knew.

"It's a great opportunity for us too," Walt continued. "Not just for the paycheck, but for the publicity."

In my mental dictionary, *paycheck* stood in big, bold, gold-embossed text. *Publicity* was the dirty word in the bottom corner of the P page.

I glanced over at Cooper, who was getting a similar lecture from Rich.

"It should be quiet for the next few weeks," Rich told him. "And if we do get called out to a fire, you'll have plenty of time to get to the station."

If Cooper shoved his fists any deeper into his pockets, he'd be tickling his toes. Firefighters craved action, satisfaction, and thrills. They also craved sweat, blood, and tears. I knew, because I'd been one myself.

But unless you had a creative streak and enjoyed hammering at your inner demons, *metal shop assistant* scored high on *sweat* and low in *satisfaction.*

And, oops. My body heated with an alternative context to *sweaty* and *satisfied.* My eyes roamed Cooper's shoulders and chest, while my imagination put me horizontal and between those sculpted arms.

Bang, bang, bang, my inner vixen giggled.

I puffed air up over my face. Hormones were a bitch.

"I can do the job myself," I assured Walt. "I just need the time to do it right."

"You will have time to do it right — three weeks, with an assistant," Walt said, then switched to bad cop mode. "You are going to do this job, Abby. You are going to do it well. And you are going to do it with Cooper's help." Then he turned to Rich with a huge smile, as if I'd actually agreed. "We're on. Starting tomorrow. That will give Abby some time to prepare."

Ha. A century wouldn't be enough.

Pablo, another of Walt's employees, was working a forge a few steps away, and I stared into the glowing embers. Step by mental step, I wandered into them, seeking refuge.

Every person had a place of mental retreat, I figured. For my sister Erin, it was gliding through the sky. For Pippa, it was shaping molten glass. When my daughter, Claire, needed to get away from it all — not all too often, thank goodness — she hunkered down under a blanket with her stuffed animals.

Fire was my refuge. Flames. Crackling, purifying heat. A place where I was invincible, where no one dared follow.

My breaths slowed, and I stroked the ink on my arms.

This is no big deal. Everything will be okay. The familiar old mantra looped around my mind, again and again. *I've survived a lifetime of hard knocks. I will survive this too.*

Vaguely, I sensed Walt and Rich shaking hands on the deal. I sensed Cooper looking at me, not at all pleased. I registered the bustle and clatter of the metal shop, a million miles away.

But it was only when Walt clapped me on the back that I slipped out of my refuge.

"So, all set to start tomorrow. Right, Abby?"

His eyes lasered into me, stern but encouraging. *You can do this.*

You will do this was more like it, but hell. I was a responsible adult now, and a job was a job.

I jutted my chin, then forced a curt nod. That was all Walt was getting out of me.

"Perfect," he announced. "See you tomorrow, Cooper. Nine a.m. sharp."

"See you tomorrow," Rich chirped.

Cooper growled. So quietly, I doubted Rich or Walt heard.

But I did. I whipped around in time to see the stubble on his chin thicken. His eyes glowed too, no longer warm brown but brick red.

Sensing my gaze, he met my eyes, and I stared.

Shifter?

His nostrils flared, testing the air.

Shifter. Definitely.

He didn't come out and growl, *What are you?* but the message was clear.

If I had a simple, one-word answer for that, I might have replied. But I didn't, being one of those rare cases where two halves didn't equal a whole.

I took a deep breath then turned away, shaking my head in dismay.

I had a few short weeks to handcraft twenty axes. *Lucky* axes that would protect hardworking people's lives. With a big, burly shifter — species unknown — huffing over my shoulder the whole time.

I could have screamed.

Instead, I flipped down my welder's mask and hit the trigger of my plasma torch, releasing a torrent of fire.

Chapter Three

COOPER

The next morning, I parked in a back lot, killed the engine... and stared at the dashboard. Back at the firehouse, everyone was prepping for the season. Testing out equipment. Running drills. Bonding.

I was at Heavy Metal Sedona on a wild goose-chase.

"Have a good day, son. And remember, what you're doing is important too." Those were the inspiring words Rich had sent me off with.

He'd been dead serious too. So were Alice and the other veterans of the Yavapai fire squad. I hadn't encountered as many delusional souls since I'd visited Las Vegas. They actually believed in the whole lucky ax thing.

So did the local police, who were investigating their hearts out, though they had no leads.

The rookies and other newbies took it in with a mixture of amusement and dismay.

"You think they're serious or just pulling our legs?" Mark had whispered.

"It pains me to say this, but I think they're serious." Chuck sighed.

I scuffed the floor. Had I really turned down job offers from three top-notch crews to join this hocus-pocus gang?

"Maybe the lucky ax has... what's it called?" Mark mused. "A placebo effect."

"As long as they don't make us do yoga..." Chuck muttered.

"Or tune in to a vortex," Mark added.

Or assist a fiery blacksmith who doesn't want help, I nearly chimed in. A blacksmith who'd spotted the animal in me at one glance.

My inner grizzly hummed dreamily. *She sure did.*

Raging fires didn't disturb my sleep, but a wisp of a woman with brown hair and green eyes had. All night long.

Auburn hair, my bear corrected. *Like maples in the fall.*

Or more appropriately, like the shadowy bases of Sedona's red cliffs.

I thought the situation over. Abby knew about shifters, though very few humans did.

She's not human, my bear concluded with a little cheer.

No, she wasn't. So, what was she?

Not another shifter, judging by her scent.

Not a vampire, because they had no scent at all.

She smells nice, my bear proclaimed. *Like dandelions and huckleberries.*

In the chaos of competing smells in the metal shop, her sweet scent had stood out like a rose among weeds.

So, not a vampire either. That left two possibilities: witch or relic — a human with a trace of supernatural ancestry.

Anything but a witch, I prayed.

Even my bear went quiet on that one.

Working with a witch was a total no-go. Not after the war they'd waged against my clan generations ago.

Okay — many, *many* generations ago. So many, I didn't know the details — not even what they'd fought over. But I knew the important part: witches were cruel, unpredictable beings and not to be trusted.

Not that I'd ever met a witch, but that was what I'd heard.

Plus, she'd forged the lucky ax. That could be witchcraft, right?

Or just superstition, my bear pointed out.

Behind me, the garage-style rear doors of the metal shop clattered open. Clenching my jaw, I headed in.

Walt introduced me to Louie the dog and three men — two youngish ones, Matt and Pablo, plus Bob, the veteran of the bunch — then left me to it.

"Abby's assistant, huh?" Pablo glanced in her direction. "Good luck, man."

"Yeah, bring a helmet." Matt chuckled. "So she can't bite your head off."

He was only half kidding, I sensed.

"Oh, come now." Bob came to her defense. "She just needs a little space."

Yeah, like the last fire I'd worked on — a few thousand acres, give or take.

"Leave her alone, and you'll be fine," Bob said, as much to me as to the other two.

I would have loved to leave her alone, but I'd been appointed her goddamn assistant.

Finding Abby's corner of the shop was easy. I followed her scent — and the noise.

Wham! Crash!

Pieces of scrap metal flew out of a container and clattered across the shop floor. I couldn't see Abby, but I could hear her mutter and curse.

"Abby, your assistant is here," Matt hollered.

A rusty crowbar landed an inch away from my toes. An old shovel came next, pinging off the cement floor before coming to rest against my boot.

Yeah, I got the message.

I circled to the less lethal side of the container and peered in. It looked like the set of an apocalyptic movie, with Abby as the earth's sole survivor crawling over wreckage, determined to kick ass against an encroaching army of cyborgs.

And, lucky me. I'd landed the part of the bad guy in that movie.

"Good morning," I said, because my mother had taught me manners.

Apparently, Abby's hadn't taught her hers. After a sharp glare, she went back to heaving metal.

"Here to assist," I added.

There. Now I could claim to have tried.

"Don't need an assistant," Abby muttered.

"Well, you got one."

"We'll see about that," she mumbled.

Not exactly a promising start.

The morning was chilly, but she seemed comfortable in jeans, a tank top, and an off-the-shoulder sweatshirt. Maybe the flames tattooed onto her arms kept her warm. They seemed to flicker between light and shadow as she moved. The shop lights glinted off her hair, and that flickered too, between auburn and copper.

And, boy. She made a hell of a lot of noise for such a thin, wispy thing. A wispy thing full of pent-up power — or anger. She was way shorter than my six-foot-two, but what she lacked in bulk, she made up in sass and brute determination. At that very moment, she put her whole body into heaving aside a piano frame.

Yes, an entire piano frame.

"Can I—?" I started.

"No," she grunted, shoving it aside.

I winced. A car crash would have made less noise. But, in terms of power-to-weight ratio, she was pretty impressive. I would have to push trucks around to exert as much force.

The banging, muttering, and tossing went on for another ten minutes. Then, quick as a cat, Abby leaped out of the container and stalked around, kicking the items she'd chosen into a rough line — everything from twisted wrenches to industrial scrap metal and rusty shovels. Chin in hand, she stood over them, considering.

I kept a safe distance, eyeing that rusty collection, then the nice, shiny steel ingots stacked by a wall. Back home at my family's lumber mill, we MacGyvered repairs using scraps all the time. But not when lives were at stake.

"You're not using fresh steel?" I asked.

She didn't even look up.

I took that as a no.

Abby picked up a wrench as big as my arm and studied it. *Seriously* studied it, turning it this way and that, bringing it close to her eyes, then squinting along the length of it.

A minute creaked by, then another.

Back at the firehouse, the crew was checking lines...familiarizing themselves with new routines...getting to know one another. But not me. No, I was a spectator to a tattooed chick who preferred metal to people.

Abby discarded the wrench and spent the next five minutes inspecting a rusty sledgehammer.

I shuffled in place. Bob Dylan once sang that a person not busy being born was busy dying. Was this really the best use of my time?

"Can I help in some way?" I finally ventured.

"Yes. Go away."

"Would love to," I muttered.

"What's stopping you?"

"Besides your stellar company?"

She shot me a dirty look and went back to the sledgehammer, tossing it from hand to hand and twirling it a few times. Either she was checking its balance or making sure I kept my distance.

I did, a safe six feet away.

Finally, she strapped on a leather apron and heated up the forge in her area of the workshop. I came up beside her, waiting. The coals turned the color of brick, then orange. Abby shoved the sledgehammer under them and waited some more.

It all reminded me of working with my uncle Rory. Patience was a virtue, and mine was severely tested.

Then again, anything Rory made lasted generations.

Also, Uncle Rory was about my size. Maybe even bigger. Abby only came to about the height of my shoulders, with the lean, tight build of a gymnast. It was hard to picture her hugging fans or smiling for cameras, though.

"So, what do you want me to do?" I asked, going for *respectful apprentice.*

"Get out of the way."

She yanked the sledgehammer out of the forge, kicking up a shower of embers.

I motioned between us. "I am out of the way."

"You're in my light," she grumbled, positioning the sledgehammer over the anvil.

Her light, not *the* light.

It reminded me of that phase my eldest sister had gone through as a teenager. My existence had been the bane of hers.

Helen is nice to us now, my bear pointed out.

Yes, but what a miserable three years that had been.

"How's that?" I shuffled back a little.

"Still too close." Abby gave the anvil a warm-up hit, exactly where my shadow fell. Then, *bang! Bang! Bang!* She started walloping away at red-hot iron.

Yeah, I got that message too.

Chapter Four

COOPER

You can learn something from any person, my uncle Rory liked to say. So, over the next few hours, I did my best to watch Abby in that spirit. She was good — very good — with efficient and accurate hammer blows that pounded the sledgehammer into submission. Wisps of hair escaped her ponytail, and sweat glistened over her tattoos, making them flicker like real flames.

When she paused for a sip of water, my hopes rose. Surely her arm was tired from all that hammering. Surely she would accept help now.

But, no. She only stopped long enough to root through a drawer, pushing scraps of colored paper aside until she found a crayon. Yes, a crayon. She slammed the drawer shut then made a few marks on the steel.

I stepped closer. "I'm here to help, you know."

"I don't need help."

"Look, I'm as happy about this as you are..."

Her grimace promised me her misery far outweighed mine.

"...but you may as well use me for something."

She regarded me silently, then thrust her water bottle at me.

"Fine. Fill this."

It was more permission than request, and not exactly the type of task I was hoping for. But, whatever. I snatched it up and stalked to the makeshift kitchen, making vows all the way. I would stick it out for today, then have a serious word with Rich back at the firehouse. Either he let me out of this ridiculous assignment or he would be down one crew member. Fire crews all over the West were shorthanded, and my experience could land me a job faster than Abby could say, *Go away.*

In the meantime, I would channel Uncle Rory's patience and try to learn something. Like what kind of supernatural she was, for starters.

I spent the next three hours watching, waiting. Gradually deciding *witch* fit.

Why? Because the flames of the forge licked at steel, but never, ever her hands, no matter how close they came.

Because a few well-placed blows coaxed solid steel into an entirely new shape — one it accepted unconditionally, like a dog eager to please its master.

Because her hammer moved with its own energy, bouncing back to deliver one punishing hit, then another.

Some kind of elemental magic was involved. I was sure of it.

Plus, she was moody as hell and definitely a renegade — two classic signs of a witch. Also, she hated people. And bears.

She hated me.

Maybe she doesn't hate. Maybe she's been let down too often, my grizzly murmured.

Possibly. But that wasn't my fault. The sooner I got back to working with people who understood concepts like *cooperation, communication,* and *cheerful,* the better.

She did work her ass off, though. By lunchtime, the stumpy sledgehammer had been transformed into a pick shape, with one lumpy end that would eventually be made into an ax head.

"You get an hour for lunch," Walt told me. "Use it."

The supermarket was only a couple of blocks away, so I set off on foot, picturing myself ambling through the woods instead of a busy main road. I flexed my fingers, imagining my bear claws snapping a salmon out of a river and my lips plucking juicy berries for dessert.

All that was a world away from the ham and cheese sandwich I picked up at the supermarket, but that was okay. I'd spent most of the off-season in bear form, tanking up on the peace of leafy forests and snowy mountains. Now, it was

fire season, which I spent predominantly in human form —
a rhythm I'd settled into ever since becoming a firefighter two
days after graduating high school.

I returned to the metal shop a few minutes shy of an hour,
plonked my unfinished carton of juice on a workbench, and
went back to "work" — i.e., watching Abby.

"Do you have younger brothers?" I asked at some point.

She looked up, brow furrowed. "Why?"

"Just wondering. You're very good at ignoring."

She snorted and turned back to work, but I caught the way
her eyes grazed over my chest first.

So, yay. I wasn't in her *little brother* category. I didn't have
a lot of hangups, but being the youngest of the Lundsven clan
was one of them.

The next two hours passed the same way as the morning.
Abby hammered away all afternoon, not flagging one bit.

At three p.m., her watch alarm sounded. She hurried to
her car, only whirling to bark an order.

"Don't touch anything."

I didn't, except for petting Louie, who commiserated with
me on the back step while Abby was gone.

At 3:25, she was back — with a kid. A really bubbly,
outgoing one holding a fluffy pink toy bunny. All the guys in
the shop cheered.

"Claire!"

The girl waved happily, showered Louie in hugs, then came
over to me, all sunny, friendly, and trusting.

"Hi! I'm Claire. This is Hopper."

"Hi, Claire. Hi, Hopper. I'm Cooper."

The most social interaction I'd gotten all day, and half of
it was with a stuffed animal.

"Do you work here too?" Claire asked.

I held back a snort. "Just...uh, volunteering..."

Abby edged closer, all mamma bear protective of her cub.

Hazy memories stirred in my mind, and I remembered my
mother doing the same to protect me in the woods, once upon
a time. Except in that case, the mamma bear really was a
bear, and I was the cub.

I smiled faintly. Next time I called home, I would have to tell my mother about that memory. She would *love* that.

Abby steered Claire over to a nearby workbench. "How about you draw a picture?"

Ah. Now, the crayons and colored paper made sense.

"Okay. Oh! I'll draw one of you and Cooper!"

Abby gnashed her teeth. "Anything you like, sweetie."

"Oh! Juice!" Claire squeaked, spotting my carton. "Can I have some?"

Abby shook her head. "It's Cooper's, and he's been drinking from the carton."

She made it sound like I had the cooties.

"Sorry, kiddo." I moved the carton away so Claire wouldn't have to look at what she couldn't have, then fetched her a glass of water.

"Thank you, Mr. Cooper."

I grinned. Polite kid. "Just Cooper is fine, thank you."

"What are you making?" Claire asked.

"A Pulaski," Abby replied.

If I'd had my eyes shut, I would have sworn a totally different person had switched places with her. Her tone was sweet, loving, and optimistic, like the world was a great place with wonderful things and nice people.

Huh. So maybe the ice queen actually had a warm heart.

Claire nodded readily. Apparently, she was familiar enough with firefighting equipment to know about Pulaskis — an ax/adze used to dig trenches and chop undergrowth. Interesting.

"Only a mock-up, though," Abby continued. "Before I start on the real ones."

Ah. Now, it all made sense.

"Like practicing?" Claire asked.

Abby nodded. "They have to be really good. Really, really good, so they do their job well and no one gets hurt."

I glanced over, catching the fierce concentration in Abby's eyes. So, huh. Maybe Rich was right about entrusting Abby with this project.

My eyes drifted over her fiery hair and fierce expression. Maybe she was a witch. Gruff as hell, but not actually evil.

I scratched my chin. Was there any such witch in existence?

One thing was for sure. There was more to this spitfire than I'd first thought.

Bang! Bang! Abby went back to clobbering the metal.

Whenever she paused to check her work, Claire bombarded me with questions.

"Do you have brothers and sisters?"

Two of each. Well, nowadays. An old ache settled in my chest.

Claire, I discovered, had no siblings.

"Do you have a dog?" she asked next.

I didn't, though she had five. Roscoe was the only one allowed in the house, though.

I learned that and all kinds of details about the other four — colors, names, sizes...

The interview paused every time Abby hammered, but the moment the noise stopped, Claire tossed out another question.

"Do you have a horse?"

None. Claire had a whole herd, though she seemed to blur the line between toys and the real thing.

"Did you know only African elephants have big ears?" she said next.

No, I didn't, but I did now. I also learned that Asian elephants had small ears.

"Are you a good blacksmith?" she asked in an abrupt change of subject.

Ha. "No. I'm a firefighter."

"My grandpa is a firefighter. So was Mommy before I was born."

Huh. I knew that about Abby, but I didn't know it ran in the family.

"My grandfather was a firefighter too," I found myself saying. "And my dad, my mom, my uncle, my cousins..."

The list stretched on for a while. Long enough for Abby to glance over, then quickly turn away.

"Wow. How many cousins do you have?" Claire asked.

I tapped the fingers on my left hand, then the right, then went back to the left again...and lost count.

"Lots," I concluded.

"I don't have any," Claire said a little sadly.

"Yeah, but you have all those dogs and horses."

Her dimples flashed, and I wondered if Abby had looked the same as a kid.

Over the next hour or so, I caught a few more hints about my temporary boss, and I wondered even more. Claire was all sunshine and rainbows. Abby was a thundercloud. Was that nature or nurture — or lack thereof, in Abby's case? What had inspired Abby to go into blacksmithing? Was she a witch? And why did her scent make my bear all dreamy?

"What was your biggest fire?" Claire asked next.

I thought it over. A tricky question, because there'd been a lot — and as many different ways of measuring them. The same went for the emotions that came with some of them.

Head back, my brother Peter yelled in my imagination. Loud enough to be heard over the roar of the encroaching fire. *I got this. You help the others.*

That had been my first season fighting fires. Peter's last.

I stared into the past. It hadn't even entered my mind to beg Peter to retreat with me, the way I'd come to beg in my dreams.

Claire's crayon stopped scratching. And, oops. So did Abby's hammering.

I blurted out whatever came to mind first. "Diablo Canyon fire."

"Oh! My friend Tana has a horse named Diablo!"

A welcome diversion. I grabbed it, asking about the horse and Claire's friend.

Things went on in that vein for a while, though the side-eyed glances Abby shot me had a softer gleam to them.

Thanks to Claire, my last hours at the shop passed more quickly than the first. When five o'clock rolled around, the other guys cleared out quickly, but Abby went on working.

"All right, now. Time to call it a day," Walt announced from the door a half hour later.

"Coming," Abby replied to his third reminder.

She didn't protest my efforts to help clean up, though she did a double take when I returned tools to their locations — like I was a complete fool who hadn't paid attention to anything all day. So, yay for me. I could go home proud of one tiny victory.

"Oh, this is for you." Claire held out a picture.

"Wow. Thank you."

Claire beamed. Me too. She'd drawn me so big, my legs ran off the edge of the paper. She'd even sketched a crooked hammer into my hands — or was that a Pulaski? The pink squiggle supervising my "work" had to be Hopper, and the whirl of a stick figure by the blocky forge had to be Abby.

"Do you like it?" Claire prompted.

I held it to my chest. "I love it. Thank you."

"See you tomorrow?" Claire asked as we walked to our cars.

I pursed my lips, not sure how to reply. Lies were always bad, but lying to a kid was even worse.

I settled for, "Have a good night, kiddo."

Chapter Five

ABBY

"So, how was your day?" my sister Erin asked over dinner.

"Apart from that disturbance this morning?" I grumbled.

Erin tilted her head toward Claire, warning me not to go there. Too late, though.

"What disturbance, Mommy?"

I refilled her water glass. "The new horses were a little unsettled, that's all."

That wasn't exactly what Erin and I had concluded when we'd compared notes before dinner. In fact, we'd both agreed that something had disturbed the magic laced into the red, rocky landscape. What exactly that was, we had no clue. Only that it didn't bode well, and we had to remain alert for trouble.

Which was pretty much our *modus operandi* anyway.

"I meant, how was your day at work?" Erin asked.

Oh, that. Not half as bad as I'd expected, frankly.

I twirled a forkful of spaghetti, considering why that might be.

It was only us four homebodies in the main house for dinner — Claire, Erin, her partner Nash, and me. Pippa and her partner, Ingo, were visiting her father in Colorado.

I briefed Erin and Nash on the fire ax contract and the assistant I'd been stuck with.

A very tall, fairly quiet assistant whose green-and-gray flannel shirt — a variation on the red one he'd worn the day I met him — brought out the color of his soft brown eyes.

A flannel shirt I could use as a blanket, it was that big.

He was that big. Not in sheer height, maybe, but layer upon layer of muscle — a detail I couldn't help noticing, especially once he stripped down to a T-shirt — extra-large but still snug in the chest and biceps. The back, twice the breadth of mine, was decorated with two crossed axes and the words, *Pine Ridge Hotshots, Wyoming.*

"All day?" Erin stared. "He just watched? How annoying."

Only for the first half hour, actually. After that, I stopped noticing. The annoying part, at least. It was hard not to notice the rest of him.

All in all, he wasn't terrible company. No boasting about firefighting prowess, no unsolicited advice on how to do my job better. Even when I'd tried to get rid of him, he'd remained even-tempered. It was a little like having Roscoe by my feet when I got some downtime in the evenings. There yet unobtrusive. Undemanding. Comforting, almost.

"He was nice," Claire said. "He's a firefighter, and he has lots of cousins."

Clearly, she found those two facts impressive. But I found his demeanor with Claire impressive. Obviously, the guy was a doting uncle. . . or was he an absentee father?

I went back to resenting him, just in case.

"Why don't I have any cousins, Mommy?" Claire asked.

I pointed my fork at Erin, then Nash. "Ask them."

Nash choked on his spaghetti. Erin patted his back. "Well, um. . . Maybe you'll get some someday."

"Soon?" Claire persisted.

Nash gave Erin a tiny, suggestive waggle of the eyebrows.

"We'll see," she said, touching his arm playfully.

A year ago, I would have rolled my eyes at those lovebirds. But Nash had grown on me, and I'd never seen Erin so happy. It was easy to picture them having a gang of adorable, noisy children who would grow up to be responsible dragon shifters like their parents. Erin would be an amazing mom and a fantastic role model. Nash would make a great dad, all patient, quiet, and indulging.

Patient. Quiet. Indulging. Now, that seemed familiar.

I caught my thoughts straying in a dangerous direction.

"Seconds, anyone?" I stood quickly.

∞∞∞∞

After dinner, Erin volunteered to read Claire a story, freeing me for a short walk.

"I'll be back soon," I murmured, holding the door long enough for Roscoe to follow. Outside, Calvin, Hobbes, and our other outdoor dogs joined us.

Stars and a half-moon lit the path to the paddock, where I paused to check our newest horses. Domino, a sway-backed pinto, nickered in greeting.

"Are you settling in okay?" I whispered, petting him.

He nudged my shoulder agreeably.

"You're in a safe place now," I assured him. "A safe home. Forever."

He and a geriatric mare named Annie had been half a day away from the kill pen when I found them. I added them to my mental list of rescues, though I'd lost count of the exact number. Twenty-six? Twenty-seven?

"You have a good home now, and everything will be okay," I murmured to myself as much as to the horse.

Domino swished his tail and let his head droop as I scratched his withers. Annie wasn't as trusting, but that was all right. She could have her space.

All seventy-eight acres of it. My heart swelled as I looked around our dusty domain. My great-aunt had left us three sisters her ranch on the outskirts of Sedona, and we were doing the best to keep the place going.

Leaving the horses with a last pat, I continued toward the mesa. Over the years, we'd worn a faint trail to the top, but I branched off to my own special spot five minutes later, stepping on flat-topped rocks to avoid leaving footprints. Once I'd turned a corner, following the contours of the mesa, I slowed at the sight of a rocky outcrop.

One of the foster families I'd lived with as a kid had been regular churchgoers, attending mass every Sunday for the three weeks I'd lasted with them. Their steps would always change as they approached the church doors, and their mood became somber, even spiritual.

The same way I approached that particular outcrop.

I ran a hand over the flat-topped rock that was my pew and gazed out over the box canyon that guarded the northeast side of the ranch. Slowly, I took a seat, resting my chin on my knees, thinking.

First, I thought about someone patient, quiet, and indulging. Had I been too harsh? Was he trustworthy? How soon could I get rid of him? Did I really want to?

Then I wrestled my thoughts around to what really mattered: the axes.

Years ago, I'd come to this very spot to mourn a firefighter's passing, fret over my loved ones, and mull over my own mortality. I'd barely slept that night and spent the following day in a fit of out-of-nowhere energy that had me banging away at steel for hours. By nightfall, I had forged the most perfectly shaped, perfectly balanced ax of my life.

Rich had wept when I'd brought the ax to the firehouse, and even Alice, the most no-nonsense member of the crew, had commented on the energy that seemed to radiate from it. I'd pooh-poohed that at the time as just another example of Sedona's overexaggerated magic.

But now, I wasn't so sure. Was their three-year lucky streak just luck, or was it magic?

Magic I'd never been able to wield... until recently.

I reached out, touching the rock beside me.

Painted Rock Ranch took its name from the art scratched into stones in a long bygone era. This outcrop only boasted a handful of pictographs, but they were enough. Especially one — the spiral symbol.

I inched my hand toward it, holding my breath. Then I exhaled and gently traced the lines, much like I'd patted Domino. Vortexes were highly unpredictable and likely to lash out if you caught them at a bad time.

A little like me.

Sometimes the vortex was dull, even sleepy. Other times, it crackled with energy — mostly angry, but on rare occasions, welcoming.

Now was one of the latter. Whew.

I closed my eyes, thinking about twenty lucky axes. Twenty trusting firefighters. Twenty lives depending on me.

Warmth trickled from the rock to my fingers, telling me I could do it.

All well and good, but how, exactly?

That was the catch — vortexes were rarely specific. So far, I'd only ever experienced two exceptions: the day our ranch had been attacked by Harlon Greene, a lightning-wielding warlock, and the night Pippa had screamed for help while battling ruthless vampires.

Both times, I'd run to the vortex, and both times, I'd been able to harness and direct its explosive energy.

Not that I ever intended to use it again. Doing so had chipped away at the inner dungeon I kept my own inborn magic locked away in. Magic I was afraid to use or even acknowledge.

But when it came to the vortex... I could trust that. I bobbed my head, thanking it silently for its assistance in those life-and-death moments.

Most of the time, the vortex simply provided silent encouragement, like now. But like the ideal parent I'd never had yet strove to be, that was it. Encouragement, but no direct guidance. More like a *You can do it, honey!* kind of cheerleading that left me to forge my own way. All I could do was sleep on it... and hope my dreams might help me.

My heart revved a little at the prospect. But getting helpful information from dreams was even more rare than help from a vortex.

Slowly, I stood and stepped away.

"Good night," I whispered to the vortex. To the night. Heck, to the whole universe and everything in it. The horses, my family... even that quiet someone who had drifted in and out of my thoughts all evening.

Then I headed back to the house and into my nightly ritual.

"One more story," Claire, now tucked into bed, begged at the end of the second one of the evening. "The one about dream weaving."

I stroked her cheek gently, regretting the day I'd told her that story passed down from my father's side of the family — the one about special people with special powers whose dreams bridged all the way over from night to day, ensuring happy endings to big problems.

Probably just a story, but sometimes, I had to wonder.

"Not tonight, sweetie." Kissing her forehead, I lay down beside her.

The ceiling wasn't scribbled with answers, but it was a comfortingly blank canvas, so I kept my gaze there for a while. Claire's breaths slowed as she fell asleep, and I sighed, relishing the simple peace of that moment.

At some point, Roscoe stirred, and I slipped away to my own bed.

It was late, and I had to get some rest. And as for the problem of the lucky axes...

I would sleep on it. Maybe even dream on it, if I was very, very lucky.

Chapter Six

ABBY

Sometime before dawn, my eyes shot open. Two startled heartbeats later, I jerked upright.

Not a bird sang. Not a cicada chirped. Not a breath of air stirred the mighty oaks by the creek. I stared out the window.

It was happening again — that rumbling. Soundless, motionless except for that violent vibration in the air.

Magic. And not just a warning this time.

I shot out of bed and ran down the hall barefoot. Halfway along, another rumble stopped me in my tracks. I gripped the bathroom door, my mind racing. The moment it stopped, I hurried to Claire's room. She was sound asleep, though Roscoe had jumped off her bed, whining meekly.

I nearly bundled Claire up and rushed her out of the house with Roscoe. But instinct promised me that rumble wasn't an earthquake and that Claire was safe here. Whatever was happening was somewhere off in the distance.

After a last look at Claire, I padded downstairs. Quickly pulling on a sweater, jacket, and boots, I stepped outside. Roscoe ventured out with me, pressing against my legs.

I sniffed the air, then froze at a rumble of a different frequency. A counterrumble, so to speak, as the earth growled back at the disturbance that had set it off. I had to dig deep to pick them apart, but the original disturbance came in shorter, lighter bursts.

Walt had once rented part of his workshop to a sculptor who'd chipped at stone to shape a hunch-backed Kokopelli with a flute and wild hairdo. It had taken days, with a constant *chip, chip, chip* as pieces of stone surrendered to the tap of his chisel.

This was similar, except that somewhere in the distance, someone was chipping away at magic.

The door to Erin and Nash's cabin opened, and light spilled over their porch.

Are you okay? she called into my mind. *Is Claire?*

I think so, I called back, using the special link we sisters shared.

What was that?

I had no idea.

A shadow loomed over their cabin, then soared overhead, making my hair flutter.

That was Nash, Erin's badass partner, a dragon shifter. Puffs of fire lit the sky as he sliced through the air, guarding us fiercely.

But was there actually a threat out there or just a disturbance?

To the northeast, a thin line of orange crept over the horizon, and I called to Erin. *Feels like it's coming from over there.*

Silence reigned while we both tuned in.

Airport Mesa? Erin asked at the very moment I'd come to the same conclusion.

I tensed through the next rumble, grabbing one of the porch posts.

In my mind, I sensed Erin moving. *Where are you going?*

Over to the cliff. Hang on...

Nash swooped lower, protecting the airspace above her.

The cliff meant the vortex — Erin's vortex. At least, that's how I thought of it. Our great-aunt had shown each of us a different vortex — or a different portal to the same vortex — years ago. Pippa's was over to the west, and mine was up on the mesa.

When the air rumbled again, I winced, imagining the earth groaning. Somewhere, someone was picking away at the magic embedded in Sedona's landscape. Stealing it, almost, like gold from an off-limits mine.

The vortex pulses at the same time, Erin reported. *Faintly, but I can feel it.*

I closed my eyes, reaching out to my special place. At the next pulse of that mysterious disturbance, my vortex reacted. Twitching, almost, like a horse irritated by flies.

Nash grumbled loudly, swooping lower.

We'll go check it out, Erin told me.

And, *whoosh!* A second winged shadow joined Nash, and they shot off toward Airport Mesa.

"Be careful," I whispered.

I tensed, expecting another ripple in the air at the same interval as the previous disturbances. But there was nothing.

Too bad Pippa and Ingo weren't home. Ingo would have shot off in his government-issued Jeep to start investigating immediately. Protecting people was his job — and his passion — as an officer in supernatural law enforcement. But he and Pippa were in Colorado.

Twenty tense minutes passed. I shuffled from foot to foot, trying to keep warm. The colors in the sky intensified as the sun approached the horizon. Soon, it would be light and too risky to fly around in dragon form.

Right on cue, Erin and Nash swept into sight, then glided into smooth landings. Erin shook out her wings, making my hair ruffle.

My sister, the dragon shifter. I was only slightly jealous, I swear.

"Did you see anything?" I called out as Roscoe cowered behind my legs.

Yes and no, she reported. *There were a couple of parked cars at the trailhead and a few people out on Airport Mesa, but that's not unusual.*

True. Folks often headed up to Airport Mesa for the sunrise.

We looked at each other. The disturbance had stopped, but that didn't put me at ease.

Weird, Erin concluded.

They disappeared into the cabin and emerged a short time later in human form and dressed, with Nash ready to race off in his vehicle.

"I'll catch up with you at work," Nash said, kissing Erin goodbye as the sun rose over the horizon.

She hugged him as if he were going off to battle.

If Pippa were here with Ingo, she would have hugged him the same way.

My arms tightened around…emptiness.

"Call the minute you have news," I called out.

Nash drove off, leaving a cloud of dust that rose then slowly scattered.

Erin and I watched him go, then split up reluctantly. Whatever had happened out there was over now, and we had jobs to get to.

I took one last, long look around, then headed inside. Another day was starting. I wondered what clarity the rising sun would bring, if any.

Chapter Seven

COOPER

At five to nine the next morning, I found myself staring at the rear entrance of Heavy Metal Sedona. When Walt rolled up the doors, he looked surprised to see me back.

Hell, I was surprised too.

"Good morning. Good to have you back."

"Good to be here," I murmured, more polite than honest.

I'd left the previous day one hundred percent resolved to give Rich an ultimatum. Either he let me prepare for the season with the rest of the team, or I would find a different crew to work for.

And yet, here I was, back at the metal shop. Why?

Well, I'd never been a quitter, and one stubborn, antisocial blacksmith wasn't going to make one of me.

Also, because a midnight ramble in bear form had given me a million reasons to spend a season exploring this fascinating landscape. How did such tiny, fragrant flowers spring up from such arid, lifeless ground? What would their honey taste like? How many intriguing little hideaways lay out there in that red, rocky landscape, waiting to be discovered?

When I returned, I'd had a good, long look at the picture hanging on the west wall of the firehouse. The one of Kevin, who'd been killed a few years ago. It blurred, though, with a similar picture hanging on the wall back at my home station in Wyoming.

Kevin had died four seasons ago, and the Yavapai Hotshots hadn't had a major mishap since. Not with the lucky ax crafted by Abby.

Intrigued? Yes, I was, in spite of my aversion to witches and witchcraft.

So, I'd decided to give Abby one more day. I could always deliver that ultimatum later.

"Morning." Bob filed in, followed by Matt and Pablo.

"Good morning," Pablo mumbled.

"Not sure it is," Matt groaned between sips of steaming coffee.

Walt came over and assigned me a locker. Had he been holding out to see if I would survive my first day with Abby?

Probably.

Pablo clapped me on the shoulder. "Congratulations! You get your own locker and everything."

Yeah, that would make up for working with Miss Grouchy Arizona. Still, it was nice to be accepted — by some people anyway.

I swapped my jacket for a thick leather apron. Wishful thinking, maybe, since Abby hadn't let me anywhere near her precious project.

Yet.

She ran in at five past nine, clearly flustered. Late to dropping Claire off at school, maybe?

Spotting me, she stopped abruptly.

"Morning," I murmured, tying my apron carefully.

She narrowed her eyes, clearly suspicious. But I wasn't guilty of anything more than sheer persistence — or ignorance. My metalworking experience mostly consisted of keeping the bellows going and handing my uncle tools. I was about as qualified for this as open-heart surgery. And like open heart surgery, there really could be lives on the line here, if Rich and Alice were to be believed.

With a grunt of — greeting? disappointment? — Abby disappeared behind the door of her locker. Yes, she was that slender. She made enough noise for a herd of mustangs, though, throwing down her bag and changing her shoes in that aggressive way of hers, like they'd personally wronged her.

"Hey, Abby. Did you feel that this morning?" Matt asked.

The commotion behind the door stopped immediately.

"Feel what?" she peeped a little too casually.

"My girlfriend said she felt the vortexes flare right before sunrise."

I made a face. Did Matt really believe that spiritual mumbo jumbo?

Abby's reply was as neutral as the cement of the workshop floor. "They flared?"

"Yeah. She said the vortexes threw out huge pulses of energy. She couldn't sleep afterward."

The dark circles under Abby's eyes said she hadn't either.

But *Huh* was all she said.

"Oh. Rich said you wanted this," I said, handing her an old ax he'd hauled out of storage.

Some women were into boxes of chocolates or flower bouquets. Personally, I could be buttered up by a jar of nice, thick wildflower honey.

Abby dug vintage axes.

Her eyes lit up, and her cheeks flushed with excitement.

My inner bear seized on that and galloped off in a totally inappropriate direction, crooning about love, forever, and destiny.

Destiny? I froze. No way.

I cleared that nonsense out of my mind. Stupid bear.

Abby snatched the ax out of my hands and turned away, shielding it.

"You're welcome," I muttered.

"Thank you," she murmured, heading off to her corner of the shop like a dog with a bone it had no intention of sharing.

She was so excited — and/or preoccupied — that she didn't react when I joined her. She just went on inspecting the axes — the vintage ax and the one she'd mocked up the previous day. So far, she'd only made the head of the mock-up. From the look of things, the fittings were on today's agenda, because you didn't just stick a steel head on a wooden handle and start hacking away — not unless you wanted that steel head to fly off and hurt someone. It had to be fitted snugly with two long, thin bars, a rivet, and several wooden wedges.

I knew this only because Abby disassembled the vintage ax. She studied each part reverently, turning each piece over in her hands and running a finger over every surface. Then she got to work creating copies for her mock-up. That took the rest of the day, and I got as much hands-on time as I had the previous day.

Namely, zero.

"How old is this?" I asked, reaching for the time-worn handle.

"Old." She swatted my hand away.

"What are you using it for?"

"You'll see."

She'd gone from a single-syllable answer to two syllables. Cause to celebrate?

I reached for the ax again, counting on my size advantage for self-defense if necessary. I nabbed it on my second try, earning a glare from Abby.

"You're the one who took it apart," I pointed out. "It's not like I'm going to break it."

"Anything is possible," she muttered. "You know, like a bull in a china shop."

I snorted. "More like a bear in a metal shop."

Abby froze.

So did I. Oops.

Her hard gaze scraped over my cheeks and beard...down to my chest, then my arms...

"Bear, huh?" she whispered.

I opened my palms to her, showing her human hands and fingers.

"Not at the moment," I replied quietly.

To my shock and wonder, she reached for my hands.

Her touch was halting. Careful. Her skin — no surprise — was callused.

Warm, my bear hummed. *Nice.*

My hands dwarfed hers, but somehow, they felt like a perfect fit.

My throat bobbed, the only movement I permitted my body.

Once, on a day off one summer, I'd shifted to bear form to wander a beautiful mountain meadow. Birds sang, and wildflowers danced in the breeze. A butterfly had fluttered by, then landed on my nose. I'd stood perfectly still, barely breathing.

Just like now.

Abby ran her hands over mine, then grasped my fingers, and—

"Ow." I jerked away when she squeezed hard, ruining the moment.

Was she checking for claws?

"Sorry." She pulled away quickly.

I rubbed my hands, wishing hers were still clasped in them.

Then I leaned in, seizing the moment. "And what about you?"

Her lips wobbled ever so slightly. "What do you mean?"

"I mean, what are you?"

The color drained from her cheeks.

"A witch?" I tried.

And, whoa. Talk about pulling a trigger. Her eyes flashed, and her hands balled into small sledgehammers. The fire in the forge sparked angrily, and I swear, the color of her tattoos intensified.

"I'm a blacksmith," she snapped. "Now, let me concentrate."

She turned back to the ax parts, but the way her chest heaved told me she couldn't focus.

I nearly apologized, but what had I done, actually?

Still, I felt like shit, because she was upset. Not with me, maybe, but upset just the same.

An hour ticked by before I found a way to make a peace offering — filling her water bottle. She accepted it without a word — her version of a peace offering?

"Are axes still made the same way?" I asked, indicating the parts, new and old, on her workbench.

"Yep." Her tone was as snippy as ever, but maybe a touch less grudging.

One thing was for sure. She had me stumped. Was she a witch or wasn't she?

"Lunchtime!" Pablo called out gleefully.

Abby whirled away from me and headed for the private corner where she had wolfed down her huge, homemade lunch the previous day. Enough food for an entire fire crew — and we were notoriously big eaters.

I sighed and repeated my supermarket run — along with my vow to quit this job.

When we returned to work, Abby was... well, not *subdued*, but... quiet. No, that didn't fit either. More focused, in any case, and not half as resentful as usual.

A good sign? A dangerous one? I kept my distance, just in case.

At some point, her watch alarm sounded, and she gave herself a little shake.

"I have to go," she said, leaving the ax on her workbench.

I glanced at the shop clock. Three o'clock. Time to pick up her daughter?

"I'll be right back," she said, jogging to her car. "Don't touch anything."

I sighed. So much for making headway.

I swept the shop floor — the entire floor, not just Abby's section, earning praise from Bob and chuckles from the others. Then, after a few sips of juice from the carton I'd bought at lunchtime, I practiced assembling the vintage ax Abby was using as a model.

Abby's car — a green Ford older than either of us — was loud enough to serve as an early warning system. I put the ax back exactly as Abby had left it.

"Hi, Mr. Cooper!" Claire called, all bright and happy.

"Just Cooper," I reminded her gently. "How was school?"

"Great! Look what I made in art class!"

"Wow! Is that Black Beauty?"

"Bucephalus," she corrected without the slightest hint of exasperation. *So* unlike her mother.

"Bu-who?"

"Alexander the Great's horse," she said, all matter-of-fact.

Wow. A kid who knew ancient history — or the equine side of it, at least.

Claire made a round of the metal shop so everyone could admire her artwork. Abby, meanwhile, took one look at the workbench and shot me a dirty look that said, *You touched, dammit.*

I met her gaze, telegraphing something like, *Yes, I did. But I handled your work with respect, and I put everything back as I found it.*

Yeesh. What was up with her? I'd grown up with five siblings, and I knew how to share. Then again, I had a mom who'd imposed law and order in an otherwise chaotic household. Maybe Abby hadn't?

Claire skipped over to her usual spot near Abby's anvil. "Oh! Juice! Can I have some?"

Abby shot me another dark look. This one said, *For God's sake, did you not hear what I said yesterday?*

Then she followed Claire's gaze... and froze.

"Sure. I got you your own." I pointed to the pint-size carton next to my big one. "If it's okay with your mom, of course."

I looked at Abby, thinking — but not daring to say — *Ha. Gotcha.*

"Can I, Mom? Can I?" Claire turned to Abby with big, irresistible eyes — luminous green, just like her mother's.

Abby stared a moment longer, then nodded curtly. "Just make sure you say—"

"Thank you, Mr. Cooper!" Claire gushed, beating her to it. "Thank you!"

I opened it, handed Claire her carton, and tapped it with mine in a toast. "You're welcome."

Claire giggled, making me grin.

"What did you do today, Cooper?"

Nothing, I almost blurted. *Your mother didn't let me.*

I settled for "Mostly, I watched your mom work."

"She's a really good blacksmith," Claire agreed, oblivious to my subtext.

Abby caught it, though. I could tell by the sharp look she sent me.

"She is," I agreed. "That's why I barely touched any of the fittings while she was gone. I wouldn't dare. You know, because metal is so fragile."

Abby rolled her eyes. Claire giggled.

"What did *you* do today?" I changed the subject.

Claire launched into a detailed description of her day while doodling with crayons. I heard all about what she had for lunch, the games she played at recess, the camper trip her friend Casey had taken with her family...

Abby's phone rang, but she ignored it.

A minute later, it rang again. And again. Cursing, she turned away to take the call.

"Hello?"

A split second later, her body stiffened. "How did you get this number?"

Uh-oh. That didn't sound good.

"I told you not to call me." Her voice was low and venomous.

Claire looked up.

"Don't you *baby* me, Jay," Abby hissed.

Claire's crayon hovered over the paper, and her sunny expression faltered.

Abby stalked out of the workshop, taking the rest of the exchange out of earshot.

I watched her go, then glanced at Claire, who'd gone pale. Shit.

I picked up a crayon, pulled up a stool beside Claire's, and sat, blocking her view of Abby pacing outside.

"Here. Let me draw you a train."

"A train?" Claire didn't sound too interested.

"Uh-huh." I lined up several sheets of paper and started sketching. "A special one."

Claire leaned around me, barely paying attention. "How special?"

My first thought was a circus train that she could fill with animals. Then I got a better idea based on what she'd said the previous day.

"It's a train that rescues animals and brings them to Sedona."

And, whew. That got her attention.

"A rescue train? Cool."

"Yep." I drew a long line of flat freight wagons, one per sheet of paper. "I'm not very good at drawing animals, though. Can you help?"

She nodded eagerly.

"So, what animals go in the first wagon?" I asked.

Horses, of course. She even had names for them.

"This is Domino, and there's Annie..."

I nodded, leaning in so she couldn't see Abby gesticulating dangerously. If hands were knives, Jay — whoever he was — would be chopped into a hundred bloody pieces.

Claire's second compartment was more of a dog kennel, while the third carried alpacas.

The next time I looked up, Abby was off the phone. She stood staring — or glaring — into the distance. She'd wrapped her arms around herself and was stroking her own arms, the way folks did when they needed comforting. Sedona's mesas and peaks rose in the background, making her look tiny. Fragile, even.

My heart tore a little.

I'd never seen anyone so...so...

Alone, my bear filled in sadly. *Lonely.*

I burned to step over and make that hug a little more comforting. But Abby barely let me near her anvil. She sure as hell wasn't going to let me close to her body.

All I could do was add another sheet of paper to Claire's train. She filled a fourth and fifth wagon — greyhounds in one, pit bulls in another— and devoted a sixth to elephants. Asian elephants, the kind with small ears.

Outside, Abby rolled her shoulders, composing herself. Then she stomped back inside.

I inched away from Claire, working on the principle of never coming between a momma bear and her cub.

Abby's eyes darkened, seeing me there, but they brightened again when she focused on Claire.

"Why don't you show your mom the train?" I whispered.

Claire scooped up the papers and scampered over to Abby. "Look, Mommy! I drew a rescue train!"

Abby's face was a mask, but a moment later, she cracked and kneeled to hug Claire.

"What a beautiful picture, sweetie." She barely looked, but that didn't stop her voice from wobbling.

I turned away, giving them space. I couldn't help hearing, though.

"Is everything okay, Mommy?" Claire asked.

The tear in my heart ripped a little further.

"Everything is fine, sweetie."

"He's not coming back, is he?" Claire went on, clinging to her mother.

My turn to ball my hands into fists. Who was that asshole?

"No, sweetie. Everything will be fine. Everything *is* fine."

The more Abby said it, the more I knew it wasn't.

Jay, I figured, was her ex. Claire's father, maybe. The guy who'd made Abby so bitter?

My bear growled.

Whoever Jay was, he was definitely a threat.

My chin itched as the stubble there thickened, and I couldn't help checking the doorway.

But there was no one there. No threat. Just the ghosts of Abby's past, invisible to me but screaming in her face, or so it seemed.

Behind us, the others started cleaning up.

"Closing time, everyone," Walt called.

This time, Abby let me help with her area. She even let me walk Claire to the car and see them off. I stood there a long time, watching the red taillights of her Ford disappear into the steady stream of commuters.

When I got into my car and paused at the edge of the road, I burned to make a left and follow her, just in case. But home for me was a right turn, and Abby hadn't asked for me to tail her.

After another long minute of indecision, I turned right.

My heart sure felt like it had taken a left, though.

Chapter Eight

ABBY

First the vortex disturbance, then Jay's call. I couldn't help thinking something was up. My sisters, on the other hand...

"I wouldn't worry about it if I were you," Pippa said.

She and Ingo had returned from their trip just in time for a sunset ride. Apache, her pinto, and Buckeye, Erin's roan, flanked my horse, Lucky. Flanking *me*, really, making it clear I wasn't alone.

God, I loved my sisters. They'd immediately picked up on my sour mood — not difficult, given the car doors I'd slammed or the way I'd thrown my phone (at the soft porch seat because I couldn't afford a new one, but still) — and had talked me into a short ride.

Ingo had promised to investigate the disturbance at Airport Mesa first thing in the morning. In the meantime, he'd volunteered to cook dinner while Nash played soccer with Claire, freeing me up for a ride with my sisters.

I gulped, glancing back toward the main house. To think those two had ever been on my red list...

Which just went to show what a shitty judge of character I was. Jay had started out on my green list. So, maybe I should start trusting every man I disliked and hating every man I trusted from now on.

Like Cooper. Did he deserve an upgrade to my yellow list?

Lucky tossed his head, making his harness jingle. Was that a yes?

The orange juice thing had gone right to my heart, and I knew the rescue train hadn't been Claire's idea. I just found myself wishing they'd drawn a carriage for me too.

"It's not the first time Jay's done this, right?" Pippa pointed out.

Unfortunately, no. Every couple of years, my ex would get it in his head that, hey, maybe he ought to be a father after all, and demand his "rightful" place in Claire's life.

The shithead hadn't even been at Claire's birth. Erin and Pippa had, and their tears of joy had matched mine when they'd held Claire for the first time. But Jay? No call to check on us. No card. Nothing.

"He's probably just trying to impress some woman," I grumbled, thinking about his last call, two years earlier.

Pippa snorted. "If he is, I feel sorry for her."

I did too — except *she* might as well have been *me*. Hell, it *had* been me. The old me, at least, who'd not just fallen for Jay's undeniable charms but plunged headfirst down a cliff — a cliff like the one our horses steadily picked their way along on the way to our favorite sunset viewpoint.

A hunk of a bull rider with twinkling, cornflower-blue eyes, Jay could have had any of the groupies who'd thrown themselves at him, but he'd wanted *me*. One look at me in the stands of a rodeo had been enough for him to hunt me down the next day and the next and the next, armed with that devastating smile each time.

No one had ever shown that much interest in me. No one.

Leather creaked as I shifted in my saddle, wishing Lucky would pick up the pace. Maybe that way, we could outrun my memories.

After a few days of fairy-tale pursuit, I'd relented and ended up in Jay's bed. I'd loved every minute of those amazing couple of weeks. Every stroke of his callused hands, every kiss, every whisper, every hot, hard thrust. He'd truly made me feel like a queen.

You had to give it to Jay: he knew how to put a woman on a pedestal and worship her.

Unfortunately, his attention span was only marginally longer than his bull rides. Before I knew it, he was on to the next cute chick who'd caught his eye — and the next and the next. Jay could staff his own rodeo, and fill the stands, with the women he'd sweet-talked into his saddle over the years.

Sorry, baby, he'd had the nerve to say when I'd found him in bed with my successor. *But, hey. We had a good time, didn't we?*

He'd dumped her just as quickly, but that was little comfort to me.

I'd been Jay's queen, but the day I hunted him down to say I was pregnant, he'd treated me like a whore.

How can you be sure it's mine?

Like I was the one with a lover at every stop on the rodeo tour.

"Maybe he's just after a free place to stay," Erin grumbled.

Equally possible. Nine years ago, Jay had been on top of the world. Now, injured and broke, he was a washed-up ex-rodeo star living off friends, dusty trophies, and rapidly fading star allure.

"He said he wants custody." My voice cracked.

"He'll never get it," Pippa assured me. "Not after what he did five years ago."

Erin shot her a look. I touched the scar on my cheek, gritting my teeth.

"He'll never follow through," Erin said firmly.

Apache's hooves scraped over rock, emphasizing her words.

"All bark and no bite," Pippa tried a joke.

"Ha-ha," I grumbled.

But she was right. Jay was a wolf shifter, and he rarely followed through on promises.

Threats, on the other hand...

Lucky tossed his head, telling me to enjoy the view while I could.

I patted his pale mane. "Beautiful."

Sunset colors split the sky into stained-glass panes of pink, orange, and red. The landscape echoed that, contributing panels of green from all the pines and oaks. The lights of town twinkled in the distance, along with the closer few dotting our ranch.

My ranch, I reminded myself. My sisters, my daughter. My life.

I raised my chin resolutely. I was the master of my fate and the captain of my destiny. I was a tough, capable woman, a respected metal artist, and a damn good mother. Jay was a nobody, and I would not allow him to steal my peace, let alone my daughter. Not now, not ever.

"Never," I whispered into the wind.

∞∞∞∞

That night, I tried dreaming Jay out of existence.

I woke angrier than ever — at him and myself. If dream weaving really was a magic power, I sure as hell didn't have it.

The only positive of Jay's out-of-nowhere call was that it put me in the perfect frame of mind to bang at steel once I arrived at work.

I turned the ingot — a block of raw steel — in my hands, getting a feel for it, reading invisible lines, and stretching it into the right shape in my mind. Then I buried it in the coals of my forge and went over my next steps. Enough tinkering. It was time to get down to business.

I picked out my favorite hammer, moved the glowing ingot to my anvil, and began.

Tap. Tap. Wham! Tap. Tap. Wham!

The red-hot metal flared, slowly succumbing to a time-old rhythm passed down through generations of blacksmiths.

Tap. Tap. Wham!

Every contact pushed the outside world further and further away, leaving just me, the metal, and the fire. *My* fire — the one beside me, and the one within.

Sweat streamed down my brow, and magic heated my veins as I slammed again and again and again.

All too soon, the metal cooled, and I had to pause to reheat it.

It was only after three more cycles — hammering away, then stopping to reheat — that I noticed Cooper there.

Which said a lot, because the guy was huge. And quiet, especially today. Giving me space. Letting me concentrate.

Or maybe just keeping himself safe?

Well, he ought to. I didn't want or need an assistant.

I opened the forge vent to raise the temperature. The burst of air ruffled the calendar pinned over my workbench, and I frowned. Three weeks left in the month, and I had twenty axes to forge. A hydraulic hammer would speed things up, but working by hand let the metal sing back to me, guiding me as I coaxed it into its new form. Working metal was like training a horse — better to guide it, not break it, especially if you wanted a little magic to seep in with every strike.

I glanced over at Cooper, then at the metal resting in the coals. Then back to Cooper — specifically, those thick, bulging arms. I'd made a good start drawing the metal out to the desired shape, but...

Well...maybe it was time to start trusting men instinct had warned me away from.

I cleared my throat and looked up at him. *Way* up.

"Have you ever worked as a smith-and-striker team?"

Warm brown eyes regarded me steadily, and he nodded. "Yes. I strike for my uncle sometimes."

I scratched my chin, then reached for my trusty twelve-pound sledge. I held it out to him, then pulled it back to my chest. Was this really a good idea?

Cooper snorted. "I can watch, or I can help. Guess which will speed things up for you."

I grimaced, then held out the tool again.

He looked offended, eyeing the larger model behind me.

I huffed, then gave in and handed him a fourteen-pounder. Men!

Even that, he took with disdain. Clearly, he was coveting the twenty-pound beast hanging on the wall behind me. Well, he could use that when he proved himself.

Which he did, real quick.

I made him practice on a piece of scrap metal first, which got me another miffed look. But there was no way I was going to let him near my project without a dry run.

"Okay. Follow my lead. I hammer first, you follow. And when I say *up*—"

He nodded, cutting me off. "I give it one more tap, then stop. I know."

I looked at him, then the metal, and began.

Bang! went my hammer.

Wham! His landed right in the footprint of mine.

I aimed a little farther right.

Cooper struck the exact same spot.

I led him through three more strikes, then blinked at the results. Wow. Solid technique, solid aim, and *really* solid blows. A single hit did the work of three of my own.

He smirked.

So, power and accuracy weren't issues. The question was, how long could he keep it up?

Plenty long, as it turned out.

I heated the metal again, and we got to work in earnest.

Bang!

Wham!

Bang!

Wham!

We went five rounds, and when I called *up,* Cooper hit one more time, then halted.

A man who could follow instructions. Yay.

As for progress... Damn. Maybe I should have put him to work earlier. The square block of steel I'd started with was already long and slender.

I heated it up, and we went another round. The metal steadily gave way to our blows.

The next time I stopped and wiped sweat from my brow, I caught Pablo looking over. Bob, too.

Walt turned away quickly, but not before I saw him grin. Hmpf. What was up with him?

Cooper used the break to shed his flannel shirt, leaving him in a snug black T-shirt. Within an hour, he was up to the eighteen-pound sledge, and the shirt was sticking lusciously — er, loosely — to his skin. The ax head was taking shape by then, though the final details would take time.

Details, like the etched lines of muscle under that black T-shirt. I only noticed now and then, though. Truly. I was too absorbed in my work.

Not just work. Teamwork, a little voice whispered in my mind.

Yes, teamwork. Smooth and practiced, like we'd worked together for years.

Bang!

Wham!

It was a rhythm. A heartbeat. A dance.

Cooper barely uttered a word all morning, and neither did I. We didn't need to. We were that in tune.

"Five-minute break," I finally murmured, snagging my water bottle. My full water bottle, though I'd been drinking like a fish.

I stared at Cooper's back as he walked off to fill his.

Then I stared a little more, because, well...wet T-shirt. Muscles. Big shoulders. Sweat glistening on skin.

I whirled away and stared into the forge. For once, I didn't feel the need to escape into it. Where I was was just fine.

In fact — much as I hated to admit it — we made a damn good team.

Chapter Nine

COOPER

My third day working with Abby started just as quietly — but a little less aggressively — as the previous two. She spent most of the morning rejigging the fittings for the new ax, making me wonder. Was she procrastinating or being really, really fastidious?

Then I thought of the portrait on the fire station wall and the responsibility she'd been saddled with. Twenty lucky axes to protect an entire fire crew.

Fastidious, I decided, wiping sweat from my brow.

By midmorning, Abby finished the fittings, assembled her glistening new ax, and headed outside, with me trailing — uselessly? hopefully? — along.

At the edge of the back lot, rough asphalt gave way to rocky ground. Abby hacked at it a few times, checking the head, then the tail of the Pulaski. Her easy handling of the tool demonstrated she really had worked as a wildland firefighter, and not just for one season.

I wondered what made her stop. Having Claire, maybe?

Either way, she had a pretty interesting — and impressive — résumé. Witch. Firefighter. Blacksmith. Loving mother. Still, so many mysteries remained.

"Here. You try it." She shoved the ax at me.

I blinked. If she had entrusted me with her daughter, I wouldn't have been any less surprised.

She gestured. "The balance is fine, but I think I angled the adze end a little too sharply."

I weighed the tool up in one hand, then chopped up a patch of soil and dragged the loose earth into a long furrow. Next, I levered up a chunk of asphalt that had dribbled off a corner of the parking lot.

The ax practically sang in my hands, and I could have gone on happily hacking at the back lot for hours. This was what I was trained for. What I was born for, it felt like. But it was one thing to chop up a chunk of wilderness to protect it, and another to turn Walt's back lot into a wasteland. So I stopped, weighing up the ax again. It was near perfect in every way. The angle was a degree or two off, but I would have been hard-pressed to identify what felt wrong if Abby hadn't mentioned it.

So, kudos to my stubborn, antisocial boss. She had a damn good feel for metal — and firefighting.

"The balance is perfect," I told her. "And you're right that the angle is a little sharp, but some like it that way. My cousin had his Pulaski adjusted to an even tighter angle."

"Cousin, huh? Which one?"

So, she'd listened in on Claire and me chatting. Interesting.

"Jack," I said as if that meant anything to her.

But, heck. She'd actually spoken to me. Not exactly sparkling conversation, but not the stone wall she'd been yesterday.

She took the tool from me and studied it for imperfections.

A neighboring shop — *Facet-nating Gems* — shared the back lot, and a salesperson in one of their signature turquoise-and-orange T-shirts paced around with a phone glued to her ear.

"Not a single one," she lamented. "Yes, I tried all of them, but not one of the gems charged." She turned and paced in the other direction. "It's as if someone switched off the vortex."

Abby's head snapped around.

"I can try Boynton Canyon, or I can wait until tomorrow." She paused, listening. "I mean, the vortexes have fluctuated before, but never like this. Even my psychic reader didn't see this coming."

I frowned. Psychic what?

Abby's brow creased, and she stared into the distance, then at the furrow I'd dug.

A minute ticked by, then another, as she grimly considered the earth.

I inched away. Just in case.

"Hang on a second," she finally said, jogging inside.

I waited in the doorway as she grabbed her jacket and called to Walt. "We'll be out for a while, okay? We need to test this ax."

We did?

Walt didn't so much as peep in protest — a testament to his trust in Abby.

She grabbed two things — Rich's vintage ax and a big burlap sack — then stormed over to her car. She unlocked it, then turned to me with an annoyed look.

"Hurry up, already. And bring that ax."

∞∞∞∞

The fifteen-minute drive that followed was one of the strangest of my life. 1990s Ford Fiestas were not made for bears, and I had barely squeezed into the front seat. In my rush, I'd stood the axes on the floor between my knees. Every time the car hit a bump, I winced, picturing the damage the handles would wreak on my private parts.

Now *that* would be a story I wouldn't ever share around a campfire.

Abby drove in fierce concentration, not uttering a word.

I considered the situation. She could be driving to a remote location to off me for all I knew. Then again, I was the one holding an ax.

"We're testing the ax...at the airport?" I asked as we sped by a sign.

"No."

That was all I got for the next mile, until she turned off into a trailhead parking lot, where she parked alongside a handful of earlier arrivals. She stuck both axes in the burlap bag, then handed it to me and set off down the trail.

"Follow me."

"Sure, boss," I muttered, resting the ax handles on my shoulder.

I'd gone from unwelcome assistant to her personal sherpa. Did that count as a promotion?

The trail marker read *Airport Mesa Vortex*. I didn't know much about vortexes, but I was sure axing them would be frowned upon. Plus, did I really want to visit a vortex with a witch?

We passed two parties coming from the opposite direction, and both gave me startled looks.

"You know how sketchy this looks?" I hissed.

"What?" Abby glanced back.

"A small, angry woman stomping away from a big guy hefting something in a burlap bag."

"I'm not small. And I'm not angry," she growled, whirling away again. "Also, you're not that big."

Ha. Tell that to the Ford Fiesta.

"You're making me look like an ax murderer," I complained.

"Well, that wouldn't be a stretch," she muttered.

Now, that hurt my ego. I was a firefighter, hero to small children and the occasional adult — especially those whose homes were surrounded by flames, as my sister had once observed dryly. That was when the average citizen upped his or her appreciation for "unskilled workers" like us.

"I could murder you and stuff your body in this sack, and no one would notice," I said just as a couple appeared at the next bend.

They stopped in their tracks.

"Just kidding," I mumbled, hurrying past.

The next twenty minutes passed silently except for the crunch of our boots over gravel. We were high up on Airport Mesa, and the views were amazing. Capital Butte, Cathedral Rock, Wilson Mountain... Everywhere I looked, rocks jutted up in jagged formations, and the scent of juniper filled my nose.

Heavenly, except for the ax murderer part.

"This way." Abby cut right, off the trail. Five minutes after, she stopped and studied the ground.

"Isn't the vortex over there?" I pointed to where a handful of hikers snapped photos slightly downslope from our position, barely visible through the scrubby trees.

Abby shook her head, then held a hand out, palm down, and followed it around.

"That's where the sign points, but the heart of the vortex is right...about...here."

She stopped, looking down.

I kept a tight grip on the ax. If she pulled anything witchy, I was out of there.

"Vortex, huh?" I didn't sense a thing.

"It comes and goes." Abby stepped back and glanced around. Her gaze narrowed on something at the edge of the clearing.

"There. Look at that."

I stepped over cautiously. "Those ashes, you mean?"

There was a whole pile of them, and fairly fresh.

Abby shook her head, dismissing them. "Lots of folks burn incense or make campfires at vortexes. They're not supposed to, but they do." Then she pointed. "I mean, that."

I turned, following a rough, arched line scraped into the earth.

The wind ruffled my hair, and a raven crowed.

"What do those marks remind you of?" Abby kept her voice low.

Okay, this was getting a little spooky.

I found myself whispering, as if someone — or something — might overhear. "Looks like a fire line."

Abby nodded grimly, then motioned for an ax. I unwrapped them slowly and handed over the one she'd made, then stepped back. It was always wise to give Abby a wide berth.

Back in Walt's parking lot, she'd hefted the ax with power and expertise. Now, she barely tapped the ground.

But, whoa. The earth shook, and I stuck out my arms.

Startled cries rose up from the tourists.

Abby looked up, wide-eyed. Then she dragged the ax a few inches, creating a faint line parallel to the one already there.

There was no sound, but I was somehow reminded of the rumbly, dangerous noise bears made when they emerged from winter dens.

Abby stared at her creation, then motioned for the vintage ax. When we swapped, I held the ax she'd forged as far from my body as I could.

Abby raised the vintage ax, aiming for the same spot.

"Um, maybe you shouldn't—" I started.

Too late. The pick end sliced into the ground, and we both waited warily. But there was no rumble this time. No disturbance at all.

Abby swapped the axes one more time with the same results. The earth groaned from a hit with the tool she'd crafted, but the vintage Pulaski set off no reaction at all.

"You try." She handed me the new ax.

A cold breeze snuck under my collar, sending chills down my back.

I stuck my hands up. This was one of those times when a smart bear would head for the hills.

"I need to see if it's the ax..." She swallowed hard. "...or me."

I stared. If I found the slightest hint of malice — or madness — in there, I was out of here. But Abby's eyes revealed a soul that was scared and confused. A lot like me.

Raising the ax slowly, I gave the earth a meek tap no firefighter worth their salt would waste their time with.

When it hit the ground, I cringed. But there was nothing. Just the quiet scrape of steel over rock.

"Try again," Abby urged. "Harder."

I did it again — and again. Still nothing.

We swapped back twice more, with the same result each time. The only combination that caused a reaction was when Abby used the ax she'd made.

Which meant... what exactly?

Witch, a voice in the back of my mind warned. *She made the ax that disturbs the vortex, and there's only a disturbance when she's the one hefting it.*

I followed her gaze as it ran along the original furrow we'd left untouched.

"That was from this morning, huh?" I asked.

She nodded quietly.

"And you weren't the one who did it?"

She shook her head, looking spooked.

Yikes. Did that mean there was another witch on the loose with another spelled ax?

Definitely time for a smart bear to make tracks. But I just stood there, wondering what was worse: a witch who knew exactly what she was capable of or one who had no clue?

Any bear in his right mind would absorb all this with a mix of fear, loathing, and disgust. But I only registered the *fear* part. Abby might be a witch, but she seemed okay.

More than okay, my bear whispered.

A little rough around the edges, maybe, but she worked hard. Plus, she was a loving mother with unwavering devotion to her child. Values any bear could relate to, even if parts of her life were kind of a mess.

"So, someone else did that," I concluded.

Another nod.

"Who?" I ventured.

She shook her head slowly. "I don't know. But they didn't use this ax."

I scratched my chin, still trying to puzzle it out. Another witch — or part witch, or whatever Abby was — and another ax? If so, which ax?

Then it clicked, and my eyes went wide.

"Someone with the stolen ax?"

Abby blew out a long, slow breath. "I hope not, but yes."

My gut twisted in warning. "So, someone using a spelled ax is disturbing the vortexes... But why?"

She blew out her cheeks, and the furrow in her brow deepened. "I wish I knew."

Chapter Ten

ABBY

Over the next two days, Cooper and I churned out five axes. The details still needed work, but we were on such a roll, we didn't want to stop. We worked all day Friday and Saturday, then dug right back in on the following Monday. A good thing, too, because at ten in the morning, Cooper's phone rang.

"Lundsven here," he said, wiping his brow.

His eyes brightened as he listened, and his whole face lit up.

"I'm on my way."

There was a wildfire, so he was off. And I swear, a kid wouldn't have run faster to an ice cream truck.

"Wait. Take this." I found myself handing him the ax we'd just completed. It wasn't polished, but it was sturdy, and something in me insisted he take it.

He stared, then slowly accepted it.

"Call it a test run. If you have a chance, I mean." I twisted my hands nervously.

Nervous because I was dying to know if the ax had that... er, special something the original did.

Nervous because every fire was dangerous, and I wanted Cooper to come home safe.

Well, I wanted that for every fire crew, every time. But him, especially.

He nodded, and our eyes met for what seemed like a lifetime. Emotions bottled up in my throat, forming a lump there.

Cooper's deep, brown eyes swirled and sparkled. "See you soon," he finally whispered.

It took everything I had not to touch him.

"See you soon," I whispered.

And then he was gone.

He stayed away two days. Enough time for me to finish the decorative details of our first few axes, but too long in every other way.

"I miss Cooper," Claire sighed on his second afternoon away.

Yeah, I did too. And not just for his prowess with a sledgehammer.

"Do you think he's okay?" Claire asked.

My heart twinged. "I'm sure he is."

But what if he wasn't?

I stared into the forge's fire, picturing him laboring away in Crow Canyon on the Arizona/Nevada border, where a midsize fire raged.

Yes, I'd been following it on the state tracker. No, I wasn't about to admit that to anyone.

I imagined the roar of the fire, the steady scrape of axes, the crackle of radios. Then I whirled away from the forge and threw myself back into fine-tuning the axes we'd made so far. They had to be perfect. They had to keep the crew safe.

Those particular axes wouldn't impact the current fire, but I worked as feverishly as if I were out in the forest with Cooper. Sweat dripped down my face, stinging my eyes as I poured all my knowledge of blacksmithing and fires into my work. I'd worked with Pippa's father, a pyromancer, for three firefighting seasons. I knew firsthand about wildfires and how they moved over a landscape. And I knew about the tools at our disposal to fight them — human tools and... er, *special tools*, as Greg liked to call them.

I didn't dare try replicating his spells. But I could let his tips, tricks, and knowledge seep into the metal I worked.

And when I really got in the zone, I could feel magic trickling from my fingers. Flowing, even. My own magic — not Greg's, not from my vortex. My own magic. And for once, I didn't try to halt or question it.

The only other time that had happened was three years earlier, when I'd worked on the original ax in a fit of emotion. This was just like that, but now, the magic was clearer and more powerful.

Keep Cooper safe. Keep them all safe. The mantra echoed in my mind, over and over. All the firefighters, all those acres of forest, all the creatures inhabiting them.

The fire in the forge flared, and my hammer sang. The metal sang too, humming at times, roaring at others. My surroundings melted away until it was just me, metal, and fire.

"Abby!"

I snapped my head up, nearly growling at the intrusion.

A *real* intrusion, judging by Louie's incessant barking.

It was only then that I noticed he'd been locked into Walt's office. And, oops. Walt had to have been hollering for my attention for a while now. A trim brunette stood beside him, dressed to the nines. Her hair was done up in a sleek ballerina bun, and her huge, glittery handbag flashed under the shop lights. Hermès? Gucci? Not my area. I was better acquainted with brands of horse feed.

A man in a dark suit and sunglasses stood beside a classy beige SUV parked outside the rear doors in a spot marked *Employees Only*. Her chauffeur or her bodyguard?

I wondered if time and space had warped, allowing this woman to take a wrong turn off Fifth Avenue and appear in Sedona. Or maybe she'd gotten lost on her way to Serenity Canyon, the thousand-dollars-a-day yoga retreat on the edge of town?

I rested my hammer on the anvil, barely changing a growled *What?* to a more polite "Yes?"

"Ms. Steinmeier here wanted to discuss a project." Walt flashed the woman a warm smile.

His eyes were a little glazed, as if Jacqueline Kennedy had just wandered into his shop. They only cleared long enough to pin me with a hard look that said, *Be nice. This is a customer with deep pockets and rich friends. We want this business.*

I shot a pointed look at Bob, then Pablo. We all had our deadlines, but mine was as tight as a corset on the nineteenth-century lady I was glad not to be. Couldn't one of the other guys humor Glamour Girl?

Walt gave a tiny shake of the head that signaled, *You humor her.*

I stared. What happened to *These axes are important? Our top priority?*

She switched her handbag to the left to shake my hand. The sparkles caught the light, making the space around her shimmer.

"Call me Liselle." She flashed a smile, showing off teeth as polished as her shoes.

"Liselle," I said obligingly.

Matt snickered. Walt glared.

"I'm Abby," I added quickly.

Liselle was about my age, but taller, more groomed, and supermodel-thin. Her blue eyes were so luminous, they bordered on purple. Colored contacts, I figured. Her beige-on-beige outfit would have fit in at a British country manor.

"I was told to ask for you. I have a special project I haven't been able to find anyone to help me with." She lowered her voice and winked. "I find that men don't really listen."

Amen, I nearly said, warming to her.

I set down my hammer. "What kind of project?"

She drew a round shape in the air at about the height of her knees. "A brazier, so I can enjoy a fire on my patio."

A patio as big as a tennis court, I'd bet, with million-dollar views of Sedona.

I tugged on the straps of my overalls as she described what she had in mind. It didn't sound complicated, but I wasn't fooled. Women like this always wanted — no, *expected* — special treatment. I'd once labored for weeks on a gate for one of those fancy new ranches — the kind with more bathrooms than livestock. The client wanted the outline of her beloved Yorkie worked into the middle of the gate, complete with the ridiculous little topknot on its furry head. It was some of my best work, but the client was disappointed that I'd chosen Pookie's bad side.

I'd barely refrained from suggesting what side that was and where the client could shove it.

So, I doubled my estimate for the time required to whip out a brazier for little Miss Vanderbilt.

"I would need about a week to do it, but I'm booked solid through the end of the month."

"Oh, that's disappointing," she sighed.

Yeah, well. So was life sometimes.

She stood there, lips pursed, waiting.

I waited too.

"I'd hoped to have it done this week..." Her eyes locked on mine.

Hope was good. Hope was comforting. But it wouldn't get her a brazier any faster.

I scratched an itch on my ear. No, the side of my head.

The coals in the forge crackled in warning. I frowned. Warning of what?

"Walt says you're the best..." Liselle went on.

Ha. Walt passed that title from employee to employee any way he found convenient.

"—and frankly, I love the idea of a female blacksmith. It can't be easy." She gave me a knowing look.

I had the feeling she knew more about boardrooms than metal shops, but hey. I could relate...sort of.

"Surely there's a way to squeeze it in..." she said, then went full steam ahead as if I'd agreed. "I'll send you some sketches. You know, to give you time to mull over the concept."

A concept, like a real artist. Cool.

Walt grinned at me from behind her in a way that said, *Good job, kid.*

I couldn't help glowing a little. This customer wanted me — me, specifically — to work on her project. Rich had also insisted on me. My boss was happy with me.

I took a deep breath. What a long way I'd come from *desperate runaway* to today.

On the other hand, yikes. That itch was *in* my head now.

Surely there's a way to squeeze it in...

Walt says you're the best...

Mull over the concept...

The words windmilled through my mind, and I found myself picturing how I might fit it in, what concepts I could develop, and what an amazing artisan I would prove myself to be. Maybe I could work on it after hours. Maybe with the time Cooper had helped me save, I could fit in one little brazier. Maybe—

Realization struck me, and I went cold all over. I barely reached for my water bottle in time to hide my shock.

Because suddenly, it all made sense. Walt's dazed expression. The shimmer around Liselle's shoulders. The soothing voice in my mind. *Surely there's a way to squeeze it in...*

Liselle Vanderbilt — er, Steinmeier — wasn't just persuasive. She was a witch. A mind-bender. Not a very good one, now that I was onto her, but still. How dare she?

The old me would have blurted that out point-blank. But the new me had learned to think before I acted, so that was what I did.

If I called her bluff, she would realize I wasn't entirely human, which might prove disadvantageous to me. I had no idea how or why, but life had taught me to keep my cards close to my vest... or my leather work apron.

But I sure as hell wasn't going to let her skip the line like a Lightning Lane guest at Disneyland — a policy that had really, really irked me the one time I'd taken Claire there after months of scrimping and saving.

"Sure. Go ahead and send some sketches," I finally replied. "I'll mull over the concept."

I would mull all the way into next month, but she didn't need to know that.

"Let me get back to you about it soon," I finished.

The dent between her eyebrows deepened, and the itch in my mind intensified. Still, she faked a bright smile.

"Wonderful. I'll give you my card..."

A card, huh? If I needed to share my details, I scribbled them on one of those free notepads handed out by real estate agents and drug stores. This lady had her own card — embossed and everything.

I glanced at the flowery logo, then tried a little mind-bending of my own.

"Now, if you'll excuse me..." I said, turning back to my project.

You can go now, I pushed the thought toward her mind. *No need to waste time here.*

I nearly cheered when she took a step toward the door. But then she caught sight of my forge and chirped, "Oh, how interesting! What are you working on?"

Up to that point, a few alarms had buzzed in the back of my mind. Now, they deafened me.

Someone had stolen the original ax. Someone could be just as interested in the new ones I was forging.

Someone like her?

I couldn't imagine why, but it seemed prudent not to share any details.

My thoughts drifted to Cooper, and my frown deepened.

Definitely prudent, because those axes could protect members of a fire crew... especially one who'd been growing on me.

Luckily, the axes we'd crafted were hidden by a pile of scrap metal. The parts in view around my anvil — the ones that held the ax head to the wooden handle — could have been anything.

"Uh..." Shit. What to tell her?

My mind came up blank, though an unconscious something ticked away in one back corner, and my fingers jerked.

Bang! An earsplitting clatter came from across the workshop.

"*Pendejo!*" Pablo cursed at the scrap metal he'd knocked off a shelf, then looked around in chagrin. "Sorry."

I glanced down at my hands, then hastily curled in the fingers that had been pointing in his direction. That little accident couldn't have come at a better time... but what if it wasn't an accident?

Liselle's phone rang, and she reached into her purse for it.

"Sorry. I'll be in touch later," she murmured, backing away.

Yeah — much later, preferably.

Still, my mind raced. I would have to talk to my sisters about this — and mention this out-of-town witch to Ingo, who worked in supernatural law enforcement. What if Liselle wasn't on his radar?

I found myself wishing for Cooper, too. He had quickly figured out I wasn't entirely human. What insights would he have gleaned from this woman?

And that was just one of many reasons I missed him.

I brought the steel back to my anvil and started whacking, willing my unwelcome visitor out the door and onto the street.

Who was Liselle Steinmeier? Was a brazier all she wanted, or did she have other plans? Could I — should I? — attempt to do something about that?

And what about Cooper? Was he all right? And when was he coming home? Er — I meant, when was he coming back?

Funny how I found myself hoping, *the sooner, the better.*

Chapter Eleven

COOPER

"Home sweet home," Vic murmured as the truck rattled along.

It's about time, my bear muttered.

From the moment we'd exited town days earlier, something had pulled me back.

Someone, my beast murmured.

Yes, someone. But I'd been doing my best to deny that all this time.

Playing it cool, I cracked my eyes open long enough to spot the *Welcome to Sedona* sign. Home was Wyoming. But, yeah. Sedona was fine for now.

Home is where the heart is, my grizzly murmured, echoing one of my mother's favorite lines.

"Great job, everyone," Rich announced. "You did good."

We had, though the fire hadn't been as tricky as the last one. But, hell. We would take what we could get. And a satisfied ride home always beat the alternative.

"On a scale of one to ten, how would you rate that fire?" Mark asked.

My bear snickered. Such a rookie question. But I probably hadn't been much different when I'd started out.

Alice shrugged. "A four, tops."

Personally, I had it at about a three. The challenge had stemmed more from the area of the fire than its ferocity.

Either way, no big deal — to the extent that a two-thousand-acre wildfire could be no big deal.

"Lucky break with that wind shift, huh?" Chuck observed.

"Yeah, and the way the fire dead-ended at that old stock-yard," Vic agreed.

I ran a finger over the handle of my ax, not saying a word but thinking of plenty. Normally, my arms would be lead after two days of nonstop digging and chopping, but not this time. And normally, it took multiple break lines to stop a fire. But it had only taken one on each of the fire's fronts. There'd been lots of fronts — one for every twist in the landscape — but the fire hadn't jumped a single line we'd carved into the earth. It had just screeched to a halt like a dog barking at the limit of an invisible fence. It had gone on raging and crackling for ages, but it never crossed those invisible thresholds.

I glanced down. Were those lucky breaks just lucky? Or was there more at play?

My shoulder brushed Vic's as the truck swung around two successive left turns. Then we creaked to a stop at the fire-house, and everyone piled out, weary yet elated. The sun was setting, and I stopped in the driveway, taking it all in.

Then a car pulled in, and before I even recognized its oc-cupants, my heart lifted.

"Cooper! You're back!" Claire waved gleefully from the window of Abby's Ford. The moment Abby parked, Claire leaped out and hugged me.

Well, she hugged my legs. I leaned over, patting her back, grinning. The only thing better than coming home from a successful firefight was having someone to welcome you back.

"Nice to see you too, kiddo."

I smiled at Abby, who had exited the car and stepped closer.

"Sorry. She insisted," Abby said, crossing her arms tightly.

Her eyes shone, though. Mine did too, judging by the warmth pooling there.

Nice to see you, my bear hummed happily.

Nice to see you too, I sensed her think, if not say. It showed in the shine of her eyes, the quiver of her lips.

"Heya, Abby." Rich waved.

Abby gazed at me a second longer, then turned to him with a little jolt. "Oh. Hi, Rich. I heard you stopped the fire before it got to Sunset Ridge. Good job."

Your average citizen remained blissfully unaware of wild-fires, unless one raged on their doorstep. But Abby had obviously been following this one. Closely. That wasn't hard if you knew where to find the information. But you had to care enough to do so.

Abby cares, my grizzly assured me.

The glow in her eyes confirmed it. Or was that just a side effect of the sunset?

Claire looked up from my legs. "You smell like Grandpa."

Right. The firefighting grandfather she'd mentioned.

"Like smoke, huh?" I asked.

Claire nodded. "Like the woods. Like dirt too."

Like magic? I wondered.

"I bet you smell a lot better," I said, and we both chuckled.

If only communicating with Abby were as easy.

"You must be tired, so we won't keep you," Abby said. "We were just driving by and couldn't help saying hi."

Heavy Metal Sedona was on the main strip. The firehouse lay on a long dead end. So, I kind of doubted they'd been driving by.

"I'm glad you did." Really, really glad.

And miracle of miracles, Abby treated me to a shy smile. Just a tiny one hidden in the corners of her mouth, but definitely there.

My stomach chose exactly that moment to rumble.

Claire patted my leg. "I'm hungry too. Can we go have pizza, Mom? Please? Oh! Can we invite Cooper?"

Abby stiffened, and I did too. Not before my heart gave a hopeful leap, though.

"I think Cooper probably needs to unwind, sweetie. He just got back from a fire."

"But he has to eat!"

My stomach growled again, and I answered without thinking. "I'd love pizza. My treat, if you don't mind waiting for me to take a quick shower."

For the record, that was my bear side doing the talking. My human side was too exhausted to think straight.

"We don't mind," Claire assured me.

Abby shot Claire a look, though the flush of her cheeks said she agreed with the sentiment.

"Um...no. We don't mind."

My bear did a happy dance.

"But it's our treat," she added quickly.

Putting off that argument for later, I rocketed away to the fastest shower of my life, fueled by a second wind.

"Hot date, huh?" Mark chuckled.

I did my best to laugh him off. "Right. With my blacksmith boss and her kid. Not exactly date material."

"It could be," Mark said. "Women love when you like their kids."

Ha. Mark practically was a kid himself. What did he know?

Still, my heart pounded, and as rushed as I was, I shaved extra carefully. Luckily, I had jeans and a clean white shirt in my locker — a nice button-up, not a free T I'd gotten from a charity event or a grateful local business. Not exactly coverboy material, but a step up from the work clothes Abby usually saw me in.

I checked my hair and beard, slapped on a little cologne — courtesy of Chuck, though he didn't know it yet. His locker neighbored mine, and he was a rookie, so I didn't feel too guilty.

Finally, I hurried outside, where Abby watched Claire hop-scotch over invisible lines.

"Ready." I closed the firehouse door behind me.

Abby looked over, then did a double take. Her throat rippled with a gulp, and her eyes traveled over my body.

"Oh! You look so nice, Mr. Cooper!" Claire exclaimed.

"Good enough for pizza night?" I asked.

"Real good," Abby murmured. "I mean...uh...fine."

I hid a grin.

"You smell nice too," Claire added. "Smell him, Mommy."

I laughed. Abby looked half mortified, half tempted. "Sweetie, we don't smell people. Not like Roscoe does."

"Well, you still smell good, Mr. Cooper," Claire insisted.

I grinned. "Just Cooper."

Alice crossed the lot just then, and she chipped in her two cents. "Huh. You clean up pretty good, Lundsven."

I did when I cared. And tonight, I cared. A lot.

Don't mess this up, my bear growled.

It made sense to take one car, and thank goodness for Claire's pleadings for that to be my pickup, where she could ride in the front seat — the only seat — with us. I added another reason to love the kid to a very long list.

She sat between us, chatting a mile a minute during the drive. She did most of the talking once we'd taken a seat and ordered, too. But that was fine with me — and Abby, too, I suspected. She wasn't exactly one for small talk.

I didn't care much either way. It was just nice to spend time with her in a place where we weren't sweating buckets or banging hammers.

Claire asked about the fire. About my home in Wyoming. About my sisters and brothers...

"Yeah, three brothers, two sisters," I said.

Claire frowned. "But you said you had two brothers."

Damn. Who knew the kid had such a good memory? And, shit. How to explain?

My expression must have given me away, because Abby's face fell.

"Claire, sweetie—" she tried, but I shook my head. My mistake, my job to fix it.

"I guess I never know how to count," I admitted. "I have two brothers now. I still have three here." I pointed to my heart, doing my best to keep the quaver out of my voice. "But one died."

"Oh. That's sad," Claire said.

Yes, it was. More than I could explain.

Abby looked down, gutted.

"What was his name?" Claire went on.

"Sweetie—" Abby cut in.

"Peter. The oldest," I said as his last words echoed in my mind.

Head back. I got this. You help the others.

Good old Peter. Keeping an eye on his kid brother, just like he'd promised Mom.

"Did he die in a fire?" Claire asked.

"Claire!" Abby admonished. "I'm so sorry," she said, then turned back to Claire. "Sweetie, people don't like talking about sad things."

"But you said talking is good. Like when Cindy died."

Abby must have caught my stricken expression, because she touched my arm. "Cindy, the dog. Not a person."

I exhaled. Whew.

"I loved Cindy," Claire said defensively.

Abby nodded. "Me too, but it's different with people."

It was, but maybe she was right about the talking part. So, I tried, for the first time ever.

"There was a big fire, and Peter didn't make it out. He made sure I did, though."

Abby bit her lip and kept her hand on my arm, and somehow, the words kept coming.

"He was really funny and really big. . ."

"Bigger than you?" Claire asked, all wide-eyed.

I laughed. "Way bigger."

Now that I thought about it, though, his old flannel shirts fit me just fine. So maybe that was just the way I remembered him.

Talking about him didn't turn out to be as hard as I'd imagined. And it was a lot better than pretending. So I kept at it.

"My other brothers would play tricks on me sometimes, but Peter would always come to my rescue. Like the time Chris lifted me up to his chin-up bar and left me hanging there. It was so high, I was scared to let go." I chuckled. "But Peter got me down. He talked me out of building a bathtub boat too, after Chris put that idea in my mind."

"A bathtub?" Abby chortled.

I grinned. "Yep. I really thought it would work, too. But Peter talked my mom into getting us a little inflatable boat for the pond."

"Oh! Can Roscoe and I have a boat, Mom?" Claire asked.

I stifled a laugh.

"Where are you going to use it, sweetie?" she asked.

"In the creek. Oh! We could take it to Lake Powell. My friend Casey went there in a houseboat, you know."

I did, because Claire had told me all about it one afternoon in the shop. Casey took lots of great trips with her parents — plural — but she didn't have as many horses as Claire.

Abby sighed. "Remind me when we get closer to your birthday."

Claire's was July fifth, I knew, because she'd told me. When was Abby's?

I pictured a cake, silly hats, and excited dogs for Abby's birthday. A small pile of presents, one from each of the sisters and "grandfathers" Claire had mentioned. One from me, too. But what would I give her?

A playground, I finally decided, because Abby was a mother, and watching her kid have fun would give her great joy, as my mother liked to say. My sister, her husband, and one of my cousins had started an off-season business designing and building playgrounds. I could get the plans from them...maybe even add a few of my own touches...

A good thing our drinks came and cut off those fruitless fantasies. Claire started slurping her soda immediately, while Abby raised her glass — ginger ale — to mine.

"To Peter," she whispered.

We clinked, and I echoed her quietly.

Abby gazed off into the distance, and it didn't take much imagination to know she was thinking of Kevin and other fallen firefighters.

"Hey," I whispered a moment later.

With a blink, she looked up.

I tapped my glass against hers. "To pizza night. In Sedona."

Her lips curled in a thin smile, and she tapped back. "To that too."

Our eyes locked for a long time afterward, and waves of understanding washed between us. Waves of all kinds of things that people who didn't fight fires had no clue about. Like sorrow, guilt, and regret — and how we'd learned to live with them. Other things too, like the terror — and thrill — of coming within spitting distance of a raging wildfire.

"I miss it sometimes," Abby whispered after a few seconds of silence.

I knew I would. As much as I loved the peace of the off-season, I always got itchy after a while. That was one reason I'd never managed to find someone willing to put up with my long absences — and my restlessness in the off-season. I'd never met a woman I was interested in who got it.

Until Abby.

But, yikes. She was a witch, or part witch, anyway.

Our pizza came, cutting off those thoughts — all thoughts, actually, because I was that famished — and we dug in.

"Watch your fingers, Claire," someone chuckled. "In case these two beasts bite you by accident."

I gulped down my mouthful of pizza and stood, belatedly catching a whiff of wolf shifter.

"Ingo!" I stood for a quick man-hug, then introduced myself to the blonde beside him. "Cooper."

"I'm Pippa, Abby's sister. And wow. I thought *she* was the one who ate like a horse."

Yeah, I'd noticed that. Like a horse left to fend for itself in an arid pasture, in fact.

"Half sister," Abby grumbled, though the looks they exchanged were packed with sisterly affection.

"Same mother, different fathers," Pippa explained cheerily as she plonked down next to Claire.

"Very different," Abby muttered.

"Heya, Claire. I missed you!" Pippa exclaimed, hugging her sideways.

"I missed you too." Claire held up her pizza slice. "Do you want a bite?"

"Yum." Pippa bit delicately. "Thank you, sweetie."

"Sorry. Didn't mean to interrupt," Ingo said.

I opened my mouth, but Pippa beat me to it. "We're not interrupting, are we?"

Abby's eyes found mine, and I sensed her sighing inside, like I was. Yes, they were interrupting. But it wasn't like this was a date. Was it?

I motioned Ingo to the chair beside me. "Have a seat."

He thumped me on the shoulder. "It's been too long, man."

Yeah, it had been. We spent a few minutes catching up, explaining, marveling. Well, I did anyway. Ingo was a lot more settled than the last time I'd seen him — settled as in *calmer* and as in *happily settled down* with Pippa. As it turned out, they lived on the ranch Pippa owned with Abby and another half sister.

I'd never had reason to be jealous of Ingo, but suddenly, I was. And not for the ranch or Pippa, nice as she seemed.

Pippa was a glass artist. The third sister, Erin, was a hot air balloon pilot. Abby was a blacksmith...

"We all love working with fire," Pippa chuckled, seeing me try to piece it together.

I smiled politely, but my mind was elsewhere. Were all three witches?

A week ago, the thought might have curbed my appetite. But having gotten to know Abby... Well, I was starting to think I ought to be suspicious of stereotypes instead.

We ordered a second pizza, and time flew. But when the topic turned to Ingo's work...

As an agent for the ADMSA — the Agency for the Detection and Monitoring of Supernatural Activity — most of his work was classified. But the vortex disturbance was the talk of the town, so we covered that too.

"Abby said you two went up to Airport Mesa," Ingo said, lowering his voice.

Pippa rolled her eyes. "Here he goes again. You're off duty, remember?"

He kissed her cheek. "I am, but seeing as it's hard to catch Cooper between fires..."

"Okay. You have a point there." Pippa sighed. "And you'll want to talk to Abby about it too, I suppose."

"Talk about what?" Claire asked.

Everyone went very, very quiet.

"About really boring stuff," Pippa finally said. "How about you and I go home and make some brownies while these guys talk about work? Your mom can catch up with us later."

"Yay! Brownies!" Claire jumped up.

Abby glanced at me, then Ingo, pursing her lips. Then she nodded and stood to see Claire and Pippa off.

"See you tomorrow, Cooper!" Claire waved.

I grinned, waving back. "See you tomorrow."

Pippa leaned in, and Ingo met her in a long, lingering kiss.

Abby rolled her eyes. Claire chuckled. I did my best to keep my bear from imagining that kind of kiss with Abby.

Which made no sense, but...

It's like Mom says, my bear rumbled cheerily. *Love doesn't have to make sense.*

Love huh?

Destiny, my bear hummed.

The more time I spent with Abby, the more I felt sure about that. But where was destiny leading us?

I watched them file out. Abby would be back in a minute, but my heart still followed her. I gulped as the door swung closed, then remembered Ingo.

I turned back quickly, catching him eyeing me.

I grabbed my drink, half hid behind it, and waved toward the door. "Claire's a sweet kid."

"The best," he murmured, still studying me. Then he chuckled. "At first, I couldn't believe she's related to Abby."

Same with me, but my heart still panged with sorrow.

"Yeah. Abby is kind of..." I faded out there. *Surly? Impatient? Unable to cooperate?*

But the adjectives I might have used a week ago seemed harsh and judgmental now.

"A tough nut to crack," I finally said.

Ingo laughed. "Yeah, if nuts were made of steel. But she's okay once she lets you in. Unlike Pippa, she had it pretty rough as a kid, so..." He waved vaguely.

My ears jumped to attention. "They didn't grow up together?"

He shook his head. "Their mother took off when they were little, leaving each dad alone to take care of his daughter. Pippa's dad is Greg Martin — remember him, the chief of the Dakota Creek crew?"

I nodded. Was that the grandfather Claire referred to?

"Erin's dad is great too. But Abby's..." Ingo's sour expression spoke volumes. "I guess she wasn't as lucky."

I glanced toward the door, slowly putting it together. All the rescued animals Claire had mentioned. The haunted look Abby got sometimes. The way she wolfed down food...

I made a mental note to tell my parents how much I appreciated them.

"She's a great mom, though," Ingo finished on a brighter note. "I have the feeling she would have been like Claire if things had been different."

"She is great," I agreed. And not just as a mom.

But, damn. Her own mother had abandoned her?

I leaned in to whisper. "Is their mother a witch?"

Ingo laughed dryly. "She's a real piece of work, but no, not a witch. A dragon shifter."

My eyes went wide. "What about Abby's father? A warlock?"

Ingo shrugged. "No idea." Then his eyes narrowed. "You got a problem with witches?"

I opened my mouth to protest, then caught myself. Did I?

"Just wondering," I said a little lamely.

Ingo's eyes bored into mine. "Pippa is a pyromancer, like Greg. A fire dancer, actually."

My jaw swung open. I'd heard of fire dancers but never seen one in action. I'd never wanted to either. But if Ingo trusted Pippa — hell, if he loved her and shared a ranch with all three sisters...

"They're awesome," Ingo assured me. "The other sister, Erin, is a wind whisperer, and her father is a weathermonger."

I stared.

"Throw out any preconceptions you have about witches and warlocks, Coop," he cautioned. "The same way we'd like folks to throw out their views on shifters."

A fair point. "Sorry. I'm getting that...slowly. It's just hard not to be on guard, I guess."

Ingo snorted. "It's not like she'll turn you into a frog."

I gave a dry laugh. "Let's just hope she only channels her magic into metal."

Ingo chuckled, then went serious. "Well, I'm glad you're in the shop with her. In case Jay decides to pull something."

My inner bear flexed its claws at the mention of Abby's ex. "You think he will?"

Ingo shrugged. "Hard to tell. Never met the guy. Pippa and Erin agree he's a shithead, but...well, these sisters..." He grinned fondly. "When they get riled up about something, they get riled up. You don't want to be on their bad side."

That much, I'd already figured out. And, yikes. Abby times three...

The door of the pizza parlor swung open, and Abby stepped back in.

I leaned back so as not to give the impression that we'd been in a secretive huddle, though we absolutely had.

Abby slid into the booth, and I rotated the pizza pan so she could reach the last slice.

"Thanks." She chomped down with the same desperate, elbows-out hunger she'd attacked her first piece with.

"So, the disturbance at Airport Mesa..." Ingo prompted her.

Abby was still chewing away, so she nodded for me to do the talking.

"We went up there a few days ago," I said. "The earth had been dug up around the vortex—"

Abby mumbled, signaling with her elbow.

"Right," I corrected, reading her sign language. "The real vortex, not the one where all the tourists go."

"And?" Ingo stirred the air impatiently.

I traced a semicircle on my placemat. "Someone cut a curved line like this, and the marks were exactly what a Pulaski would make."

Ingo frowned, and Abby motioned to me.

"*Exactly* like a Pulaski," I emphasized.

Ingo's brow furrowed as he looked at me, then Abby with an expression that asked, *You can actually understand that mumbling?*

Of course. Couldn't he?

He studied the two of us a moment longer, then continued his interrogation. "Really exactly?"

Abby made a chopping motion while I filled in the words. "*Exactly* exactly. I'd put money on those marks having been made by a Pulaski."

"But how..." He trailed off into a lightbulb moment, then leaned in. "You think it was the ax stolen from the fire station?"

We both nodded.

"The lucky ax?" Ingo made air quotes around *lucky.*

We nodded again.

"The lucky ax you made?" He stared at Abby.

She gulped, then nodded slowly.

"The lucky ax someone stole," I added, just to be clear.

Ingo stared at Abby. So hard, I could see her squirm.

"Sorry, Abby, but I have to ask. What magic did you weave into that ax?" He sounded a little fearful of the truth.

Like me.

"Nothing!" Abby blurted, then hung her head. "Nothing intentional. I swear!"

I'd never seen a person more torn, though I was torn myself.

As a kid, I'd been taught to avoid magic at all costs. But I'd also been taught to stand up for what was right. To fight for the truth, even when it hurt. To help, to protect, and to think for myself.

And just like that, my mental scales tipped.

I found myself growling at Ingo. *Hear her out.*

His eyebrows jumped up, but he nodded slowly.

We both waited, giving Abby time and space.

The whole time, my bear growled to me, reminding me, *Whatever she says, you hear her out too.*

Chapter Twelve

ABBY

I squirmed in my seat, wishing I hadn't been so defensive. But there was a good reason for that. I was guilty as hell, albeit unintentionally.

I hung my head in the blazing spotlight of Ingo's inquiring eyes. "Nothing I was aware of. I swear!"

"It's not an accusation, Abby." His voice was soft, even apologetic. "I'm just trying to understand what's going on."

That made two of us. Or three, given the way Cooper sat on the edge of his seat.

I studied my hands for a long time, half hoping Ingo would abandon the topic. But he was right to ask, and I knew it. Claire was right too, about talking being better than pretending.

I glanced at Cooper. If he could talk through the hard stuff, maybe I could too.

I took a deep breath, then started very, very quietly.

"I have magic. I know I do. But I've always done my best to suppress it."

Cooper nodded along, while Ingo's look was uncomprehending.

"Why wouldn't you use it?"

"Because it comes from my father, and I refuse to be anything like him. In any way. No matter what it takes." My voice cracked a little. Then I jutted my chin. "If you met him, you'd understand."

To Ingo's credit, he didn't ask. He sure looked like he wanted to, though.

And, damn. I found myself burning to explain. To finally get it off my chest. *My mother took off when I was a baby, and unlike my sisters, I didn't have a great dad to fill in the gaps.*

Lots of gaps. Chasms, more like.

But expanding on all that would be complaining, and I'd vowed to move on from bitterness. Claire deserved better. So I stuck to the point.

"But sometimes, a little magic slips through. Without my noticing, even. That's what must have happened when I made that ax for Kevin." I gulped. "It's been happening more lately."

Cooper's expression was impossible to decipher, and I ached to read his thoughts.

Ingo leaned closer. "What kind of magic?"

I kept my eyes on his. How much did I dare reveal to a man whose job required him to report on supernatural activity? On the other hand, Ingo was a good man who'd chosen to overlook a few things when it came to the interests of our family versus the interests of his job. But how much could he afford to disregard?

"Elemental magic," I finally whispered. "You know — earth, air, fire, water."

"All four?" Cooper asked, looking pained.

Oh, I was definitely pushing his limits here.

"Just earth... and a little bit of fire." I did my best to make it sound insignificant.

"Earth, as in...?" Cooper asked.

"Let me guess," Ingo interjected. "Metals."

I nodded, keeping my eyes down.

"A hephto... er, hephaesto—" Ingo struggled with the official term.

"Hephaestid," I whispered.

The word stemmed from Hephaestus, the Greek god of fire, blacksmithing, and forges. I loved the idea of a god dedicated to blacksmiths, but I'd always denied having any such powers.

Until lately.

Ingo dropped his voice to a whisper. "So, you think some magic slipped into the ax you made?"

"It must have," I admitted.

Over the years, I'd erected a brick wall against the magic that pulsed inside me. But some snuck through, especially when I was worked up. And I'd definitely been worked up the day I'd made Kevin's ax.

Lately, though, that magic had been flowing more freely. And, yikes. What did that say about the axes I was making now? All I intended was for them to be effective in firefighting — but what if someone used them for a different purpose?

Happily, Ingo seemed focused on Kevin's ax...for now.

"So, what exactly is that ax capable of?" he asked.

I bit my lip. "I'm not sure."

Silence weighed over us, heavy as lead.

Finally, Ingo eased back and flashed a tight smile.

"One of many things I've learned from Pippa is when to call it a night." He grabbed the bill, paid the whole amount despite our protests, then leaned in, serious again. "Thanks for the info. I'll take it from here." He gave me a pointed look. "Call it my case now, okay?"

I hated men telling me how to run my life. But Ingo had saved my sister from vampires. He'd helped save our ranch. He would risk his life for my daughter, I knew.

Also, I was a blacksmith. He was an agent in supernatural law enforcement. It was pretty clear whose jurisdiction this fell under.

So, no protest. Just a slightly forced nod.

Ingo stood to go, and we followed. Outside, he thumped Cooper's shoulder fondly. The force would have sent me reeling, though Cooper barely moved.

"Let's make next time sooner," Cooper agreed. "You know, to use the chance while we can."

Ingo's eyebrows shot up. "You're not planning on staying past this fire season?"

My heart jumped into my throat.

Cooper glanced at me, and a tsunami of emotions swirled between us. Then he tore his gaze away, and I looked at my boots.

"I guess we'll see," was all he said.

"For the record, my vote is for you to stay." Ingo chuckled.

My vote too, though, unlike Ingo, I didn't voice it.

Ingo drove off with a wave, leaving me alone in the dark lot. Well, with Cooper, but dark thoughts dragged me into a lonely cave of doubt.

Why someone had been messing with the vortexes, I didn't know. But they had used the ax I'd forged, so it was partly my fault. I'd forged magic into that ax. Magic with a dark side, I feared, despite the luck it had brought. Dark magic someone now sought to exploit. But who? How? Why?

The questions assailed me, a hail of piercing arrows from every side. . . except one. The side where Cooper stood.

When he touched my arm, I blinked. And for a moment, I felt warm. Comforted. In the storm of my inner turmoil, someone had my back.

A very big, very badass someone. Someone who cared.

I gulped at the unfamiliar feeling, then looked up.

"Don't beat yourself up about it," he murmured.

Huh. Since when were bears so good at reading minds?

I managed a thin smile. "Hard habit to break."

The moment I said it, I cringed. God, that made me sound so damn. . . weak.

A few quiet seconds ticked by, followed by something completely unexpected.

A hug.

A great big, cautious one, because Cooper knew me by now. Moving slowly, gently, he reeled me into the world's warmest, safest, most impenetrable hug. I slid into it the way I would slide into the creek on a warm summer night.

For the first second, I was tense as a bow. Then I exhaled.

And exhaled and exhaled, letting everything go. Everything but the feel of his soft flannel shirt. . . his clean, woodsy scent. . . his steady, beating heart.

My pulse slowed to match his. I nestled closer. . . and closer. The way I felt when I mentally crawled into fire to hide from reality, I felt now. The difference was that fire crackled dangerously, cutting me off from the world. But this hug — this bear hug, ha-ha — tugged me into a peaceful, friendly place where I wasn't alone.

Then, *zoom!* A car rushed by on the adjacent road, blaring its horn at a truck. They were gone within seconds, but we slowly pulled apart.

I took a deep breath, tempted to duck back into Cooper's arms. Instead, I stepped away, dragging my hands along his arms.

"Um, thanks. I needed that," I admitted, trying not to meet his eyes.

Failing, and glad for it, because they were two glowing gold coins, an unexpected treasure in this small adventure of a night out.

"Happy to help," he rumbled quietly.

I stood watching his eyes glow — and wow, sparkle — for the next long, quiet minute, imprinting the wonder of it all into my mind.

This man had been kind, just because. He didn't exploit my moment of weakness. He'd helped me move past it.

I cleared my throat, erasing the thank-you on the tip of my tongue. I'd already said that, right?

"Time to go, I guess." He gestured to his car in a way that invited me to come up with a better idea.

I had dozens, but I couldn't get any of them out. So, we went.

I kicked myself the whole drive back to the fire station, where we slid out of his pickup and stood by my car.

Last chance, a voice screamed in my mind.

I pursed my lips. Cooper stuck his hands in his pockets. Neither of us wanted this night to end, but habit drove us through the motions.

"Thanks. That was really nice." His voice was low and controlled, but his eyes still glowed.

I nodded. "Yeah, it was."

I didn't want to go. I didn't want this night to end.

"Glad you got back safely," I said, then tried covering up. "I mean, all of you. I mean..."

His lips curled, and his eyes twinkled. "I'm glad too."

I clutched my keys, reminding myself of all the bad choices I'd ever made. Telling myself to get in my car and drive away, fast.

My lip wobbled as I looked up — and up.

"I'd better go," I whispered, though I didn't budge.

"I guess you should," he murmured, just as quietly and just as immobile.

I nodded because, there. We were in agreement.

Agreement about something else too, as it turned out. Like a kiss.

Because instead of leaving, I rolled onto my toes and looped my arms around his neck. Cooper dipped at the very same moment, and our lips met.

My soul sighed, and every muscle relaxed — except the ones that made my lips dance over his. Giving. Getting. Exploring. Then a few other muscles kicked in, making my hands caress his broad back.

Our noses bumped, so I angled my head. And, oh. That was even better. Warmer. Rougher, then softer when my lips reached the small square of skin framed by his beard. That left my cheek nuzzling his beard, where the prickly sensation was just right.

I cupped his face, deepening the kiss. An amazing, confusing kiss. No fireworks, no jolt of lust. Just a feeling of rightness. Of connection. Of home.

Cooper murmured something, changing the angle, and whoa. *There* was the jolt of lust. I slid my free hand down his back and pressed closer. And, yep. *There* were the fireworks.

The whole deal. Everything I'd ever felt with Jay, but more — way more — without the warning flags.

Hot, pulsing need filled my veins, and Cooper made a little choked sound. I pressed forward, feeling him go hard. Wanting that, exactly that. Needing it...

Then I stiffened, remembering Claire waiting for me at home.

I dipped my chin slightly, breaking the kiss but staying close. I panted into his chest for the next minute or so, and he held me the whole time.

"Claire..." I whispered, wondering if it was an excuse.

Just a little longer, a man like Jay would say. *She'll be fine.*

Cooper nodded, proving he was not that man.

"Got to tuck her in, huh?" he said, respecting the sanctity of that. Encouraging it, even.

I eased away, nodding. "And read her a story."

He grinned. "Then another, then another..."

I laughed. Boy, did he know the deal.

"Always one more for her," I said.

He smiled, then pulled me in for a quick hug. "Well, read her one for me. Maybe something about a bear?"

I thought over our options. "*Goodnight Moon* has a bear."

"That'll do." In the muffled universe of his hug, I felt his chest rise and fall in a sigh. Then he gently released me. "See you tomorrow."

My heart stuttered at that reminder of the real world, where I would have to stay on guard. A place where I had to be impatient and annoyed. Where I had to make cutting remarks to ensure everyone knew I was not to be messed with. Where I would have to—

I trailed off there. Did I really have to? This parallel world was a much kinder, gentler place. A dangerous place, too, because the pain set off by letting down my guard was much, much worse.

I stepped away quickly and all but jumped into my car.

"Bye," Cooper whispered, pivoting aside.

I waved, unable to speak past the lump in my throat. Then I drove off.

∞∞∞∞

"Well, that was fun," Pippa said once I'd arrived back home. Claire was already in her mermaid pajamas and in the bathroom, getting ready for bed. Then Pippa waggled her eyebrows. "And, wow. If Ingo didn't exist, I would *so* go for Cooper."

"Yeah? I guess I didn't notice."

97

She snorted. "Ha. You noticed, and you know it. I saw your whole body notice, in fact. And those goo-goo eyes you made at him—"

"I did not make goo-goo eyes!"

But, damn. My cheeks heated, and my inner vixen was still yowling for him.

"I nearly called you to offer Claire a sleepover at our place. You know, so you and Cooper could—"

I cut Pippa off before she verbalized precisely what I'd fantasized about.

"Not necessary. Not now, not ever," I growled.

I hated how Pippa's eyes pitied me.

"All good, all good," she covered up quickly, aiming for a lighter tone. "Have a good night." She bid Claire goodnight, then headed for the door, where she paused.

I braced myself for sisterly advice — something along the lines of *You only live once* or some such nonsense.

But Pippa just pointed to the table. "Oh — Erin picked up the mail. There's a letter for you."

With that, she headed out into the night. I listened to her footsteps scuff, then fade as she walked toward the converted barn where she and Ingo lived.

"I'm ready, Mom!" Claire hollered down the stairs.

"I'll be right there, sweetie," I called, reaching for the letter. Something official-looking. Something from Claire's school, maybe? Or a bill?

Law Office of Watson, Hernandez, and Gray, the printed envelope said.

I frowned. Now what? Something about our property value or water rights?

I pulled out the letter and started to read. *Dear Ms. Carson...*

Seconds later, the breath went out of me, and my knees shook.

Our law office represents Mr. Jay Wilson in matters pertaining to the custody and welfare of your daughter...

All the blood drained out of my cheeks.

Mr. Wilson has decided to pursue legal action seeking joint custody...

Over my dead body! I nearly shouted as I speed-read the next parts.

...petition being prepared...filed with family court...proposed custody schedule...

My hands shook. How could this be happening?

Mr. Wilson wishes to establish a parenting arrangement that ensures he can actively participate in Claire's life and provide her with love, guidance, and support...

Support, my ass. Jay was broke. And love? Jay only loved himself. As for guidance, I wouldn't trust him to lead a blind horse away from a ditch. The man had never shown any interest in Claire's well-being before. Why now?

The paper wrinkled under my grip as I read the closing line.

We appreciate your attention to this matter and hope to work toward a resolution that is in Claire's best interest.

Claire's best interest was to have just enough contact with her biological father to understand why she was better off without him. And that, she'd already had.

Under the signature was an addendum.

Enclosure: Notice of Intent to File for Custody.

My pulse raced. Fuck. Was Jay serious?

"Are you coming?" Claire called from the top of the stairs.

I thrust the paper behind my back. She couldn't see from there, but I was that panicked.

"Yep. Coming."

I stuffed the letter on a high shelf and went upstairs to read a bedtime story. *Goodnight Moon*, with special emphasis on the bear. On the outside, I was the calm, loving mother Claire knew, rhyming lines like *Room* and *balloon*... *Mush* and *hush*... *Kittens* and *mittens*...

"Bear and Claire," she giggled.

I hugged her tightly.

On the inside, I was raging — and thinking a mile a minute. Jay didn't have the money to hire a lawyer. He didn't have the interest either.

Had he found out about an inheritance that came with the stipulation that he finally clean up his act?

Fat chance.

Had he found God and decided to repent for his ways?

I really, really doubted it.

There had to be something in all this for Jay — and that *something* wasn't the pleasure of Claire's company. Something tangible, like money. Enough to recoup the cost of a lawyer.

But what? Why?

"Goodnight everyone and everywhere," Claire helped me finish. Then she hugged Roscoe. "Goodnight, Roscoe. Goodnight, Mommy."

"Goodnight, baby. Sweet dreams."

She smiled. "Will you weave me a good one?"

Ah, if only I could.

I stood and kissed her. "I'll do my best, honey."

Chapter Thirteen

ABBY

A fretful week passed, and the metal shop was my sole refuge. If only the rest of the world were a place where problems could be solved with a few slams of the hammer.

The shop was my happy place. There, I could control things, from the temperature of my forge to the number and force of hammer blows that went into shaping the axes.

At work, I could pretend the outside world didn't exist.

I also had the world's best assistant there. Cooper, who'd been teaching me what good company a bear shifter could be. With him, it was easy to lose myself in a steady rhythm.

Bang!

Wham!

Bang!

Wham!

"Up," I murmured.

He struck one more time, then waited while I reheated the metal.

We'd fallen into a perfect rhythm over the past few days. So perfect, we barely spoke — in a good way. Instead, we communicated with our eyes. With hammer taps. With silent, barely perceptible gestures. We were that in tune.

On the flip side, our bodies were a little too good at silent communication. Every time we bumped, my body heated. Every time I paused to wipe away sweat, images of a different hot and sweaty activity poured into my imagination. Every time Cooper came close, my toes curled. One time, I backed right into his groin, and a wild, untamed part of me yowled before I stepped clear.

"Oh, I should warn you," Cooper said at one point. "My mother is passing through town today, and she might drop in to say hi." He made a face, like he was really, really embarrassed.

"Your mother, huh?"

He blushed. "Yes, because I *give her great joy.*" He made air quotes. "I'll keep it as short as possible."

Ha. I knew a good son when I saw one.

"Oh, and do me a favor," Cooper went on.

I tilted my head.

"Promise me you'll banish any nicknames you might hear from your memory."

I broke out laughing. I might even look forward to it.

"No promises."

He grinned, and we went back to work.

So, when the bell over the shop door chimed about an hour later, I turned, expecting to see Cooper's mother — a stout woman with warm brown eyes, no doubt, and an easy smile, just like her son.

Instead, I spotted a tall, wiry man with long silver hair pulled into a loose ponytail.

His eyes landed on me with a thump, and I wobbled backward. Then he strode over with that commanding presence of his. Matt, Pablo, and Bob all shrank back, staring. A good thing too — that kept them from noticing that little bits of metal in the shop slid forward to pay homage to their master.

Or, more accurately, my father.

If Ingo had been there, he might have whispered, *Warlock. Hephaestid.*

Walt opened his glass office door but didn't venture out. Neither did Louie, for all he loved to growl and bark. The only two souls who didn't instinctively cower were Cooper and me.

I kept my hammer clutched at my side. Cooper bristled, and a wave of moss-scented air wafted through the shop. He was that close to shifting.

"Abby." My father grinned, stepping toward me.

The grin wasn't for me, but my name — the only part of me my father took pride in. Abby, as in Edward Abbey, one of the few humans my father admired. He also loved that our last name happened to be the same as Rachel Carson's, the pioneering environmentalist.

Yeah, my father was a real hoot that way.

He powered up to me — *right* up to me. He would have crowded me the way he always did if Cooper hadn't stepped in the way. Towering at about the same height, they glared at each other like a couple of Rottweilers in the split second before all hell broke loose.

The air grew thick with magic, and the hair on the back of Cooper's neck thickened.

I reached out to touch Cooper's back, whispering, "All good."

A lie, because my father was never good news. I even peeked behind him in case the law was hot on his heels.

But, no. Not this time, at least.

Thanks to Cooper, my heart rate didn't skyrocket, but it did thump hard enough to rattle every corner of my body. All the more so when I noticed the quiver in Cooper's arm.

He'd rested his sledgehammer on his shoulder when my father approached. Now, an electric crackle filled the air, and Cooper's muscles bulged.

Dammit. My father was wielding magic, trying to force Cooper to put down the weapon — er, tool.

My father's eyes blazed into Cooper's, demanding submission. But the stubborn bear wouldn't budge. That sledgehammer sure wanted to, though. I could feel it heat under the force of my father's magic.

Bits of steel started sliding across the floor, and screws started rattling in drawers against the wall. Tools hanging against the wall leaned toward him at a gravity-defying angle.

"Cut it out, Ed," I ordered in a low, even voice.

The man had always insisted I call him by his first name. So, no, we didn't exactly share a warm father-daughter relationship.

The air grew heavy with magic. My father's nostrils flared. Sweat broke out on Cooper's brow. Their eyes glowed and lasered into each other's.

"Stop that right now, Dad," I growled before this turned into a full-fledged standoff.

My father's eyes flicked to me, and I socked him with my hardest look.

Finally, the air stopped crackling, and Cooper lurched forward when the invisible pressure halted.

His wide-eyed glance asked, *That's your father?*

I sighed. Unfortunately, yes. Not that I said that aloud.

"What are you doing here?" I demanded.

"Can't a guy check in on his daughter once in a while?"

I crossed my arms. "Is that what you're doing?"

Because Claire, I'd noticed, hadn't made his list.

The thought made my heart ache, but it was better that way. She already had one self-centered, unhinged supernatural trying to intrude on her life — Jay. She didn't need a second one.

Ed shrugged. "Yes, to check in. And also to..." He trailed off with a look that said, *Walls have ears, you know.*

Ha. Especially the bear-sized wall standing a few inches away, ready to claw my father to shreds.

I'd never been more inclined to hug Cooper. But I couldn't. Not with my father there.

"Out here." I waved to the back door.

Cooper took a step to follow, but I put a hand on his chest.

"I'll make this quick," I whispered, hoping it was true.

That night at the pizza place, Cooper's eyes had glowed softly. The light that shone in them now was about a thousand watts higher and hotter. More dangerous. He crossed his arms, still glaring at my father.

I patted his chest softly. "Thanks. I mean it. But I have to do this. It won't take long."

This was hearing out my father's latest rant, then sending him on his way before I got dragged into one of his crazy schemes.

Cooper leaned forward, pushing against my hand. Did he even feel it there?

"Are you sure?" His eyes searched mine.

Sure about getting rid of my father? Absolutely. Yes.

Sure about that hug I owed him later? That too.

I nodded, then followed my father outside. Cooper remained in the doorway, every stiff hair on his body communicating, *Try something, and you're dead.*

"Stupid bear," my father muttered when I covered the twenty steps to his side.

My blood pressure doubled. "Do you ever have anything nice to say about anyone?"

And, ouch. I winced at my own pot-calling-the-kettle-black moment.

Maybe I took more after my father than I'd thought. Or maybe I was just jaded. Either way, I made a mental note. *Say nice things to other people. Especially Cooper.*

My father shrugged. "I tell it like it is."

I crossed my arms. "No, you judge based on one look."

Ouch again. I made a second mental note.

Then I made an exasperated sound. "Good to see you and all..." (another lie) "...but as you can see, I'm at work. You know, work? The way I earn a living?"

Ed snorted. "You're just caught in the rat race like the rest of them."

Them was the general population, for whom my father had nothing but contempt.

But there was no arguing with him, so I bit back my cutting reply.

"The point is, I can't just walk out whenever I want, so please get to the point."

My father frowned. "Since when are you so begrudging?"

I snorted. "Since the time you dropped me off at Aunt Carrie's when I was seven. Or maybe the second or third time, when I begged you not to. Even when I told you about Uncle Carl..."

My voice wavered there, and even my father made a face. Carl had been a bad man. I'd avoided the worst by pushing the dresser up against my door every night. Carl's own daughters hadn't been as "lucky."

"I made sure he got what he deserved," Ed grunted.

"Yeah — five months later, when you came to pick me up. Great parenting."

"What kind of parent would I be if I let all the fools out there make a mess of the world?"

There were earth-huggers, and there were eco-warriors. My father had long since crossed both those lines. The ends justified the means, even when the collateral damage included human lives. So, eco-terrorist was more like it, with arson and sabotage as his favorite tools. A blaze at a GMO lab, cut gondola lines at a ski resort expansion. . . not to mention his special passion for halting mining operations. . .

I sighed. Pippa's father was a firefighter. Erin's designed custom motorcycles.

Mine was on the government's watch list.

I threw up my hands before my mind went any further down the long, ugly list of Ed's crimes.

"Why are you here?"

"Because something is wrong." My father took me by both shoulders. From the corner of my eye, I spotted Cooper lunging forward, barely restraining himself.

The man deserved a medal, but all I'd ever hung around his neck was scorn.

I made yet another mental note.

"Something is definitely wrong. I can sense it," my father emphasized.

My heart swelled. Had my father finally paused his quixotic quests long enough to put me first, like Erin's and Pippa's fathers always did? Had he sensed me fretting about Jay? Was he finally coming through for me?

I blinked, holding back happy tears.

"It's that damned Edelweiss Corporation again," Ed continued.

My bubble burst, crashed, and burned.

"Edelweiss?" I fumed.

"Yep. More development. Right here in your hometown." He swept a hand over the surrounding buttes and mesas.

I loved Sedona. I really did. I hated development. But at that moment, all I saw was red.

"You're here for *that*?" I hissed.

Cooper took a step closer, ready to charge.

My father blinked in a way that asked, *What else would I be here for?*

Not me, that was for sure. Not for his granddaughter either. I cursed my stupid, wounded heart.

Twin flames lit in my father's eyes, and he shuffled closer. "You mean, there's another big corporation trying to muscle in here?"

The air started pulsing with energy again, and he rubbed his hands eagerly, itching for a fight.

"No!" I barked, though *Probably* was more like it. Sedona was always under siege from developers, including a warlock who'd targeted my own ranch. But that wasn't the point right now.

I shook my head, trying to clear it. "You know what, Ed? I've had it."

He nodded briskly. "I know how you feel. They stole this land from the Native Americans. They stole it from the small-time farmers. Now they want to steal some more, so they can build their goddamn strip malls—"

I gripped my hair to keep from shoving him away.

"No, I've had it with *you*," I cut in. "I know I'm not as important as all this." I waved at the stunning scenery just outside our back lot. "But a daughter should be that important to her own father, at least once in a while."

He frowned. "How is this about you?"

I bared my teeth in a snarl. "Because for once — just once — I deserve to have you care about me. But you've never managed that. You've never even tried."

He held up his arms. "I do care. That's why I—"

"Land yourself in jail? Abandon me with friends and relatives because you have better things to do?"

"It's not like your mother did any better," he grumbled.

Which was why I resolved to give her the same speech the next time she came sauntering through town. But he didn't need to know that.

"I'm talking about you, Ed, and the things in your control."

"Yeah, well, these developers fall right into that category." He dropped his voice. "They've been bought out by a couple of magic-wielders. A whole fucking family of them."

I could have screamed. At least that was one family that was whole.

"Then bring it to the goddamn ADMSA," I snipped. That was the Agency for the Detection and Monitoring of Supernatural Activity, as my father well knew. He was on their watch list, too. "I even know one of their agents. Want me to put you in touch?"

It was more threat than offer, and he knew it.

But he didn't know that agent was Ingo, who lived on my ranch with my sister Pippa. Oh, and that Erin's man was a former agent too.

I'd never been so tempted to invite my father over for a family meal. Then again, I'd never been tempted to invite my father over for a family meal, ever.

"Another fucking government agency?" he spat. "You can't trust any of them. Did I teach you nothing?"

He had the nerve to sound disappointed, and that was the final straw.

"Oh, you managed to teach me plenty. How much it hurts to be alone. How bad hunger burns. How far the future is when just getting through a day is a marathon." Cooper inched forward as my voice rose. "But there was so much more you *didn't* teach me about. Like what love feels like. How trust works. What it means to rely on someone."

Cooper moved again, and just like that, a definition for each of those formed, crystal clear, in my mind. Love. Trust. Reliability.

The thought took the wind out of my sails, and I gasped for air. I was truly finished with Ed — and desperate for him to leave, but too wired to make that happen without creating an even bigger scene.

Enter Cooper, my own private Ivanhoe.

"I—" my father started.

"You're ready to leave?" Cooper cut in. "Good. I'll show you out."

Technically, we were *out* — in the back lot — but I'd never loved a man as much as I did in that moment.

Okay, okay. I'd never loved a man, period. Jay was infatuation. But here and now, looking into Cooper's deep, safe brown eyes. . .

My pulse skipped, and my racing heart slowed a tick.

"Can a man not talk to his daughter—" my father started.

"Not when he talks like that. No, sir." Cooper pointed to the door.

My heart fluttered. Tough but polite. I would have to travel to Wyoming someday to see if every man was raised that way there or just the Lundsven boys.

My father raised his hand and curled his fingers, stirring up another spell.

I made a chopping motion, one for every word. "Don't you dare, Ed. Don't. You. Dare."

My father's eyes — moss-green like mine, but not at all like mine — flashed, then dimmed.

"It saddens me to see you like this, Abby," he finally said, turning for the door.

I snorted. "It should sadden you that you only see it now, Ed. It's been years."

With that, I turned to the grandiose scenery, the endless blue sky.

Behind me, two sets of heavy footsteps sounded — my father's and Cooper's. The back door of the metal shop creaked open, then slammed shut.

I counted the seconds, one for every step it took my father to stalk through the shop and exit out the front. A car engine roared to life, then peeled out onto the main road. Angry beeps followed, and I closed my eyes.

Minutes passed before the back door opened, more quietly this time. Without a word, Cooper came up beside me and slowly, carefully, slid an arm over my shoulders. The weight of it ought to have pressed me into a slouch, but instead, his warmth slipped over to me, giving me the energy to stand tall.

We stood there for a long time, neither of us uttering a word.

Chapter Fourteen

COOPER

I stayed in the back lot with Abby for a good ten minutes after her father left. Out of sight, but clearly not out of her mind. Abby balled her hands into fists that quivered at her sides. Then she blinked a few times, tilted her head back, and closed her eyes.

My dad did that too. The tough-guy substitute for crying, I supposed.

He would like Abby, I decided. Witch or no witch.

For some reason, the thought made me smile. I hid it before she noticed, though.

"I'll just check the forge," I finally murmured, giving her space.

It was hot — plenty hot — by the time she joined me five minutes later. Her face was blotchy, her eyes trained on the floor.

I handed her a hammer, shoved the ax head a little deeper into the flames, and gripped my sledgehammer, ready to begin. She was like my father in that way too. Work was the best medicine. In the months after we'd lost Peter, my dad had built an entire barn.

Abby's throat bobbed, and her eyes met mine.

I dipped my chin, acknowledging her silent thanks. Then I nudged her.

"Fifteen axes down, five to go," I murmured.

It was amazing how far we'd come and how fast. Abby had even found the time to finish the etching on most of those. Several were decorated with flames, others with more abstract, swirling designs, and no two were alike. One even sported a snarling dragon head — a hat tip to her mother, maybe?

After a nod — and a long exhale — she took the hammer. Then she moved our latest ax head to the anvil and got back to work.

Bang! Her hammer punished the metal with twice the power of my twenty-pounder. And punished and punished. . .

The next time she stopped to reheat the metal, I caught Matt and Pablo exchanging concerned looks. I pretended not to notice. Clearly, this was not one of those times when *talking* beat *pretending.*

Abby didn't let up for hours, not even for a lunch break. When the shop door opened with a new arrival, she tensed.

"Brace yourself," I whispered as an older woman walked to Walt's office, stooping to pet Louie.

Walt pointed me out, and I waved as she looked over.

My mother clapped her hands to her heart before hurrying over. "My baby! There you are!"

"Baby?" Matt chuckled.

I sighed. I could live to eighty or ninety and still be a baby to my mom. Regardless, I returned her huge hug and let her rock me from side to side, like she had when I was a kid.

"Hi, Mom."

Ten years earlier, I might have found the open affection embarrassing. Now, I knew to cherish it — especially after witnessing Abby and her father. My mom loved the hell out of me, and that was a true gift.

So I hugged and hugged and told her *I love you* back.

"Oh, Cooper. You give me such joy, you know," she whispered, as she always did.

"I'm glad, Mom."

Abby, standing to one side, went from startled to amused.

I waggled my eyebrows, indicating *I did warn you.*

Abby grinned openly.

That was another plus of my mother's visits. She had a way of lifting everyone's mood. So, totally worth it, even if I got teased mercilessly afterward.

My mother let go, looked at me, then hugged me again. Finally, she eased away, though that took some effort. She'd always had a catch-and-release policy when it came to us kids, but ever since losing Peter...

"Nice to see you," I said gently.

It was. It really was. But doubly so for a mother who'd lost one of her kids. Another reason I would endure any amount of hugging she wanted — or needed.

My mother proceeded to stage two of her greeting, patting me on the arm in the same way she patted my eldest sister's baby on the bottom whenever she got to hold the little guy, which was a lot.

"So good to see you," she whispered again, then moved her pat to my shoulder and looked around. "Well? Aren't you going to introduce us?"

That was stage three of Mom's greeting, and it encompassed anyone in a hundred-foot radius. Mom *loved* meeting the people I spent time with.

She turned clockwise, so I introduced her to Bob first, then Walt (who she'd already met, but never mind), then Matt and Pablo, and finally...

"This is Abby." My voice went a little thick there.

"Abby!" my mother exclaimed as if she was meeting someone I'd told her all about — which I absolutely, positively had not — and threw her arms around my boss.

Abby stood stiffly, arms trapped at her sides, gripping her hammer tightly.

"Um...Mom..." I warned.

"Oh, shush, child," she chided softly.

"Not everyone likes hugging strangers," I pointed out.

"Nonsense. Everyone needs a hug."

I didn't point out that if she wanted to be consistent, she ought to hug Walt, Bob, Matt, and Pablo too.

Finally, she released Abby and clapped her hands together. "A female blacksmith. I love it."

Abby was still recovering from the hug, so I filled in for her. "She was a firefighter too."

And, oops. My mother snatched her into an even tighter hug. Every firefighter was a member of the family as far as she was concerned.

"Oh, that's wonderful! Which crew?"

"Dakota Creek crew," Abby wheezed from under the hug. "In Colorado."

"Oh! Under Greg Martin?"

Abby looked up from her trapped location by my mother's shoulder. "You know him?"

"Of course I do. We met ages ago. Wait. You aren't that lovely daughter of his, are you?"

I winced, because that would be Pippa, and being compared to her was probably like being compared to Peter. You had no chance of ever meeting that standard.

Then my mother saved the day by correcting herself. "Oh, wait. You must be the lovely stepdaughter he always gushes about."

Abby's eyes went from guarded to surprised to. . . happy and a little moist.

"I guess I am."

"Wonderful, wonderful. What a pleasure," my mother said, absolutely sincere.

I hid a grin. Good old Mom.

"Pleasure's all mine," Abby said.

And, wow. A rare compliment, coming from Abby. The shine in her eyes said she meant it too.

My mother turned back to me. "I thought you were here to fight fires. But isn't this lovely! You can help Uncle Rory even more next time you're home."

God, I hoped not. Working with Abby wasn't half as bad as I'd expected. Actually, I'd come to enjoy it. . . a lot. But that had more to do with Abby than the forge.

"Oh. Dad sends his love," my mother continued. "So do Helen and Christopher and Hattie and Parker and. . ."

She rattled through the whole list — all my siblings, cousins, aunts, uncles. . . Most of whom made up Wyoming's Pine Ridge fire crew at one time or another.

Abby's eyes went wider and wider.

"Greta sends her love too," my mother added with a heavy undertone.

Abby's face fell, and I rushed to set the record straight.

"Did she, or are you just saying that?" I asked.

My mother flashed that *Mother knows best* expression she did so well. "Well, Greta would send her love if you sent yours."

I ran a hand through my sweaty hair. One of these days, my mother would stop trying to fix me up with the nice she-bear from next door. Greta made tasty cookies, and she liked to share. She wasn't moody, and she didn't cuss.

But she didn't hammer steel or weld or operate a forge. I would bet she couldn't dig a decent fire line either.

My eyes half closed, and I inhaled Abby's dandelion and huckleberry scent.

For a few blissful seconds, I imagined myself in a different time and place. Then, with a little shake, I opened my eyes.

My mother's eyes drifted from me to Abby and back again.

"Tell Greta and the rest of the neighbors I said hi," I answered quickly. There. That ought to clarify things for Abby.

"Well, I'm a little late for lunch, but I stopped off for some snacks." My mother pointed to the huge bakery box she'd left by Walt's office. "Can you take a quick break?"

I'd been expecting that. The only thing that gave my mother more joy than seeing her children was seeing them eat... and eat and eat. Preferably home cooking, but takeout — a total taboo when we'd been kids — was okay too.

"That would be great, thanks."

"Perfect. Would you like to join us?" My mother turned to Abby, whose eyes filled with a dozen emotions at once. Hope, joy, fear...

"I brought plenty," my mother added quickly.

Ha. That went without saying when it came to my mother.

"Um... I'd—" Abby started.

Walt leaned out of the office with a phone in his hand, one hand over the receiver. "Hey, Abby. Come on over. It's that woman — the one who wants the brazier." His stern expression said, *Don't mess this up.*

Abby made a face, then stuck on a smile for my mother. "Thanks, but I have the feeling this will take a while."

"What should I do while you're gone?" I asked.

"Keep away from my anvil?" she joked.

I stuck up my hands. "I wouldn't dare."

She flashed a wry grin.

"Seriously, though," I went on. "What can I do that's useful?"

She thought it over. "Maybe work on some handles? You know woodworking, right?"

My mother patted me on the shoulder. "He's an excellent woodworker."

"Thanks, Mom," I sighed. Nothing better than a sweeping endorsement from your own mother.

Still, my eyes lit up, all golden retriever who'd just spotted a ball. Abby trusted me. She'd even given me my own job. An important one. I could finally prove myself to her...

She pointed. "You'll find some hickory over there, and Pablo can give you any tools you need."

"Great." I couldn't believe my luck.

"Abby!" Walt gestured impatiently.

She sighed and turned toward him. "Sorry. Gotta go. It was nice to meet you," she told my mother.

"Nice to meet you too. Tell Greg hello. Oh, and grab something on your way out."

"I will, thanks." Abby smiled and walked toward Walt.

My eyes followed, and my soul stretched with every step she took, until, like a rubber band, it snapped back.

"Nice girl," my mother whispered.

Fascinating was more like it. The more I learned, the more I wanted to find out.

"She is," I murmured, trying to suppress the longing in my voice.

Chapter Fifteen

ABBY

I stalked over to Walt, not at all pleased. It wasn't often that I got invited "out," even if that was just snacks in the metal shop. The urge to accept the invitation was even more rare, but this time, I really wanted to stay. Dinner with Cooper had been great, and I wouldn't have minded more downtime with him — even with his mother there. Besides, seeing his mother exude unequivocal love switched on my inner anthropologist. Normal families were a source of endless fascination to me.

But no such luck. Not with Walt gesturing me over.

"Yes... Absolutely..." He nodded to the person on the other end of the line. "Not a problem."

I stomped to the threshold of Walt's office just as he concluded the call. "Perfect. I'll send her over right now."

I bristled. Whomever he was sending had better not be me.

Walt jotted an address on a slip of paper and handed it to me. "That was that woman — Miss Steinmeier. You know, the one who wants the brazier."

"The one who'll get her brazier *next month,*" I corrected.

The witch, I nearly added, but I kept that to myself.

Walt shook his head. "You're ahead of schedule with the axes, thanks to Cooper's help."

True. But we were on a roll. Why stop now?

"We can't afford to lose her," Walt said grimly.

For one fire pit? I frowned. Could witches cast mind-spells over the phone?

He rattled a set of keys. "Here, take the van. Whatever she wants, make it happen. You got that?"

"Listen, Walt—"

My boss stuck up a hand, definitely not in an indulgent mood. "The axes are important, but this is too. Now, go." Every line in his face said, *Don't mess this up.* Then he lightened up a little. "She says she has faith in you. I have faith in you too."

Hmm. Was that Liselle's mind-bending, or did that come from the heart?

Still, it was like I'd told my father. A job was a job, and there was only so far I could push my boss. Also, Liselle was a third-class witch at best. I had nothing to fear from her. I just had to watch my step so she wouldn't figure *me* out.

A glance at the clock — two p.m. — had me hurrying along. If I was going to fit in this house call before picking up Claire from school, I had to get moving.

"Thanks so much," I said, selecting a cinnamon doughnut from the box Cooper's mother offered on my way out. At the door, I turned back to look at Cooper. Our eyes met one more time. And, oh. So much longing, so much said without uttering a word.

"Abby..." Walt grumbled.

Dammit. I did an about-face and marched to his van, munching the doughnut on the way.

The more I drove, the more bitter my mood became. First, my father, then having to turn down a nice invitation, and now this. I cursed all the rubbernecking tourists who drove at painfully slow speeds, and I grumbled at every McMansion and golf course I passed along Jacks Canyon Road. A golf course. With grass. In the desert.

I made a face. Okay, so maybe my values aligned with my father's in one small way.

My frown deepened as another thought struck me. Did witches play golf?

I mulled that over, only half concentrating on the road. When a pickup sped by in the opposite direction, something caught my eye, and I whipped around. I turned back to watch it in the rearview mirror, unable to make out whatever it was that had caught my attention before it faded out of sight.

Shifting in my seat, I did my best to focus on the task ahead. Several twists and turns later, I pulled up to the entrance of a gated cul-de-sac, where a security guy leaned out of a little shed.

"How can I help you?" he asked.

I checked the address Walt had scribbled down. Wow. Maybe he was right about hanging on to this customer, witch or no witch. The development screamed big money — really big money, judging by the way houses backed on to the immaculate golf course. The helicopter landing pad in the middle of the development was another clue. Whoever lived here had the cash to buy magnificent views and major privacy.

"I'm here to see Liselle Steinmeier," I said, going for an *I so belong here* vibe.

The guy glanced at the logo on the side of the van — so much for belonging here — and ran his eyes over a list. "Name?"

"Abby Carson."

He made a check mark, then pressed a button to retract the gate. "Third villa on the right."

Villa, indeed. I stared at the four-car garage, then parked in the vast, open space beside it. Shortly after, I rang the doorbell and stepped back, trying not to look awed. But, hell. The villa was a beauty, blending traditional adobe with modern lines and huge panes of glass that reflected Courthouse Butte. Not bad.

The door opened, and I half expected a uniformed butler to appear. But no. Just Liselle Steinmeier, the lady of the house. She might be a witch, but no black dress and pointy hat for her. More like fashion fit for the cover of a magazine, with her peacock-blue-and-white striped shirt and matching white pants. Tiny blue studs sparkled from her earlobes. Sapphires?

"Oh, hello! Thanks for dropping by!" She waved me in as if this were a social call.

Entering a witch's den was one reason I hesitated at the threshold. The other was the spotless white rug. I dragged my feet over the doormat six times, then followed her through the house. Cavernous rooms branched off both sides of the long hallway. Living room, parlor, study, office, music room, library, den...

I ran out of words for big rooms with impressive furniture, each sporting several couches with mountains of throw pillows. Lots and lots of throw pillows in every color of the rainbow.

Liselle Steinmeier — or her decorator — was definitely going for a bright, playful look.

The house was eerily quiet, though. Either everyone was out golfing, or Ms. Steinmeier lived alone.

Out golfing, I decided. Women like me might live alone — or as alone as a single parent got. But women like Liselle — young, rich, perfectly done up — had to have a dozen suitors to choose from, especially with a little magic to back them up. Famous race car drivers. CEOs. Up-and-coming artists. Fellow trust-fund babies...

I caught a faint whiff of leathery cologne, and *charming rodeo jock* ran through my mind. Then I spotted a leather couch and laughed the image out of my mind. If a woman like this ever had a fling with a guy like Jay, she sure as hell wouldn't invite him or his dirty boots into her house. She would take a walk on the wild side and follow him home to his trailer, which she would find quaint for the brief duration of their crash-and-burn affair.

I peeked into the massive kitchen. Not a cauldron in sight, nor a broom. That didn't put me at ease, though.

Eventually, we exited onto a terrace at the back.

"So, this is the spot." She pointed to four couches forming a square around a metal frame blackened by the ashes of a recent fire.

A brazier, in other words. I looked at my hostess.

"It's beautiful at sunset, and when the stars are out..." She looked around dreamily.

I nodded impatiently. Yeah, yeah. The stars shone over our ranch too. The point was the brazier.

"So, I see you already have one..." I tried moving things along.

"Yes, but I want another one. Exactly the same, but smaller, so it's portable."

I glanced around. The property was huge, with several nice spots for a fire. Also like our ranch, in fact. But one big fire pit suited any urge we got to sit around a fire under the stars. Why bother moving your fire around?

Unless, perchance, you were a witch.

I gulped, picturing her chanting over a fire. Could she summon spells that way?

My warlock father didn't, and neither did Erin or her father. Not even pyromancers like Greg and Pippa did. But there were many types of magic and different types of witches with very different powers. Maybe some needed fire to weave spells.

Then it hit me. Hadn't there been ashes near the dig marks at Airport Mesa?

My throat went dry. All my life, I'd done my best to distance myself from magic. Now, I half wished I knew more about that secret world.

I fumbled for my measuring tape and clipboard and started sketching before Liselle noticed my unease. "You want one identical to this?"

"Yes. Almost exactly. Those slots along the top edge are especially important. I love how they make the smoke swirl."

Did she just love how it looked, or did that feature play a role in casting spells?

She watched me closely for any reaction.

"Got it," I said as neutrally as possible, still sketching away.

I squatted for a better look, though my mind spun. Someone had recently disturbed the vortex at Airport Mesa. Someone who'd started a fire *and* used the lucky ax — an ax with magic woven into it.

Liselle?

I glanced at her from the corner of my eye, then at the tool shed across the yard.

On the other hand, third-rate witches were a dime a dozen in Sedona, and the town occasionally attracted powerful supernaturals too. Dangerous ones, even. Liselle was just one possible suspect in a fairly large pool, and I doubted her magic was strong enough to cause any real trouble.

But if her magic combined with whatever I'd inadvertently woven into Kevin's ax...

I made a mental note to talk to Ingo — and soon. Meanwhile, I sketched the design that ran along the body of the brazier.

"Very *Lord of the Rings*," I joked, though my mind was thinking, *Runes.* Magic runes?

Liselle laughed. "Lots of people say that. They're actually Norse."

I did my best to sound dumb. "Oh wow. Is it a good-luck rhyme or something?"

Something like that, her scheming eyes said. Or was I imagining that?

"I'm not sure, actually." She chuckled. "Maybe I should check in case it's a curse."

We both laughed. Ha-ha. Such a hoot.

Ash smeared my finger as I traced the pattern cut along the brazier's upper lip. Liselle tensed.

Me too, because, yikes. A warm current ran through the metal, as if it was wired to a live battery. Very faint, but definitely there.

Someone had been using this brazier for more than just fire.

I forced myself to drag my finger nonchalantly along the design. Then I started a second sketch to detail the runes on the other side.

"So hard to get this just right..." I muttered for show. "Do you have a copy of the design I can work from?"

"Let me check..." She wandered into the house, then returned, flicking through a tablet. "Maybe I still have it..."

She took forever, and my eyes strayed to the clock on the wall. Two thirty-five. Still enough time before school let out, even allowing for the longer drive from this location.

"Here's one..." She showed me the tablet. "Oh, wait. That was just the draft. Let me see..."

She flicked through her files. Lots and lots of files. The clock ticked.

"I liked this one too, but it didn't fit..." she murmured, going off on a tangent.

I inched toward the door. "You know, just take your time. You can email Walt when you find the design."

"Well, I'd love to get this settled right now," she murmured, still flicking away. "It should just take a moment..."

Another minute dragged by. Then another, punctuated by exclamations now and then.

"Oh! Here it is." She would smile, then frown. "Oh, wait. Not that one..."

One dead end after another ensued. I scratched my head and checked the clock.

Then I froze, sensing an itch in my mind — just like that day Liselle had visited the shop.

Beep! Beep! Beep! My watch alarm sounded. I stared at it, then the wall clock.

My watch said three. The wall clock said a quarter to.

Liselle followed my eyes, then shook her head. "Oh, sorry. That always runs late."

My eyes nearly bugged out as I rechecked my watch. The few minutes that had ticked by were more like twenty. Shit. Liselle had managed to mind-bend me after all.

With a yelp, I headed for the door. "I have to go."

"Oh, sorry. Did I keep you too long?" Her voice had a victorious note to it.

I nearly turned to glare, but I didn't have time. Departing the metal shop at three o'clock gave me a sufficient buffer for picking up Claire. But I was an additional fifteen minutes away here.

The van tires screeched as I tore out of her driveway.

Liselle waved me off cheerily. "I'll send you that design."

Witch. Bitch. I cursed all the way to the front gate, where the security guard leaned out of his hut.

"In a rush, huh?" He hit the button that retracted the gate.

I fumed as it inched aside. Yes, I was in a rush. I couldn't be late to picking up Claire. I just couldn't. Not just because the school frowned on that, but for myself. I'd sworn my daughter would never experience the utter dejection of being too low in someone's priorities to be picked up on time. I'd waited hours sometimes. I'd even been completely forgotten, and no amount of kindness from teachers or the police officers they eventually called made up for that.

Damn that Liselle for making me late!

I froze. Making me late... purposely?

I revved impatiently as the gate slid aside, then raced down the road.

Dammit, dammit, dammit. Why would Liselle want to make me late?

My heart twisted. Claire. She would be alone. But why?

I couldn't fathom why Liselle would care. Still, panic coursed through my veins.

I sped around several corners and onto the main road, blaring my horn. The school would only release Claire to those listed on an official form. That meant me, my sisters, Greg, and Mike. So, Claire would be fine, right?

Still, I grabbed my phone, desperate to reach Pippa, who would be nearest the school. But she didn't pick up, and neither did Erin, who I tried next.

I darted into the oncoming lane to pass a huge camper, then cursed, trying to think. Who else was close enough to hold the fort at Claire's school until I got there?

I hesitated, then dialed a different number. A familiar voice answered on the third ring.

"Heavy Metal Sedona. Walt speaking."

My words came out in a rush. "This is Abby. Can you get me Cooper?"

"Cooper?"

"Yes, Cooper. Right now."

Walt caught the urgency in my voice. "Is everything all right?"

I sped down the road. God, I hoped so.

Chapter Sixteen

COOPER

The minute Walt called me over, I knew something was wrong. Abby's breathless words confirmed it.

"I need someone to get over to Claire's school right now," she begged over the phone.

Abby never panicked. But she sure sounded close.

"I'll be about fifteen minutes late, but I need someone there until I arrive," she said. "Just in case. Please..."

I had no idea what that *case* might be, but it didn't matter. If Claire needed something, I was there.

"I'm on my way," I told Abby, running for the door.

The good news was, my mother had already left, so I could run out without a word of explanation.

The bad news was... Well, everything else.

The school was just off the main road and easy to find. Navigating release-time traffic was a little tricky, but most folks were leaving, so it wasn't hard to find a parking spot. I slid out of my truck and hurried toward the entrance, a few steps behind a guy I assumed was picking up his kid.

As it turned out, I was right — and not in a good way.

A stout, no-nonsense woman waited at the top of the stairs with a couple of kids. She wasn't wearing a badge, but her sensible suit and *in charge* aura screamed *principal.*

The guy sauntered up the stairs and lifted his cowboy hat, all smooth and cocky.

"I'm here to pick up Claire."

Claire cringed, making my bear growl. I flew right up the stairs, passing him.

125

Claire dashed over and latched on to my leg. "Cooper!"

"Heya, kiddo." I leaned over to shield her. Whatever was going on here, it wasn't good.

"Now, just a minute," the guy and the principal barked at the same time.

I stuck a hand in the air to indicate no ill intent. The other hand, I kept around Claire, who pressed her face against my thigh, a ghost of the happy, trusting kid I knew.

"Who the hell are you?" the guy demanded.

The principal gave him a scathing look that said, *Watch your tongue, young man.*

"I'm Cooper Lundsven, ma'am," I kept my eyes on the principal, refusing to acknowledge the guy.

Not just a guy. A wolf shifter, my bear warned, catching his scent.

"Claire's mom is on the way," I said, leaning down to echo that to Claire. "She's on her way right now. Don't worry," I murmured, patting her back.

Her hands clutched my jeans. She was worried, all right.

A tiny nod was her only reply.

The principal checked a clipboard. "I don't see you on the authorization list."

"No, ma'am. I'm not. Claire's mom just asked me to wait here until she arrives."

"Well, I'm Claire's father, and I'm here to pick her up," the guy declared.

I nearly bared my teeth. Make that, my fangs. This jerk was Claire's father?

Brown hair, cold blue eyes. The guy was tall and athletic, but he had that worn-out look that said his glory days had been at least a decade back.

"Name?" the principal demanded.

"Jay Wilson."

"You're not on the list either," she said.

"What list? I'm her goddamn father!" he bellowed, advancing a step.

The principal was a head shorter and thirty years older than him, but she didn't retreat an inch.

"School policy. Students may only be released to adults on the authorized pickup list. It's for their own safety. I'm sure that's your priority, too."

I wasn't all that sure, judging by the way Claire clung to me.

"My priority? My fucking priority?" he hollered, making heads turn. "She's my kid. Give her to me."

His tone was that of a guy trying to claim an impounded truck. So much for parental warmth.

"It doesn't work that way, sir." The principal turned to me and bent down. "Claire, honey. I need you to come to me, please."

Claire shook her head, and I gave the lady an imploring look. "I don't want to take her anywhere. I'm just here to wait with her."

Jay looked like he was about to punch me. I growled under my breath. *Let him try.*

But not with Claire there. I turned sideways, putting myself between him and her.

"I'm her father!" Jay yelled. "Who the hell do you think you are?"

The principal signaled to a pudgy security guy, who spoke into a radio before joining her.

Great. Jay was going to get us both arrested — and worse, traumatize Claire.

"I'm just a friend," I said as calmly as possible. "Like I said, Abby will be here soon."

Jay's frown suggested he'd hoped to be gone — with Claire — by then.

"A friend? A fucking friend?" He shoved at my shoulder. "Well, let me tell you something, *friend.* You can sleep with that slut all you want, but you can't have my kid."

My fingernails ached as I fought to keep my bear under control. This was not the time or place to shift. But damn, did I come close.

"Now, Mr. Wilson..." the principal snipped. "According to our records, you don't have custody."

He scowled. "Custody? I'm getting it. I got me a lawyer and everything."

Ha. I would love to see a lawyer argue his case, especially after this scene.

"Well, that's a matter for the courts," the principal said. "This child goes nowhere without an authorized adult."

I nodded vigorously, making it clear I was on her side.

"I'm her fucking father!" Jay insisted. "You want ID?"

"I want you to stop raising your voice." The principal couldn't have known she was facing a wolf shifter, but even if she did, I doubted she would back down. The woman deserved a goddamn medal.

Things went on in that vein for a while, with Jay barely acknowledging Claire. My heart bled for the kid, who wrapped herself around my leg, boa constrictor style. I kept a hand on her back, letting her know I wasn't going anywhere.

Over the next few minutes, parents hurried up to pick up the other three kids waiting with the principal. Loving, polite parents who apologized profusely and gave Jay a wide berth. Smart folks.

That left just me, Claire, Jay, and Wonder Woman.

The line of cars exiting the school gradually trickled out. I watched for Abby, but a couple of squad cars appeared first.

Shit. If Jay's bullshit got me arrested, I would flip. On the plus side, they might lock me in a cell with him.

My bear snarled, vowing to make him pay for causing Claire distress. No kid should have to endure a scene like this.

"Police are on their way," the security guy murmured.

That call was about all he'd contributed so far. Useless. The gray-haired principal, on the other hand, could hand Jay his ass, I was sure.

"You called the fucking police?" Jay backed away.

Wisely, they didn't answer.

Jay watched the approaching patrol cars for another few seconds, then cussed and backed down the stairs.

"Don't you worry, kid. I'll be back," he told Claire.

Her fingers dug into my leg. Oh, she was worried, all right. *And you,* his eyes blazed at me. *I will make you pay.*

I let my canines extend a little bit to say, *Try me, asshole.*

A big group of fifth or sixth graders with sports bags exited the school from a side door and filed into a bus. That slowed the patrol cars' approach, allowing Jay to rush to his truck. When the police finally got through, they approached us.

"Everything under control here?" one asked.

Jay sped away on the far side of the school's circular drive.

"It is now," the security guy murmured.

I snorted, watching Jay go. No, things weren't under control. Not with Jay in the area. But at least he was out of Claire's face.

When I squatted to check on her, she threw her arms around my neck and hung on.

"It's okay," I whispered again and again. "Everything is okay."

Chapter Seventeen

ABBY

My hands were still shaking that evening, hours after I'd arrived at the school to find Claire buried in Cooper's arms. She'd hugged me tightly when I rushed over, and I'd held her a long, long time.

I'd thanked Cooper and the principal so many times, they begged me to stop.

I promised Claire everything would be all right just as often, but she clung to me for hours.

Too shaken to work, I swapped cars at the shop, took the afternoon off, and headed home. Cooper followed us most of the way, just in case — a case I really, really didn't want to think about.

Before splitting up, I thanked him another hundred times, and every time, he'd murmured the same two words.

"All good."

Words I repeated to myself for the next few hours, letting his deep voice echo in my mind.

All good. All good. Somehow.

Claire put on a brave face, and feeding and grooming the horses helped too. But even after I'd tucked her into bed that evening, she wouldn't let me leave her.

Good, because I never wanted to go.

"I don't have to go with Jay, do I?" she whimpered.

My heart bled. Like mother, like daughter — we both called our fathers by their first names.

"He said he was getting cusdody," Claire fretted away.

Cusdody. She couldn't spell it, but she sure knew what it meant.

"No. Never. I won't let him." Then my voice cracked. Words couldn't capture how I felt, but I tried. "I'm so, so sorry I was late, sweetie."

She patted my back. "It's okay, Mommy. Cooper was there."

I held on to her, wishing Cooper were part of that embrace.

"I'm so glad he was," I murmured.

"I'm glad too."

The understatement of the year. Cooper was convinced the principal could have held Jay off on her own, but Claire would have been doubly traumatized without her big, strong buddy there.

I held her tightly, cursing myself again and again. I'd let her down. My own daughter. How could I?

"Go to sleep, sweetie." I kissed her. "Dream good dreams."

I caught myself too late to reel back the words.

"Will you help me?" Claire clutched my hand.

My heart cracked. She really believed I could. Once upon a time, I'd believed too. But not anymore.

On the other hand, I had woven magic into Kevin's ax. I'd drawn power from the vortex on our ranch in times of need. And the new axes I was making now practically hummed with magic. So maybe...

I settled down beside Claire, then stroked her cheek gently. "You bet I will, sweetie."

∞∞∞∞∞

It was late — very late — when I finally wandered downstairs, but Pippa and Ingo were still there.

"Hi," my sister whispered, forcing a smile.

My reply was all scratchy. "Hi."

A shadow fell over the moonlight filtering in through the window, and I peeked out.

"Erin and Nash are keeping an eye on things, just in case," Ingo explained.

I watched the dragon pair glide through the inky night, illuminating it with small puffs of fire.

I'd always been grateful for my sisters — and for their partners — but I was doubly grateful two of them could shift into dragon form and two into wolves. The world's best neighborhood watch program, right here on my ranch.

Plus one bear, a little voice whispered in my mind.

I pursed my lips, silently thanking Cooper. Dreaming, even, for him to come join us someday.

I took a deep breath. Did I dare weave that wish into my own dreams sometime?

But it was one thing to fill your mind with pleasant images for a night or two. It was another to make those dreams jump dimensions and come true — and living with the disappointment when you failed.

"Okay to talk?" Ingo asked softly.

I bit my lip. Did I look that unapproachable?

Yes, I realized. I did.

The thought filled me with shame.

"Yes. Please," I added quickly. "Thanks."

Some of the tension went out of his shoulders. "What can you tell me about this Liselle?"

I told him everything, down to any detail that might prove significant. Being in supernatural law enforcement, Ingo knew much more about such things than I did. So, I described the woman, her house, the brazier she wanted, and the mind-bending I suspected her of. I showed him the sketches I'd made, along with her card.

Ingo frowned at the runes. "Mind if I take a few pictures and send them to the agency?"

I gulped, looking at Pippa. As an agent of the ADMSA, Ingo was required to report suspicious supernatural activity. But as a member of our family, he had a duty to protect, and protect he did — including protecting us from the attention of that agency.

"Can you keep it incognito?" I asked.

"I'll call it a routine check, and if they ask, I can say I have to protect my source. But I can't promise that no one will start putting two and two together. I'll do my best, though."

I looked at Pippa, then nodded.

"Do it." Then I hastened to add, "Thank you."

While Ingo submitted the pictures through his phone, Pippa fingered Liselle's business card.

"Very fancy," she muttered. It wasn't a compliment. "Embossed and everything."

I nodded. "Some kind of flower, I think."

A weird, spiky flower.

"Edelweiss," Pippa mused.

My blood ran cold, and I stared.

Pippa tilted her head. "What?"

I snatched it out of her hands. "Edelweiss? Are you sure?"

"Well, I'm no Heidi, and I've never been to the Alps, but yes, I'm sure." She typed into her phone, then held up the image her search had turned up. "See? Edelweiss."

I stared, then started sputtering. "My father stopped by the shop today—"

Pippa's eyes went wide. "Your father was here?"

I made a face. "He was passing through, and he dropped into the shop." I dug through my memory for what he had said.

It's that damned Edelweiss Corporation again. They've been bought out by a couple of magic-wielders...

I explained to Ingo, who started typing into his phone.

"Edelweiss Corporation..." He waited, frowning at the screen. "Luxury property development with projects in Colorado, New Mexico, Montana, Oregon... All over the West, it looks like." Another pause as he skimmed through what he'd found. "New partnership announced a few months ago with Steinmeier Associates..."

I made a face. "That would be that bitch, Liselle."

I chastised myself, then decided it wasn't snippy if it was the plain truth. What kind of person messed with someone's child?

Ingo set his phone aside. "I can't access classified agency files from here. We'll have to wait until tomorrow to run a background check." Then he rubbed his jaw and looked at me. "Actually, I could drive into town now if you don't want to wait."

My heart panged. Ingo truly was a good man. To think he'd started out on my red list...

Which only served as a reminder of what a bad judge of character I was and what other men I might have misclassified...like Cooper.

"Thanks, but it can wait," I said.

Pippa tapped her lips. "Then there's the question of Jay..."

That shithead, I nearly growled.

"Is it a coincidence that he turned up now? With a lawyer, no less?" Pippa went on.

My mind saw evil connections everywhere, but maybe I wasn't the best judge. So I did my best to stick with the facts.

"Two things don't sit well with me," I started, though *several hundred* would be a closer estimate. "Jay hates lawyers. He would never get it in his head to hire one. And he certainly doesn't have the money to pay one."

"So, who would?" Pippa scrunched up her face, thinking. "And why? What kind of person would bother getting involved with someone else and their kid?"

"Someone who cares about Jay's relationship with Claire?" Ingo tried.

I snorted. "Jay doesn't care about his relationship with Claire. Why would anyone else?"

"Good point," Ingo conceded. "That leaves someone who stands to gain from all this."

We all went quiet, stumped.

Then Ingo's expression changed, and he looked at me.

I tilted my head. "What?"

He hesitated, like I was a dog who'd snapped at him too many times. And, hell. I probably had.

Finally, he spoke. "What if we turn the proposition around? Maybe it's not about who gains from Jay getting custody, but who stands to lose."

"Claire," I answered immediately.

Pippa and Ingo looked at each other, then at me.

"Claire and *you*," Pippa said gently.

True, but I couldn't follow her train of thought.

"Awarding custody would give Jay power over *you*," Ingo emphasized.

"Why would he want that? What do I have control of that he — or someone else — wants?" I asked.

Pippa paled, and a heartbeat later, I did too.

"The ranch," we both said at the same time.

Ingo took it from there. "That warlock — whatshis-name..."

"Harlon Greene," I practically spat.

"Right. Him," Ingo agreed. "If he was interested in this property, then another witch or warlock could also be for...er, similar reasons."

Ingo was putting it delicately, but we all knew what those *reasons* were. The secret vortex — or vortexes — on our property.

The room went quiet. So quiet, I could hear the horses nicker outside.

"Maybe Harlon told someone else about the ranch." Pippa looked at Ingo. "Is there a way to check on his closest associates?"

Ingo looked grim. "Another thing I need the agency database to check."

They both looked at me.

Impatient as I was, I shook my head. "Tomorrow."

"The good news is, Erin called her dad, and he's on his way," Pippa said, pressing a cup of tea into my hand. "Mike will be here as soon as he can." Her tone softened. "You know my dad would rush over too if he weren't leading a fire crew."

I nodded past the lump in my throat. I owed Mike and Greg so much. Claire did too.

I knew what they would say. *You're family. Of course we would do anything for you*

"But he'll come if we think we need help," Pippa assured me.

Ingo patted her hand. "I don't think that will be necessary, though."

I prayed that wouldn't be the case. But only time would tell.

Chapter Eighteen

ABBY

"You're sure?" I asked, holding my daughter's hands.

"I'm sure, Mommy." She tugged away impatiently. "We're having pizza and everything."

It was 3:20 the next afternoon — a Friday — and school was letting out. No Jay in sight, thank goodness, though I had brought Cooper with me, just in case.

But I hadn't popped over from the shop to pick up Claire, only to see her off.

"It will be fine, I promise," Lana Hawthorne, one of the top-ranking wolves from Twin Moon Ranch, assured me with a warm smile.

We'd only met a few months before, but our daughters had become fast friends, and they'd been planning a sleepover for weeks.

I promise it will be fine, too, Lana's big, badass mate, Ty Hawthorne, echoed with a thunderous look.

Their home was a forty-minute drive away, and unlike our modest property — population six — Twin Moon Ranch was a huge place packed with over a hundred shifters. Most were tough-as-nails wolves willing to battle for life and love, as they'd proven over a few tumultuous years. Things had calmed down since then, and strong leadership had allowed the pack to prosper. More than a ranch, the place was a community with business interests across the state.

Jealous? Maybe a little. But our tiny setup suited me fine, especially since my ambitions only extended to *peace*.

Cooper stood beside me, hands shoved deep into his pockets, quiet as a mouse. A six-foot-two mouse whose bulk more than made up for Ty's greater height.

A damn good thing they were allies, not enemies. *My* allies.

My heart warmed, and my grip on Claire's hands loosened. She would be as safe — or safer — on Twin Moon Ranch than at home. She had also slept long and peacefully, waking without a trace of the fear Jay had left her with.

She hadn't reported any dreams, but hey. A good night's sleep was miracle enough after what she'd been through. So, why ruin her chance at a sleepover with a friend?

"Sorry. Just being clingy, I guess." I kissed Claire, hugged her, kissed her again for luck, then hugged her...

"Mom..." she protested.

I forced myself to step back. "Have fun, sweetie. I'll see you tomorrow."

"Bye!" she called, running toward the Hawthornes' Jeep Wagoneer.

"Love you," I called past the lump in my throat.

"Love you too." Claire waved happily.

I stood stiffly, reminding myself to let my daughter live the normal childhood I'd once dreamed of, with a good home, friends...even sleepovers. Stability, in a word.

I waved a long time after the Hawthornes' Jeep disappeared down the school drive.

"Come on." Cooper tapped my shoulder softly.

My feet were stuck in tar, or so it seemed, but with a great deal of willpower, I managed to shuffle away. It helped that Cooper took my hand and tugged.

He didn't tease or make light of it all. He just nudged me along like an old horse. The metal shop was only a seven-minute drive, and we were quiet the whole time. The quietest we'd been all day, actually, since we'd spent most of it hammering at metal.

Well, Cooper had hammered. I'd done more slamming and banging. But, hey. It got the job done.

So, I picked up where I'd left off when we returned. Seventeen axes done, only three to go. We really were on a roll.

Normal closing time was five, but I was close to finishing the latest ax head, so I stayed in the shop long after Walt and the others had gone. Cooper stuck by me, faithful as an old hound, and by six p.m., our tally was up to eighteen ax heads.

"Looks good," Cooper murmured, turning our latest masterpiece under a light.

"That handle looks good," I emphasized.

Good was an understatement. Cooper had spent the previous afternoon — the one I'd taken off — crafting handles for our axes. He might not be a metal master yet, but he sure could work wood.

I ran a finger along the grip. "Really. It's so smooth, and you got the fit just right."

A proud twinkle lit his eye, though he shrugged off the compliment. "The whole ax looks good. Feels good, too." He weighed it in one hand, then passed it back to me.

I gave it a swing. "Perfect, if I may say so myself."

Cooper stuck up a hand. "High five."

I laughed and reached up — way up — to smack his hand. "Good job."

I looked at the clock, then at the next half-crafted ax head, estimating how long that might take.

Cooper must have read me like a book, because he winced.

"You go," I urged him. "I'll just get started on the next one."

He mulled it over, then shook his head. "Nah. Got nothing much to do tonight anyway."

Ha. Sedona wasn't big on nightlife, but a young, good-looking firefighter could still find plenty of fun — and plenty of women to have fun with — on a Friday night.

I, on the other hand, was a single mom. Quiet nights in were my norm.

But Cooper refused to leave. In fact, he gave every impression of having a good reason to stay.

I couldn't help entertaining the fantasy that that reason might be me.

We kept the big rear doors open, the better to see another spectacular Sedona sunset, with rays of orange and red illuminating the sky. We kept them open a while after that, because the stars were a treat too. By seven, Orion was high and bright, perfectly framed by the doors. Cooper had another handle finished, and I had made great progress on the next ax head.

"Takeout?" he suggested when we both paused. "My treat?"

"My treat," I insisted.

The fifteen minutes he was away to pick it up seemed like a lifetime in the desert — long and empty. I stood in the garage-sized doors, thinking of Claire... and trying not to think of Jay or Liselle. With a shiver, I retreated inside, intent on finishing that ax head.

"Okay, boss. Dinnertime," Cooper called a short time later.

With him around, the whole shop seemed brighter and cheerier, like the colorful bag from the Cactus & Curry Thai restaurant.

I threw Cooper a smile, then turned back to my anvil. "I'll be right there. Almost done."

"My uncle always says that. You know what my aunt says?"

"What?"

Cooper gave me a pointed look. "*Almost done* is the best place to quit for the night. It makes starting the next morning that much easier."

I laughed. "Very wise. But seriously, I'm really close."

"My uncle says that too," he sighed, sounding a lit-tle... exasperated.

I stared at the ax head, knowing exactly where the next few blows would go. But my heart thumped in warning. I stood to finish one ax or lose a friend. Which was more important?

I put down my hammer and flicked off the forge.

"Sorry. I'll be right there." I untied my apron to show him I meant it.

As I scrubbed my hands, Cooper dragged something across the floor to one of the rear doors. Then he scurried back and forth a few times. What was he up to?

Leaving the bathroom, I stepped to the shop's kitchenette, but it was empty. I shifted my gaze toward the rear doors, and—

My breath caught.

"Okay with you?" Cooper asked.

He'd pulled a workbench to the threshold and set out dinner there. And not just dinner.

"It's beautiful," I breathed, taking in the flickering candles, yellow placemats, and purple napkins, all under a backdrop of the starry night.

He blushed. "The guy in the restaurant insisted on throwing all this in."

"He did not."

"He did!" Cooper swore. "He said, life is short, so live big."

"Smart man," I murmured while making an inner pledge to send all my future takeout business, modest as it was, to the Cactus & Curry.

"Not too chilly here?" Cooper asked.

I shook my head. Not with happy vibes warming my body and soul. "All good."

I sat slowly, soaking it all in. When was the last time someone had treated me to something like this?

Well, Claire sometimes did, with handcrafted notes and baked goods Pippa helped her with. My sisters and their fathers were great about making a big deal out of my birthday, too.

I gulped, reminding myself how lucky I was.

Still, the point remained. When was the last time someone outside the family had done something like this for me?

"Chicken mango for you..." Cooper handed over my order. "Beef stir fry for me..." Then he set out a tiny wine bottle. "Non-alcoholic. You'll have to excuse the juice glasses, though."

Ha. It beat drinking straight from the bottle, as Jay would have done.

I frowned, then banished the man from my mind.

When Cooper took a seat, we raised our glasses.

"To...uh..." His eyes twinkled, but he held back whatever he'd meant to say.

To hell with the red list, my gut said. *To big guys with big hearts and a soft touch.*

To us, Cooper's eyes said.

Outside, cicadas chirped, and the stars shone bright.

"To living big," I whispered at last.

He touched his glass to mine, making it ring. The sound hung in the night, as clear and pure as the desert air. Our eyes met, and seconds ticked by. Then Cooper reached for his fork.

"Well, dig in, I guess."

Amen, the never-sated corner of my mind said, and I did.

Dinner was delicious, and Cooper was gracious enough not to comment that I gulped my food down like a starved wolf. But, hey. He shoveled his down pretty quickly too.

I pictured a big family around a big dining table, and for once, I wasn't jealous. Just glad Cooper had gotten that.

Then I thought of his brother, and my heart ached.

My eyes darted to my workbench and the almost-finished ax. My fingers twitched, and I burned to run over and release that burst of magic — or determination, or whatever it was — into the ax.

Instead, I took a deep breath, trying to capture the feeling. I couldn't count on luck to forge "lucky" axes. I had to learn to control and apply my own magic reliably, as my stepfathers had once advised. At the time, I'd refused to listen. But when I thought about what good magic could achieve when applied carefully...

I dragged my mind back to the present. The Cactus & Curry guy was right. Life was short, and I had to live big. That meant enjoying every moment of fine dining under the stars.

And enjoy, I did. More than I'd enjoyed anything in a long, long time. I savored every bite of sweet mango sauce over chicken and rice. I laughed at the stories Cooper shared long after we leaned away from our empty plates.

The candle closest to Cooper flickered, highlighting his lips. The next time it flickered, it illuminated his eyes. They glowed brighter than ever, a sure sign of his shifter side.

A side I yearned to meet, because that was part of him too.

"Oh! Look!" Cooper pointed to the stars.

A shooting star flashed across the sky, and we jumped to our feet.

"There — another one!" I said, standing just outside the shop doors. "Quick. Make a wish."

I thought for a moment, then decided not to make one. Enough wishes had come true for me, and asking for more might be asking too much.

I glanced at Cooper, wondering what his wish was.

Oops. He was looking at me, his eyes glowing ultra bright.

And, oh. We'd ended up standing pretty close. Nice and close, actually.

"Such a clear night," I murmured, just to have something to say.

He nodded absently. "Beautiful."

The big wall clock behind him ticked, telling me it was getting late. But for the first time in a long time, I didn't have anyone to rush home to. On the contrary, I had good company right here. Someone I was tempted to stay with.

Very, very tempted.

So tempted, I slid a little closer. And closer...

The candles ought to have been burning low by then, but they flared high and bright, waving like so many flags.

Cooper's hands found mine. His lips moved.

I held my breath, then told myself, *Yes.* With no one waiting for me at home, and someone I could trust right here, right now...

Cooper's lips moved again — this time moving over mine.

Within the space of a few heartbeats, I'd melted in his arms, and those candles were dancing wildly.

Chapter Nineteen

COOPER

I tried taking things slowly, but I failed. Within seconds, I'd backed Abby against the shop wall in a series of kisses that rapidly grew out of control. Abby didn't seem to mind, though. Not judging by the happy sounds she made and the way her hands roamed.

Still, I slammed the brakes on long enough to check.

"Too fast?" I panted. I wanted her that bad.

She shook her head and tugged me closer. "I want this. I want you."

If I were in bear form, I would have reared up and roared. But my human body could do better, like kissing. Touching. Exploring.

And, wow. Maybe Abby had a secret shifter side, because she was as uninhibited as a bear. In no time, her hands had wandered down my body and worked my belt loose.

She stopped suddenly. "Uh... too fast?"

I couldn't help laughing, and she gave me a play-glare. "Are you suggesting I couldn't have my wicked way with you if I wanted?"

I grinned. "I know there are no limits to what you're capable of."

She looked pleased.

"Luckily, I'm all in with your evil plan," I finished, diving into another kiss.

"Evil plan?" she said between stuttery breaths. "Says the guy who put on a candlelight dinner."

"That was the restaurant guy's fault," I mumbled, working my way down her jaw.

She tipped her head back, directing my nips and kisses to her neck.

"Was he cute?" she asked.

My laugh bounced off her skin and back at me. God, did she smell good.

"Didn't notice," I mumbled back. "I have too much of a thing for my boss for that."

"Your boss, huh? Isn't that kind of taboo?"

Ha. Not as big as the taboo bears held against witches. But I was long over that.

"To hell with taboos," I whispered.

"Me, I have a thing for a firefighter," she admitted. "Kind of a cliché, huh?"

I slid my hands up from her waist, bumping over the edges of her ribs before reaching a soft field of flesh.

"I don't know," I mused, cupping her breast. "Is he cute?"

She laughed, then shook her head. "Nah. Not sure what I see in him, actually."

I laughed, but a second later, she tensed. "Wait. Stop."

I froze, terrified she would call this to a halt.

She put her face in her hands, then jerked up again. "I take that back. Bad joke. I see so much in you. More than I deserve. You're kind and sweet and patient. You know when to help and when to back off. You listen — you really listen — and you don't play games with my heart."

All that came out in a torrent, and I stared, not sure how to respond.

Her eyes shone with near-tears. "But me... I'm not nice. I say bad things. Mean things, sometimes. I'm quick to judge, and I don't judge well."

I took her hands because, damn. Wasn't she being a little hard on herself?

"I don't know," I whispered, going for a joke. "I think you're judging pretty well right now."

She flashed a thin smile, then hid her face against my shoulder. "First time in my life, maybe."

I hugged her tightly. "I doubt that. And as for deserving... You deserve as much happiness as anyone. More, maybe, for all you have to deal with." Then I winced. Why highlight the hard parts of her life? So I quickly added, "Like the world's worst apprentice. A bear, no less."

"Nicest bear I know," she whispered, hugging back.

I was probably the only bear she knew, but hey. I would take what I could get.

Gradually, my pounding pulse calmed, and hers did too. A minute later, she raised her head. "Sorry. Didn't mean to ruin this. Can we maybe... um... move on?"

Relief washed over me. Holding her was great, but loving her was even better.

"Absolutely. I think we were right... about... here," I said, easing my lips over hers.

She opened her mouth under mine, and just like that, I was on fire again. The best kind of fire.

"Actually, I think you were more like here..." She guided my hand back to her breast.

"And you were about here..." I tugged her hand to my jeans.

The metal shop was stiller than ever, while the night pulsed with life. Cars passed on the main road, but the building buffered the sound, pushing the rest of Sedona far, far away. The night was chilly, but my body blazed with need.

We belong together. Forever, my bear roared, high on the scent of desire.

"Cooper..." she whispered, pressing her hips against mine.

Well, she tried, but with the height difference...

I hoisted her up, and she wrapped her legs around my waist.

"Perfect." She surged against my body.

It was perfect, because with the wall at her back, I could press in close and hard. Closer...

Her breaths came faster and faster, and she changed the angle of her legs.

It was heaven, but it was hell, because we were close but still fully clothed.

Abby fumbled with my shirt, then growled in frustration and dropped her legs to the floor.

"Call it a technical time-out," she murmured apologetically while shoving down my jeans.

I went for hers, but she wrapped her fingers around me first, and my brain short-circuited. I stuck a hand against the wall to fight the sharp bite of need.

She chuckled. "Don't forget to breathe."

A smart aleck answer popped into my head, then vaporized when she switched from stroking down to up. Slowly. Agonizingly, deliciously, brutally slowly, in the best possible way.

When she switched again, I croaked. "You're killing me there."

"Want me to stop?" Her cocky tone said she had her money on *no*.

She would be right. This was the kind of death a guy could die a thousand times, with no complaints.

"Don't you dare."

She laughed, stretching out her next stroke. "I did warn you about my wicked ways."

"Wait till I get my turn."

Her breath hitched, and I felt her pulse skip.

Just wait, my bear vowed, and I grinned.

"I'll look forward to that," Abby assured me. "But first..."

She changed direction, moving a little faster.

My breath rattled as I rocked against her hand.

My eyes were closed, but I imagined ribbons of fire twisting around us like a cage. Or maybe *sanctuary* was a better word, because I never wanted to leave. All around me, flames pulsed, danced, and swayed.

Then my bear growled, and I grabbed Abby's hand to stop her.

"As I see it, we have a few choices," I said, panting hard.

Abby's eyes sparkled. "Other than what we're doing right now?"

"More like where," I managed.

I'd been dreaming of this moment for too long to let it all go by in a rush. But sex was like a wildfire. It dictated its own pace, and sometimes, all you could do was go along for the ride.

"Like what kind of where?"

I took it as a good sign that her sentence structure was off. My mind was just as incapable of coherent thought.

"Like a bed, maybe?"

"Overrated." She reached for me impatiently.

Still, I held her back.

She made an exasperated sound. "For the first time in years, I have a night off — and a guy I want. I *need*." Her voice cracked, and she tilted her head to the right. "Seriously. We could do it on that workbench for all I care."

Which was exactly where we found ourselves seconds later, feasting in an entirely different way. Abby perched on the edge of a workbench that was the perfect height — for more than just pounding metal, as it turned out. While I moved the candles aside, she'd stripped out of her lower layers, lightning-fast, and even done a contortion act inside her shirt.

"Here." She handed me her bra and lay back.

I chuckled. "My teenage fantasy just came true... about fifteen years too late."

Then she winced. "I don't suppose your teenage fantasy comes with condoms, does it?"

"As a matter of fact..."

I tore myself away from her long enough to riffle through my wallet. The condom had been in there, untouched, for a long time. I'd had plenty of offers to use it, but none of those women had really tempted me. But now...

My hands shook as I tore open the packet and rolled it on.

Her chuckle was husky. "I get to do that next time."

Next time. I liked the sound of that.

I leaned over to kiss her, shuffling nice and close. So close, my cock ached.

"You sure?" I whispered over her lips.

"Well, let's triple-check." She guided my hand down to her slick, warm core. Her inhale cracked into pieces when I slid one finger in, then two.

"Definitely need to triple-check," I murmured, making good on my vow to shatter her self-control.

Abby arched, biting back a moan. She danced under me, then clutched my shirt and panted.

"If this doesn't count as ready..."

I grinned. "That was double-checking. You said triple, right?"

It was only half a joke. She was pretty small — not that I dared say so — and I was pretty big. For this to feel as good for her as it did for me... Well, triple-checking made sense.

"I didn't mean it literally—" Her protest broke into a gasp when I slid a third finger in, but then she exhaled. "Okay, maybe another minute of checking is good..."

Her body danced under my touch, assuring me she meant that in a good way.

"Oh... Ah..." she murmured, moving in time with me.

A car pulled into the lot next door, and we froze. We were out of sight, but not by much. Then, whew. It made a U-turn and pulled out.

I exhaled, then chuckled.

Abby looked at me. "Not an exhibitionist, huh?"

"No. Plus, do you realize how sketchy this looks?"

She waited, grinning at that echo of our trip to the vortex.

"A small woman under a big guy in an empty workshop at night..."

She stuck a finger at my chest in warning. "I'm not small. And you're not that big."

"Not big?" I brought her hand to the straining condom to illustrate my point.

"Okay, medium." Her eyes sparkled with the thrill of a challenge, and she slid her leg up along mine. "You think I can't handle you?"

"You can handle anything," I said, dead serious.

Her expression softened, and she cupped my cheek.

"You, Mr. Lundsven, are a good man." Then her eyes sparkled, and she slid her left leg around my waist. "And if you don't screw me senseless right now, I will scream."

I grinned, then pressed over her for a kiss. A kiss that quickly grew deep and desperate. I pressed closer...closer...

Then I pushed into her, and she gasped, throwing her head back.

The candles I'd moved to one side flared, and their flames blurred.

Slow, my bear warned as I slid deeper into her hot, tight sheath.

How the beast thought *slow* might be possible, I had no idea. Still, I forced myself back an inch.

Abby ran her hands up my chest. "Much as I love this shirt..."

She meant the flannel, not the Henley shirt I wore underneath. I yanked off both in one move and tossed them aside.

"Better?"

"Definitely." Her eyes roved for a moment before she gave herself a little shake. Then she grabbed my ass and yanked me back in no uncertain terms, howling as I pressed back in.

I plunged deeper...deeper...up-to-the-hilt deep. I gritted my teeth, then withdrew and pushed back in.

"Oh..." Abby cried, bucking against me.

We didn't gain momentum so much as having momentum grab us and sweep us away. But that wasn't too surprising. We'd had plenty of practice in achieving perfect rhythm over the past few weeks. Why not now?

"Yes..." Abby groaned.

The playful ribbons of fire I'd imagined grew into towering flames. They roared in my ears, urging me on. Our pace quickened, and our movements grew sharper. Louder, too, with each hard thrust punctuated by a heady moan or cry — hers and mine.

Usually, I fought fires. But this was one inferno I was happy to surrender to.

"Yes!" Abby cried out, tensing in her high.

I powered in one...two...three more times, then exploded with a roar.

We clutched each other, blind to the world, unable to speak, move, or think.

I was just about to slump over when Abby arched in after-shock. Not a time to leave your woman hanging, so I obliged by pressing hard and deep. Bears knew duty when they saw it, dammit. That brought us both to a whole new level of pleasure, which whirled around my soul for a while.

The next thing I knew, I was lying down, savoring Abby's scent with every panting breath. She trailed her hands absently over my back, then wrapped her arms around me and squeezed me tightly.

I nuzzled her cheek and squeezed back. If she thought I was going anywhere, she was wrong. When bears loved, they loved good, long, and hard.

Forever, my grizzly whispered inside.

I kissed her, then grinned. "We'll have to compliment Walt on his workbenches on Monday."

"Don't you dare."

"I don't know," I teased, tracing the grain of the wood. "Not just sturdy, but multipurpose too."

She grinned. "Metalworking, dining, sex..."

We kissed, then slowly straightened. I pulled Abby to a seated position. Her hair was a mess, and her shirt was twisted to one side from our...er, haste. I didn't dare tell her how beautiful she was, but it was true.

"I have a proposition," I finally said, choosing my words carefully. This was a woman who kept her heart in a fortress. Too much, too soon, and she would spook.

She waited, watching me closely.

"There's this thing in the cabin I rent," I continued. "I think they call it a bed."

She laughed, and the little bit of tension that had threatened to arise evaporated.

"A bed, huh?"

"Yep. Not as multipurpose as this, but more private and probably just as sturdy."

She gave me a saucy look. "Does that mean you haven't tested it yet?"

I shook my head. "I never had anyone to help run a test."

"And you want me to help?"

I nodded while my bear leaped and pranced. "I do. If you were okay with that."

"Hmm. Going home with a stranger..." She tapped her lips.

"A stranger?" I motioned to the ax heads we'd made, stacked neatly on a shelf. "After sweating through all those with you?"

Her eyes twinkled, and she ran a hand over my hip. "Sweating, huh?"

My cock twitched.

"I guess we'll have to test that too," I said.

I kissed her, then turned away to grab the clothing we'd left littered around.

"Promise me I get to take this off next time," I said, handing over her bra.

"I promise." She grinned.

Thirty seconds later, we were speeding down the road toward my place.

Chapter Twenty

ABBY

It had been a long time since I'd had a night to myself. I was giddy with delight but riddled with guilt too. Shouldn't I be at home, missing my daughter?

No, I told myself firmly. I should be enjoying the best night I'd had in years.

Cooper, in the vehicle ahead of me, waved. I could just make out his silhouette.

I grinned and flashed my lights in reply.

Yes, I'd insisted on taking my own car — and going to his house, because I wasn't ready to bring a man into Claire's and my private space. And as for taking my car... Well, a smart woman kept an escape pod handy, no matter how nice a guy seemed. Still, it was hard to imagine Cooper as anything but sweet and sensitive. If there was any problem, it would be me.

My knuckles turned white from my tight grip on the steering wheel.

Don't ruin this, I ordered myself, again and again. *Just loosen up and have fun.*

But I was out of practice and scarred by past mistakes.

What I needed was a pep talk, and now. I grabbed my phone, hit a button, and waited for my sister to reply.

"Hello?" Erin's voice crackled over the speakerphone.

"Hi. It's me."

My sister, bless her, went right on high alert. "Is everything okay?"

Very okay, my girl parts sighed happily.

"Yes. Claire is at her sleepover, and Lana texted to say they're having a great time. I just wanted to ask if you could...um...uh..."

Erin waited as I stuttered, then finally cut in. "Are you sure everything is okay?"

"Yes! It's just that I might need you to feed the animals tomorrow morning, in case I'm...um...uh...not home."

"Not home? Where else would you— Oooh." She stretched the word out in slow realization, making my cheeks heat.

Still, that was better than Pippa's reaction would have been — a squeal, no doubt, followed any a cheer of *You go, girl! Enjoy every minute of your night.*

Yes, there was a reason I'd called Erin, the oldest and calmest of us sisters, instead. She wouldn't begrudge the favor either. She'd been encouraging me to "find a new friend" for years.

Pippa tended to put it less delicately. *When are you finally going to get laid?*

Well, here I was, doing just that. On my way, anyway.

"Feeding can wait until you're back from work," I hastened to add, just to get past the weighty pause that ensued.

"Um, sure. I should be back by ten." As a balloon pilot, Erin worked ridiculously early hours.

"Okay, thanks. Bye."

"Have fun," she said softly.

"Bye," I repeated and hung up before I died of shame.

Still, I continued fretting. Was I being a negligent mother? A cruel animal owner? Was I doing the right thing?

Doubts stacked up on one side of my mind, but anticipation — and a revving libido — tipped the scales all the way over to the other side. And when I replayed what we'd just done...

The engine revved, and I had to hit the brakes not to slam into Cooper's truck from behind.

Yeah, I wanted this all right.

I followed him out of town, down a side street, and along a long, bumpy road, where modest homes sat on three-acre plots. A few kept horses, and most had cars that could almost pass as landscaping, thanks to the thick greenery springing up around the tires. Cooper pulled into the driveway of the last "house" on the left — a neatly kept trailer home — but didn't stop there. A faint track continued past it, winding around scrub and trees to a small cabin in a private corner of the property.

Cooper parked, slid out of his car, and waited for me.

My heart pounded. I wanted this. I deserved this. But part of me wanted to spin into a U-turn and run back to my safe place.

He stuck his hands deep into his pockets, waiting patiently.

My heart warmed. The man was a saint.

Well, okay, maybe not a saint, because they weren't supposed to succumb to carnal desires in metal shops. But a very good man, indeed.

I parked in the spot next to his and slid out, trying not to overthink this.

"Wow," I breathed, sidetracked by the view.

He found my hand and squeezed. "Pretty nice, huh?"

Trees sheltered the driveway side of the house, but the other side was open to the views. And what a view! Soldier Pass, Brins Mesa, Coffee Pot Rock...

"Wow," I said again.

Seeing familiar landmarks from a fresh angle was like seeing them for the first time. I turned to Cooper, and that was similar: same guy, different setting. A very private setting, at his home.

He kissed me, then led me inside.

"It's not much, but it works. You know, for a season," he said, flicking on the lights.

His cheeks went a little pink, and my heart fluttered too. Would he really leave after only one season?

Or as long as I decide to stay, his eyes seemed to add. Even plead.

I want you to stay, I burned to reply, but I couldn't squeeze out the words.

"It's nice," was all I managed to croak.

We glanced around for a long, quiet minute, trying not to look directly at the bed pushed up against the opposite wall of the one-room cabin. The entrance was behind me, and a fireplace and kitchenette took up the remaining two sides. A beat-up sofa faced the hearth, and an old braided rug separated the areas of the house.

It needed updating, but it sure had character.

Cooper stepped to the fireplace, lit the kindling already set over the woodpile, and returned to me once it was crackling quietly.

"Nice," I murmured, tossing my jacket over a chair. A bad move, maybe, because I didn't know what to do with my hands after that.

My eyes slid to the bed, then back to Cooper. Where exactly did we start?

"Sorry. I'm a little out of practice," I finally admitted.

He flashed a shy smile. "Me too."

I snorted. "You're talking to a former firefighter here. I've seen the groupies, believe me."

Loneliness was not a common ailment among young, buff firefighters. Not on off-duty Friday nights, at least.

He shrugged. "Not my thing."

"No?" I winced at an unwelcome thought. "What about what's her name — Greta?"

His expression was one of stoic suffering. "My mom has been trying to get us together for years. That way, I can move in next door to my parents and live happily ever after, adding to their collection of adorable grandkids who grow up to become firefighters. Never mind that I'm not actually interested in Greta, or that Greta isn't interested in me."

"Hmm," I mumbled, trying not to reserve judgment. But, yikes. How dumb was Greta?

Then I caught myself. How dumb was I for hemming and hawing when I had a chance at a very nice night?

I took a step closer, then another, keeping my eyes on his chest — an unmissable target that kept me focused.

My heart skipped, and my body heated just from the proximity.

"Greta's not into firefighters, huh?" I whispered, resting my hands on his ribs.

"Not this one anyway." His voice was a low rumble.

"Maybe when she discovers what an ace blacksmith you've become..."

He laughed, looping his arms around my shoulders. "An ace assistant, at best."

The best, my soul whispered.

I raised my eyes to the level of his chin... his lips... his nose... and we eased into a kiss. That meant rolling to my toes and pressing against his chest.

Whoosh! Flames fanned through my veins.

Cooper smoothed his hands over my back, then cupped my head gently, deepening the kiss. And, wow. The man was a master of combining *soft* with *hard* and *gentle* with *sheer power.* Which fit, I supposed, for a man who could turn into a bear capable of killing — or cuddling.

His tongue brushed over mine, and when he ran a hand down my back and over my rear, I nearly moaned.

I ran my hands over the soft fabric of his shirt, exploring the hard planes of muscle underneath.

"Much as I love this shirt, it's coming off."

Still, I went on stroking, tracing the contours of his chest through the material, then sneaking my hands underneath.

"I love it too." He chuckled. "It was Peter's."

It was an offhand comment, not a heavy revelation, but my heart still ached.

"You think he would mind?" I asked, trying to keep the mood light.

Cooper shook his head. "I think he would approve."

For all the sorrow the notion must have brought, a smile played over his lips. I cemented it into my mind. We all had tragedies and regrets. But we all had to carry on, and Cooper's way of going about that sure beat moping or feeling sorry for himself.

A girl could learn from that.

I ran my hands over the cloth one more time, then worked it up toward his shoulders, along with the long-sleeved shirt underneath.

"Well, then. This all needs to come off," I ordered, getting back on track.

"Yes, ma'am."

I managed not to stare as he shucked those upper layers, but I did peek before we got back to our kiss. His shoulders were roped with muscles. His chest was a sun-warmed boulder to lean against, and I did. And farther down... Let's just say those parts were equally warm and hard.

"Much as I like these jeans..." he murmured, running his hands over my ass.

I chuckled. "That's my line."

"Mine now," he said, all low and growly, like he didn't mean just the jeans.

It didn't take long for more layers to follow, and soon, I found myself floating down to the bed in his arms.

"All good?" he whispered, easing down over me.

The man had definitely seen that video on *Tea and Consent.*

"Very good. Except this part." I tugged on his boxers.

I helped him roll them away and jumped on the opportunity that presented itself.

"All good?" I echoed, wrapping my fingers around his shaft.

His head sank to the mattress, and he eased down beside me with a little croak. "Yes, please."

The answer didn't match the question, but I got the gist. I nuzzled his cheek while my hand worked its magic on him.

No, not *that* kind of magic. The kind any woman could wield with the man she loved.

My breath caught. Wait. Love?

"Don't stop," Cooper breathed, and I got back to "work."

Still, my pulse jumped. I was no expert in love. Was that really what this was?

Cooper's breath rattled, and his, er...um... Well, my grip filled.

"Oh. Condom?" I hated to break the mood, but I had to ask. I would never regret having Claire, but if I were ever to have another child, it would sure as hell be planned.

"Got one." His voice shook a little as he opened a drawer in the bedside table.

"Just one?" I joked.

He grinned. "Well, maybe more than one."

The package was new and unopened — an encouraging sign. It was also a ten-pack, which was even better. I pulled one out and left it on the table, then went back to stroking its destination.

Cooper made another low, rumbly sound. Then he turned to kiss my neck... my collarbone... my chest...

He slid a finger into the cup of my bra, and my body burned in response. Then he pushed the shoulder strap aside and kissed his way to my nipple, distracting me from my mission.

I arched, closing my eyes. Up to that point, we'd proceeded in a fairly civilized manner. But now—

I bucked and cried out as his lips encircled the tight bead and rolled. Hard.

"Oh..." I clamped my hands over his head, demanding more.

His huge hands bunched and kneaded the flesh of the other side.

A damn good thing my bra had already become unclasped. I might have ripped it off otherwise. In a preemptive maneuver, I wiggled out of my panties too, then flopped back the way Roscoe did when he wanted a belly rub. A belly rub was not what I was after, though.

"Here," I whispered, guiding his hand down.

Call me demanding. I could live with that.

Happily, Cooper could too. He slid one hand down and made me very, very happy, very quickly. I closed my eyes, surrendering. Trusting, for once in my life.

Luckily, I had a man who was not only gentle, but also highly skilled. He knew just how to work me up to the edge and exactly when to ease back. Not teasing so much as bringing all systems to "go."

"Promise..." I whispered, though I didn't know what I was asking.

"Anything," he rasped into my skin. "Anything."

As vague as the request was, he satisfied my every need — and many I'd never known I had. I was heated metal on his forge, happy to bend, twist, and stretch under his touch.

"Oh!" I cried as he discovered yet another patch of virgin territory. Who would have guessed I had any of those left?

Briefly, I thought of Jay. The man was nowhere near the master lover he thought himself to be. Then I erased him and every other thought from my mind and simply enjoyed.

"I felt guilty," I managed between happy gasps.

Cooper stopped long enough to rest his chin on my chest and look into my eyes.

"Guilty? Of what?"

"Being selfish."

His laugh tickled my skin. "I could say the same thing."

I threaded my fingers through his hair, wishing he were close enough to kiss. "Well, then don't stop what you're doing."

His sunburst of a smile warmed my soul. "Happy to proceed."

The man was as good as his word — and then some. I tossed my head from side to side as he went back to where he'd left off. Finally, he scooted higher, claimed my mouth in a bruising kiss, and whispered, "Like this."

A light touch told me to roll, giving him my back. I started to rise to my hands and knees, because doggy style certainly worked for me. But Cooper pushed gently on my shoulders.

"Just there. Flat. Okay?"

I wiggled my ass in reply. "Definitely okay."

His weight shifted as he reached for the condom, then fumbled with it. As he repositioned himself, I took a deep breath.

A damn good thing, because when he slid in—

I gasped, though the mattress muffled the sound.

He backed away immediately. "Too fast?"

I slapped a hand blindly over his hip, begging him to come back. "Just right."

He kissed my shoulder, then pushed back in. And, oh. That angle was heavenly — a blacksmith's version of heaven, powerful and pounding.

The sounds I unleashed must have made that clear, and Cooper soon settled into a rhythm. Slow, but powerful, like giant bass drums that boomed, then let the sound vibrate through space before booming again... and again.

My hands went from clutching the sheets to braced against the headboard. That was even better, giving me leverage to push back into his thrusts.

Cooper groaned, while I howled into the sheets. Again and again, until, overwhelmed by lust and pleasure, I came. Cooper tensed and shuddered, exploding a few heartbeats after me.

We froze, unmoving, a statue carved from stone — the kind museums didn't always display.

How long we stayed there, I had no idea. But at some point, my muscles unwound, and Cooper melted over me. His short, hard breaths tickled my hair. He stretched his legs slowly, and I hooked my ankles over them, keeping him close.

The weight of his body pressed mine into the mattress in the best possible way. My heartbeat slowed, and I'd never felt so happy, warm, or fulfilled. So protected. So loved.

A good thing we weren't face-to-face. I could keep my face firmly against the pillow and fight the flood of emotions, telling myself it was okay not to think straight at a time like this — or not to think at all.

Cooper nuzzled my shoulder, bringing our statue to life, then murmured apologetically. Slipping away, he disposed of the condom, then hurried back. I waited, not budging, until he returned to exactly the same place. Getting smushed into a mattress shouldn't feel good, but it did.

I patted his hand, then the mattress. "This bed gets a ten out of ten."

Cooper got an eleven out of ten, but I kept that to myself.

"I agree." He wove his fingers through mine, telling me I was a ten — or eleven — too.

The fire crackled behind us, and I gradually worked up the nerve to turn and face him. I hated letting my guard down, yet there I was, totally at his mercy — emotionally and physically.

But when Cooper — sweet, silent Cooper — cupped my cheek, I couldn't help smiling back, and my pounding heart settled down again.

Neither of us said anything for a long time, and my eyelids drooped. Cooper tugged at the sheets, then softly cursed the tangle.

I helped him straighten them, then tuck us in together. With a flickering fire, a comfortable bed, and a bear shifter to snuggle with, I'd never been cozier.

"Oh. Am I stealing your side?" I asked. "Do you even have a favorite side?"

He shook his head. "No. Just inside." Then he broke out in a crimson blush. "I mean, inside my bed. With you."

I grinned at the rare chance to watch a big, confident guy get all tongue-tied.

"Better watch out. I might be hard to get rid of, you know," I warned.

I meant it as a joke, but maybe it wasn't.

He slid a hand down to my waist. "Maybe I don't want to get rid of you."

I patted his hand, fervently wishing he never would. Because this feeling — of love, acceptance, and possibility — was pretty damn good.

So good, my mind filled with dangerously blissful dreams.

I laced my fingers through his and listened as his breathing slowed and stretched into sleep.

Chapter Twenty-One

COOPER

Years back, my brother Chris had stumbled back to the fire-house after a weekend off with "the most amazing" woman, claiming his life had permanently changed. Over the next two weeks of firefighting, he'd done nothing but croon about destiny, love, and forever.

At the time, we'd laughed him off.

Now, as I lay in the darkness, holding Abby close, my inner bear crooned the same way.

Destiny... True love... Forever...

Chris had made a beeline for Mara the minute we'd returned from our next forty-eight-hour break and came back engaged. Nearly ten years on, his enthusiasm hadn't waned one bit. If anything, he was happier than ever, the proud dad of three kids, and cheerfully looking forward to forever together with his mate.

I nuzzled Abby's shoulder, inhaling her floral scent. Just enough moonlight filtered into the room for me to make out the flames tattooed along her arm. Her chest rose and fell under my arm, and her auburn hair cascaded over my hand, half covering her bare breast.

Seeing Abby at rest was a little like glimpsing a UFO. I felt super special — and I doubted anyone would believe me if I told them. Not that I planned to spill the beans, of course.

I held her a little closer. I would never, ever betray her trust.

Will never, ever leave her, my bear declared.

I never wanted to, but did she feel the same?

I nuzzled some more, marking her with my scent. Thinking. Wondering. I'd never thought I might end up with a hard-talking, tattooed, single mother from what Mom would call a "broken" family. And I'd never, ever imagined myself with a witch.

Then again, I'd never, ever imagined I might find myself a woman who could fight blazing fires — along with her inner demons — and work solid steel, not to mention raising a really sweet kid.

Would all hell break loose if I brought Abby home as my mate, or would everything fall into place as easily as it had for Chris?

I took a deep breath, telling myself this was a little like working a two-week shift. Whatever would happen, would happen. In the meantime, the best thing to do was catch some rest.

I closed my eyes, snuggled Abby closer, and drifted off to sleep.

But what felt like only a second later—

Bam! I jerked upright, completely disoriented except for Abby's tight grip on my arm.

"What's wr—"

She cut me off with a sharp gesture, staring out the window, where the stars were beginning to fade.

It wasn't quite dawn, but not far off. Was some foe on the prowl out there? My inner grizzly growled.

Abby tensed again, and her fingers clamped down on my arm. Her eyes were wide and wild, and her breath hitched.

A moment later, her shoulders loosened a little.

"You didn't feel that?"

"Feel what?" I asked.

She opened her mouth to explain, then froze.

"Not that either?" she asked when it passed.

I looked around. Earthquake? Thunder? A landslide? I'd felt nothing, but Abby looked like she was ready to bolt.

"Look." She pointed to the water glass I'd left by the bed.

Seconds ticked by.

"Watch wha—" I started, then froze.

Concentric rings rippled through the water as Abby tensed again.

Okay, that was weird. Like an earthquake that had hit Abby, the glass, and nothing else.

A tiny dust storm whirled by outside, and a tumbleweed rolled past.

Then my eyes fell on the fireplace. The fire had long since burned out, but suddenly, the embers flared. The points of light reflected in Abby's eyes.

"What's going on?" I whispered.

"A disturbance." She stared into the distance, cocking her head to listen.

Finally, I put it together. Someone, somewhere, was stirring up magic. Magic that humans and shifters were oblivious to, but not Abby. Magic that affected fire, water, air...

Elemental magic, the back of my mind whispered.

It wasn't coming from Abby, though. Who, then?

"Like the other day, when someone was messing around at the Airport Mesa vortex?" I asked.

"Messing around *with* the Airport Mesa vortex," she corrected.

She stood and stared out the window, her slim figure half lit, half shadowed by the predawn light. I couldn't help picturing a fairy or a goddess from a Greek myth.

She tensed again, then turned and grabbed for her clothes. Mine, too — whew. Wherever she was going, she was taking me with her.

Good.

She tossed my pants to me, sounding grim. "Come on. We need to find out what's happening."

∞∞∞∞

The only plus side of being ripped out of a peaceful morning in bed with Abby was that urgency — and the low clearance of her Ford — put her in my pickup with me. I drove over back roads while she spoke in hushed tones over the phone.

"Not Airport Mesa this time," she said to her sister, then waited. "No, not Cathedral Rock either. Somewhere around the back of Soldier Pass...maybe Mescal Mountain?"

They debated for a while. Erin and Nash couldn't miss work, and Pippa and Ingo had already rushed off to investigate Boynton Canyon, where they had no reception. That left Abby and me to check out the area behind Soldier Pass.

"Be careful," I heard Erin admonish Abby over the phone. "And keep trying to reach Ingo."

"Will do," Abby replied, just as terse. Then she hung up and pointed right. "Turn here."

A damn good thing my copilot knew every back road in town. After many more turns, we reached the junction of Dry Creek and Boynton Canyon Roads.

Abby closed her eyes and did whatever it was that allowed her to home in on the disturbance.

As for me, I was running on pure faith, unable to feel a thing. But it was a little like blacksmithing. It might seem like a dark science to me, but Abby knew what she was doing. All I had to do was go along for the ride and keep my eyes peeled for trouble.

"That way." Abby pointed me into a left turn.

We'd barely gone a hundred yards when an SUV came roaring around a bend ahead, swinging into my lane as it raced in the opposite direction. Two heads swiveled toward us, and one of them — a man — gestured angrily, as if I was the lunatic who'd drifted over into his lane. I barely caught a glimpse of the woman beside him, but when I did, my blood ran cold.

Abby whirled, watching the vehicle speed away.

"Shit. That's Jay."

I barely heard her. My mind was in overdrive. Was that Lisa I'd just seen?

I took my foot off the gas pedal and looked at Abby. Should we follow the bad guys — and I was sure *bad* was right — or continue to the scene of the crime?

"Dammit," Abby muttered. "What the hell is Jay doing out here? And who was that with him?"

"Lisa," I grumbled. "I think."

Abby cocked her head. "You mean Liselle?"

After quickly comparing notes, we decided, yes, we were talking about the same woman. Brown hair, blueish-purple eyes. Rich, stylish, entitled.

But was that who we'd seen rush by with Jay? Neither of us had gotten a clear glimpse, but we both agreed the vibe fit.

"So... Lisa or Liselle?" Abby asked. "And, wait. You know her?"

I nodded curtly. "I wish I didn't, but yes." Then I motioned over my shoulder. "Do we follow them or keep going?"

Clearly, I'd internalized our roles. She was Batman to my Robin, and I would follow her wherever she went. I just hoped that didn't get us hexed or killed.

Abby thought for a moment, then pointed ahead. "Keep going. I know where Liselle lives."

She sent a text to update Ingo whenever he was back in cell phone range. Then she motioned for me to pull into a trailhead parking lot. Once there, she jumped out and scanned the landscape.

It was stunning. Quiet. Timeless. But eerie and foreboding too.

"The disturbance was out there." She pointed down a trail lit by the predawn light.

"What's out there?"

"Devil's Bridge."

Even more foreboding. Great.

Abby set off briskly, and I followed.

"Is there a vortex there?" I asked, remembering our last sleuthing trip.

"Not a permanent one, but from time to time, there are reports of an upflow. I've never felt it myself."

"And now?"

She puffed out a concerned breath. "I guess we'll see. I can feel the disturbance, though. Whatever they were doing out here, the vortex isn't happy about it."

I tried to picture a happy vortex, but a swirling, angry force was easier to imagine — and much scarier. So, why exactly were we heading to one?

My bear grumbled. *Because if Lisa is involved, that means trouble. And with Jay around, Claire could be in danger too.*

I clenched my hands, resisting their urge to turn into claws.

There was a lot to puzzle out, but walking and talking didn't work — not at the scorching pace Abby hit, and not over the loud crunch of gravel as we jogged down the trail.

After a brisk twenty minutes, the flat trail turned uphill, and a short time later—

Abby pulled up and gestured. "Devil's Bridge."

I stuck up a hand, blocking the sun. A bulky mesa reared over the terrain ahead, and the first ray of sunshine had just broken over it, pointing directly to a long, slender natural arch.

This wasn't a sight-seeing tour, but we couldn't help stopping to soak it all in. Sedona was stunning no matter where you looked, but wow. This really was a superlative spot. The air smelled of pine and juniper, and my bear longed to explore at a leisurely pace.

Some other time, because Abby took off again, heading for the natural bridge. She strode right out onto it, then stopped in the middle and looked around.

I followed slowly. We bears liked to keep solid ground beneath our feet, and a bridge that slender — even if it was rock — wasn't a natural choice, especially if a witch had been poking around out there.

Like Abby, I studied the ground. The rock was scraped, just like the vortex at Airport Mesa had been.

"So, the vortex..." I whispered as if it might hear me and attack. And, hell. Who knew?

Abby stretched out her arms, palms down, the way folks absorbed the heat of a bonfire in winter, and moved around.

"It's weak and diffuse. And it's pulsing a little, like it's angry."

Yeah, well. Who wouldn't be with Lisa around?

She scanned our surroundings, then kicked at the ashes on the ground. They whirled into the air and puffed over the edge of the rock arch, which was only a few steps across.

I sniffed around. Bears had some of the best noses in the world, and even in human form, that sense was finely honed.

"That fire is recent," I said, then sniffed some more. "Two people came through maybe an hour ago. Jay and Lisa."

"You mean Jay and Liselle," Abby muttered.

"She was introduced to me as Lisa," I said, scowling. "I met her during a job in Nevada. The Clark Canyon fire."

Abby nodded, and I went on.

"She came over to my crew when we were eating out one night after things had settled down a bit. She offered to pay for the meal and invited us to her place — an amazing house overlooking Lake Tahoe..." I made a face, remembering her pointing it out. "Of course, we couldn't accept..."

Locals usually treated fire crews well, bringing us home-cooked goodies and hanging huge thank-you signs wherever we pitched camp. We got a lot of dinner invitations too, but we had to turn those down as a matter of policy. As government employees, we weren't allowed to accept gifts.

"We explained that to her, but she kept insisting. Eventually, she invited herself to our table and chummed around for a while, too."

"Chummed around?" Abby's eyebrows drew together.

I made a face. "Hitting on the guys. I was all the way at the far end of the table, but she went after my brother Peter real hard. He was polite but totally uninterested, and he kept turning her down."

"Let me guess. She was very insistent." Abby's voice was bitter, like she'd experienced that too.

"More than insistent. She wouldn't take no for an answer, and she was really mad when we left."

I'd hated her then, and I hated her now, because the ugly memory overshadowed what should have been good memories of my brother.

Abby waited a moment, then asked, "Then what?"

I shrugged. "She made a big scene in the parking lot. But that was it. The fire flared up overnight, and we went back to work." I cleared my throat, skipping over the tragedy that had ensued. "Anyway, we never saw her again. Hard to forget her, though — and I don't mean in a good way. She's the type who stirs up trouble wherever she goes."

"No kidding," Abby muttered. "She was the one who held me up the day I was late to Claire's school."

Alarms went off in my mind. "What did she want?"

"A brazier," Abby said, staring at the ground. "A portable one..." She knelt and rubbed fresh ashes between her fingers.

"For what?" I asked, more alarmed than ever.

Abby dusted off her hands and moved around, studying the ground. Then she scowled and gazed into the distance. "I don't know. I know she's a witch, though."

"A witch?" I spat out the word, then stopped at Abby's affronted expression. Oops. "I mean, a bad one?"

Abby flashed a thin smile. "Yes, a bad one. Not especially powerful, but if you're not on guard..."

Her eyes flashed, and I wondered if — when? — Abby had let her guard slip.

The next minute passed in ponderous silence. We both scanned the area, but there was no one around. Finally, Abby sighed, sat, and flopped on her back, grumbling. "Damn, is it early."

"Um... What about the vortex?" I asked, anxious to get back on solid ground.

Abby made a cutting motion. "It stopped. All quiet now."

I looked around a moment longer, then sat beside Abby. Like her, I stared up at the sky, thinking. And, wow, was it blue. That was the thing about nature. Even when the world was a mess, its beauty still shone through.

I snuck my hand over to Abby's, and she wrapped her fingers around mine. I tugged a little to kiss the back of her hand, and she smiled.

"Now I have an extra reason to hate Liselle," she murmured.

I looked down, waiting for the punch line.

Abby sighed at the sky. "We could still be in bed."

In bed, but not asleep, my bear chimed in.

I grinned. Good to know Abby mourned the missed opportunity as much as I did.

I leaned over to kiss her. Just one little kiss before we got back to sleuthing — I swear! But the kiss took off with a drive of its own, and soon, my heart was pounding — and hers too.

She slid her hands over my back, while mine found the dent of her waist. Abby broke off the kiss to smile at me, and what a sight.

"Not exactly the most private place..."

No, but now that we'd started, it was hard to stop. I kissed my way down her neck, driven by instincts wired into my DNA.

"By noon, this place will be crawling with tourists, you know," she warned.

"Good thing that's hours away," I mumbled into the smooth curve of her collarbone.

Abby tilted her head back, giving me space. Then she laughed and looked down.

"This is all your fault, you know."

"What's my fault?"

"Getting me off track. Again."

I looked up with a chuckle, and she grinned back. The wind ruffled her hair, and she pushed it away from her face. Then her eyes caught on something in the sky, and her smile faded.

"What the...?"

I rolled away to look, but my nose caught a scent first. Something wild and feline.

I jumped to my feet, pulling Abby up with me. Her eyes were on the sky, but mine were on the trees at the end of the natural bridge.

A growl built in my chest, echoed by a faint snarl from the trees. Shadows flickered as something slunk around, just out of sight.

I backed up a step, pulling Abby with me.

"Where did that come from?" she murmured, gazing north.

I glanced up. *That* was a dark cloud stretching across the horizon. But that wasn't the only thing that had snuck up on us.

A cougar stalked out of the bushes, keeping low to the ground in attack mode.

I grabbed Abby's shirt to get her attention.

"Oh. Wow," she breathed.

No, it wasn't every day you saw a cougar. But that wasn't an ordinary cougar, and I knew it. Especially when two more emerged from the bushes.

Chapter Twenty-Two

COOPER

Abby's breath caught, and she backed away. I followed her, keeping my body between her and the cougars.

But, shoot. We didn't have much space to retreat into. The rock arch connected smoothly to the landscape at one end — where the cougars were — but it crumbled off at the other. To escape in that direction, we would have to jump a six-foot gap over a fifty-foot drop.

A fourth cougar appeared at the cliff face near that end, cutting off that suicidal option.

"Aren't cougars supposed to be solitary?" Abby murmured.

I nodded slowly. "Cougars, yes. Shifters, no."

Their scents made that clear — a musky feline scent mixed with a faint trace of human sweat.

Abby's hand tightened around mine as she checked the sky. "It's getting closer."

I didn't look, because so were the cougars.

We were running out of options fast.

I pulled my shirt over my head and thrust it at her. "Hang on to this, please."

That was Peter's shirt, and I'd hate to ruin it in a shift.

The cougars closed in, snarling.

I yanked off my boots next, because those would be a bitch to kick off halfway through a shift.

"Wait!" Abby protested when I stepped away. "What are you—"

My back hunched, and I snarled. It was all garbled, though, because my bear pelt broke through my skin, and that stung like hell.

"Oh," Abby mumbled.

Not exactly a cheer of approval, but at least she hadn't screamed in horror.

My bear ripped to the surface, and I found myself on four feet and awash in scents. I wrinkled my nose at the smell of the felines. How had I not caught that earlier?

Angry with myself and them, I reared onto my back legs and roared.

"Whoa," Abby murmured.

A good thing Abby was Abby and not most folks. Otherwise, she would have run for the hills. Not that she could, though, with that fourth cougar blocking our only avenue of escape.

The three felines at the near end converged and stepped onto the first part of the arch, one in the front and two at its flanks.

Definitely shifters — with military training, I would bet.

A leaf fluttered by, then another, and the wind picked up, whispering through the trees. The dark cloud was nearly upon us, more orange than gray now.

"Dust storm," Abby warned. "Not far off."

Well, neither were those cougars, though one at the back glanced toward the storm in concern. It grumbled at the others and dropped back. The leader turned to hiss at it, then tried to impress me with his long, curved fangs.

Ha. I pulled my lips back to show off mine with an ear-splitting roar.

Three of us and only one of you, his snarl implied.

Yeah, well. I was three times their size, and the narrow bridge would make it hard for them to attack at once.

A gust of wind tore over the bridge, and I dropped back to all fours. Even the cougars put their bellies to the ground, while Abby crouched.

Then the leader leaped forward, catching me off guard. Claws parted my thick fur, but only two sliced my skin. I roared and swung back. We slammed together, and I heaved to one side.

"Watch out!" Abby yelled as momentum carried me toward the edge.

The cougar scrambled wildly, and I thrust my front paws out, barely managing to hit the brakes before skidding over the edge.

With a panicked yowl, the cougar tumbled past me and disappeared. The wind lulled just long enough to let the sound of a sickening thump reach us from below. Then the wind kicked up again, howling like a living, breathing thing.

My hair stood on end.

Magic, my bear hissed.

The second cougar stopped, swishing its tail. The third anchored itself against the wind with a wide stance and yowled, not at all enthusiastic about being so exposed.

Abby hunched and turned away from the wind. "Oh. Ow. Ouch."

Tiny pricks slammed at my nose. The dust storm was about to hit — and hit hard.

The wind howled, and I stumbled sideways, digging my claws into the ground.

"Get down!" Abby yelled.

The hell I would. Not with those cougars there.

But the wind buffeted them too, and they swayed against the force of the wind. Seconds later, they turned and raced for cover.

I glanced over in time to see their buddy disappear into the trees.

"Hang on!" Abby cried over the howling wind.

I roared back as it blasted over us. I was heavy, but Abby was light — light as a feather to those hurricane-force winds.

As quick as I dared, I shuffled over and hunched, keeping my claws sheathed as I scooped her against my body with one paw. Then I curled up like a momma bear caught in a blizzard with her young, with Abby nestled against me. Dammit. How had we not seen this coming?

Abby wrapped her arms around my front leg, holding on. Sand pelted my back, and wind flattened my fur.

In the midst of the dust storm, lightning flashed, and *Boom!* Thunder cracked.

My teeth rattled — the lightning was that close. My back leg twitched, and I found myself an inch closer to the edge. Abby was even closer to the abyss.

Shit. What next? Fire?

Somewhere out there was a witch or a warlock, and it wanted us dead.

A witch like Lisa — er, Liselle?

Abby stirred. I grumbled, keeping her close, but she wiggled through my grasp.

"Hold still!" she hollered in my ear.

No way. I reached for her, wishing for human hands to grasp with.

"Trust me, dammit!" she whispered — or yelled — next.

I wanted to, but I'd seen Abby mad, and mad made her impulsive. Explosive. Dangerous to everyone in a hundred-yard radius.

Then again, explosive and dangerous might come in handy right now. I sure as hell wasn't accomplishing much. A bear could vanquish almost any foe, but witchcraft was kind of a stretch.

So, I did my best to shelter Abby as she struggled up to her hands and knees, leaning into the wind — and me. She didn't have much body mass to lean with, though. My mother would definitely not approve. If we survived this, I vowed to take Abby home to Wyoming, introduce her to my entire family, and let my mother stuff her with home cooking to put some meat on those bones.

But right now...

Through the howling wind and dust, something colorful whipped around. My shirt, I realized. Well, Peter's. Abby had wrapped it around her arm like a talisman.

Gripping fistfuls of fur, she worked her way up my body, stopping when the wind blasted, then fighting onward. When she reached her knees, she sucked in a deep breath and stabbed one hand into the storm.

The wind screamed, knocking into her. Abby wavered slightly, then reached higher. Higher...

Heaving to her feet, she stood and thrust a hand out against the storm. The other hand clutched my fur, and the shirt wrapped around it whipped in the wind.

Stop, her gesture said. *I order you to stop.*

It didn't, but sand stopped stinging my eyes, and the heavy curtain of dust that had enveloped us thinned.

I turned my head, watching her battle the wind. Her hair streamed out behind her, but a pocket of air cleared in front of her face. She rotated her hand, slicing the wind like a knife.

The storm raged on, but it split around the blade of her hand, letting the air pocket around us expand. My body was Abby's trench, and her arm was a rifle protruding into the battlefield. The shirt wrapped around her wrist flapped so hard, I thought it would shred.

The air crackled with magic. Lightning flashed, and thunder boomed. Whoever was on the other end of that storm was really, really mad.

But so was Abby, and she was stubborn as hell. Gritting her teeth, she hung on.

The storm raged all around us, but a bubble of calm expanded, inches from our skin. Sand flew through the air, blurring my view of straining trees and whipping shrubs. Thin rays of sunlight burst through the clouds, blinding me briefly before clouds wiped them away.

Gradually, though, the sun won out, and thin slices of blue sky became wide swaths. The wind faded, letting sand and dust settle to the ground. The shirt wrapped around Abby's arm stirred a while longer, then went limp.

Abby sagged over my body. Her heart pounded against my side.

I rolled slightly and looked up, quietly chuffing at her.

Releasing a fistful of fur, she patted my side. "I'm okay."

I chuffed again, not satisfied.

"Really. I'm fine," she whispered, creaking to her feet.

Sand rained from her clothes, and her hair was a mess. But she seemed fine — until she realized she was face-to-face with a grizzly. Me.

I kept perfectly still, like she was the butterfly in that mountain meadow, a long time ago.

Her throat rippled with a gulp, and she patted my side tentatively.

"Um... Good bear. Nice bear..." She backed away.

A mournful rumble sounded in my chest, and she froze. Then she inched closer and rested a hand on my side.

"Sorry. And thanks. And...er...wow." She moved her fingers over my fur.

I nosed a little closer and wiggled my ears. They were much softer and nicer to pet. Would she get the hint?

She did, moving her hands to my head, then my ears.

The rumble changed to a hum, and she chuckled.

"Whoa. You're a bear."

Well, obviously. And she was a witch. But, hey. Once again, we'd proven ourselves a good team.

I flopped back, exposing my belly.

She laughed and scratched there next. "If you were human, this would be totally inappropriate."

My gut warmed. We'd spent a hot, sizzling night together. Did appropriate even apply any more?

Abby's eyes sparkled, and I was sure she was thinking the same thing.

A bird darted by, making Abby glance around.

The storm had faded to nothing, but the landscape was still in a hushed, batten-down-the-hatches mode.

"We ought to get out of here," she whispered.

I looked around, then dipped my head in a nod. Still, I couldn't help giving Abby a quizzical look.

"What the hell happened?" she echoed the question my expression had asked. Then she gritted her teeth and took a step toward the trail. "I don't know. But I intend to find out."

Chapter Twenty-Three

ABBY

We were both silent on the hike back to the car. Not that I'd
expected Cooper to be chatty in bear form.

I wedged his boots under one arm and shook out his shirt,
releasing a cloud of orange dust. We'd found his jeans — or
what was left of them after his rapid shift — tangled in a bush,
and I carried those scraps too.

So, it was a damn good thing we didn't meet anyone else
on the trail. What would they think of a woman and a bear
toddling along?

And, wow. It wasn't often a girl got an escort like *that.*
Cooper's massive shoulders swung as he walked, and his fur
glinted under the sun. The upper half of his body was golden-
brown, his legs tree-trunk brown — and about as thick. His
paw prints were the size of plates, and where they overlapped
with my footprints, well. . . goodbye footprint.

Whoever came along the trail next would have a field day
with *that.*

But that was the thing — we didn't meet a soul, despite
the popularity of this trail. A few hardy souls usually trekked
out to Devil's Rock for sunset, and by noon, dozens of visitors
crowded the place. Had Liselle — if she was the one responsible
for the storm — spelled the area in a way to keep people away
too?

I sniffed the air. Cooper kept his nose to the ground, vac-
uuming up scents.

"Anyone you recognize?" I asked.

I took his grumble as a yes.

"Liselle — or Lisa, I mean?"

Another grumble.

"Jay too?" I asked.

Cooper's eyes shone with pure hate, and he showed his teeth.

Yep. Jay had been here, all right. But what the hell was he doing with Liselle?

Back at the car, I fished the car key out of Cooper's jeans pocket. Then he shifted, and I froze, mesmerized by the sight.

My mother was a dragon shifter, and watching her shift — the few times I had — was mind-blowing, to say the least. Because, well... Wings. Leathery hide. Sharp teeth. In comparison, Cooper's shift — from one type of mammal to another — was less abrupt. More... natural, if that was the word. The air around him shimmered, his fur thinned, and his body morphed gracefully. One minute, he was down on all fours, and the next, he was human and rising up to two feet.

Naked, too.

My eyes drifted down, and it was all I could do to jerk them back up. But, heck. That was a mighty fine man there, and he'd just been a bear. I could be excused for ogling a bit.

I handed him his shirt as casually as I could.

"Thanks." His voice was low and growly. A sign of emotion or an aftereffect of his shift?

I nodded quietly. Keeping hold of his shirt during the storm had been a challenge, but there was no way I was going to let the wind rip it away. Not a shirt that had belonged to his brother.

"Sure," I murmured as he pulled it over his head. A damn shame, because I'd been enjoying the view.

He grimaced at the remnants of his jeans, then gave up on them and tugged on his boots. Then he looked down at himself and sighed.

"Great."

It did make for an unusual sight — a grown man wearing nothing but boots and a flannel shirt that barely covered his rear, let alone his, er... front.

"I don't know," I tried a joke. "It's kind of cute."

"Cute?" he protested.

"Adorable, even."

"Exactly the look I was going for," he grumbled, swinging into the driver's seat.

Did I peek at the prime vista that afforded? Yes, I did. How could I resist?

He turned on the engine, then the wipers. That sort of backfired, though, because the wiper fluid turned the thick layer of dust into orange sludge.

"Great," Cooper griped as the mud swished back and forth, back and forth.

A few more squirts cleared the glass — mostly — and we started cruising toward town.

"Didn't you say Liselle wasn't all that powerful?" he asked after the first dusty mile.

"I did. And she's not."

"Then what was that?" He jerked a thumb behind us, more an indication of time than place.

I mulled it over. "Three possibilities. One, I was wrong, and she's more powerful than I thought."

Cooper's eyes flashed. "Let's hope not."

"Two," I continued, "she wasn't that powerful, but now she is."

"How?"

I tossed my shoulders in a frustrated shrug. "By siphoning power from the vortexes, maybe."

"With the stolen ax?"

"Maybe." My frown deepened, because we hadn't only found ax marks. There'd been ashes too. "Or with fire, or both." Then I cursed.

Cooper swung his head around, and it was such an echo of the same move in bear form that my mind went blank. The guy behind the wheel of the vehicle could turn into a bear. Make that, the guy I'd slept with.

The thought terrified as much as it thrilled.

Then my brain got back into gear, and I picked up where I'd left off.

"Liselle wanted a brazier. A *portable* one," I said.

Cooper's jaw went hard. "Not just to barbecue, I take it."

I shook my head slowly. "I think not."

"Does that mean she can't make fire?"

"You mean, like a pyromancer?" I shook my head. "I don't think so. Why?"

"Just wondering," he muttered.

Just wondering, my ass. What was he thinking?

Cooper went painfully quiet, and when he finally spoke, his voice was gruff. "What's option three?"

I bit my lip, not sure if I liked it any better than the other two.

"That Liselle wasn't the one kicking up that dust storm — or, at least, not alone."

His face clouded. "Another witch?"

"Or warlock."

"Great," Cooper muttered again. Then he sighed. "Who else around here is capable of kicking up lightning, thunder, and a dust storm?"

Other than my sister and Mike, who couldn't possibly be responsible? "I don't kn—" I started, then froze.

Cooper tensed, waiting.

"Months ago, the ranch was attacked by a warlock," I said. "Harlon Greene. Lightning, thunder, the works." I flicked my fingers to illustrate.

And, yikes. Thunder rumbled in the distance.

Cooper stared at my hands, and I did too. Cause and effect or coincidence?

I stuck my hands under my thighs as he drove on. "Where were we?"

"Harlon Greene," Cooper said a little hoarsely.

Right. "He was after our ranch."

"You mean, to develop it?"

My mind spun. Development. Edelweiss Corporation. Could Harlon be involved? I made a mental note to ask Ingo. Then I replied to Cooper.

"Yes and no. Harlon wanted access to the vortexes there."

"Vortexes?" Cooper's tone stressed the plural.

I nodded stiffly. This was not going well.

"What happened?" Cooper finally asked.

I skipped over some of the details, like Erin throwing lightning bolts with help from Pippa and me, and said, "Harlon was arrested by the ADMSA and submitted to a restraining spell that overrides his powers."

"For how long?" Cooper demanded.

"Forever, I assumed," I said.

In truth, I'd never looked into the details. I pulled out my phone and dialed Ingo again, then cursed. Still no answer.

And no end to the questions in my mind. Was Harlon back and at full power? Was he involved with Liselle?

"Given that the lucky ax is missing..." Cooper started, then trailed off. After a heavy pause, he continued. "So...I'm about to say something you might not want to hear."

I waited, digging my nails into the seat.

"You need to be real careful using magic if you don't know exactly what it's capable of."

I gulped. He had a point there.

"I do. I will. I mean, I'll try," I stammered.

Which pretty much summed up my problem, didn't it?

Cooper looked at me, and I looked at my feet.

Silence settled over us, so thick and heavy, it pressed over my body.

A few minutes later, we turned onto the main road, and not long after, Cooper pulled over in a supermarket parking lot. All the vehicles parked there were covered with a layer of dust. A young guy walked up to his van and shook his head, then drew a smiley face in the rear window. Another person cleared their windshield with an ice scraper. We watched them in silence.

Finally, Cooper spoke. "Well, you did a good job fighting off whoever was responsible for that storm."

I looked at my feet, proud but frightened too. "I have no idea how."

A little like the lucky fire ax, I supposed.

Chills went down my back. What if I was inadvertently throwing magic around? What if others could capitalize on that somehow?

And, shit. There was a very thin line between *inadvertent* and *negligent*. What would the ADMSA have to say about that?

Cooper looked at me. "No idea at all?"

I shook my head. "No. Metal, fire — I can work with those. But not weather."

"And yet, you stopped the storm."

I closed my eyes, trying to replay what I'd instinctively done. "All I did was deflect it for a little while."

He snorted. "That's 'all,' huh?"

My shoulders sagged. I prayed Cooper wouldn't ask me *how* I'd done that deflecting, because I wasn't sure. I'd just acted on instinct.

The upholstery of the pickup's front seat squeaked as Cooper leaned over and slid an arm across my shoulders.

"Sorry." He tipped his head against mine. "Not accusing. Just trying to understand."

I laced my fingers through his and held on tightly, praying all this magic wouldn't drive him away.

My phone rang, and I grabbed it, eager to hear from Ingo.

But it wasn't Ingo calling. It was Claire.

"Hi, Mommy!"

Rays of sunshine illuminated my soul, and my heart fluttered on angel's wings.

"Hi, sweetie! Did you have a good night?" I asked.

Cooper looked over with a faint smile.

"The best!" Claire launched into a detailed description of everything she'd done on her sleepover at Twin Moon Ranch.

"Wow... Great... Amazing..." I interjected at appropriate intervals.

A few syllables from someone like Jay could ruin my day, but a few words from Claire made me an optimist again.

Then Claire launched into a long, feverish sales pitch about why she really, really ought to be allowed to stay one more night. Apparently, Twin Moon Ranch had an old-time covered wagon, and all the kids were going on an outing that day.

"Please, Mommy. Please?" Claire pleaded.

Wow. A covered wagon? As in, pioneers? I'd never gotten to ride in a covered wagon. I'd never gotten to do a lot of things. All the more reason to say yes now, no matter how much I would miss her.

Claire passed the phone to Lana, her host "mother" for the night.

"It's no trouble, really," Lana assured me. "The girls are having a great time, and we can bring Claire home tomorrow — Sunday." She chuckled. "I'm sure you can use a day off."

A day off was fine. And another night with Cooper...

A gutter cut through the parking lot, and my dirty mind jumped right into it.

Oh yes. I had a few ideas on how to fill the time.

My cheeks heated, and I exhaled upward, reminding myself to get real. We'd been ambushed by a gang of cougars *and* a dust storm. How could I think about getting down and dirty at a time like this?

But think, I did.

And honestly — was that so wrong? No one had ever made me feel so...special. Capable. Interesting. Was it crazy to want to dive in and paddle around that pool for a while?

"I guess I could," I told Lana. After profuse thanks — and a last, quick chat with Claire, I hung up and stared at the phone.

Cooper had to have caught the gist of the conversation, though he didn't say a word.

I'd never been shy when it came to speaking my mind, but for once, my tongue was hog-tied. Maybe because I'd never wanted to say something like, *I have the rest of the day and the whole night off, and I'd really like to spend them with you.*

And not just that, but *I really like you.*

I made a washing motion with my hands, then caught myself and stopped. *Nervous raccoon* was not an attractive look.

Or maybe it wasn't so bad, because Cooper gently tugged my hands apart and clasped them in his.

"So, I was thinking..." he started.

My heart leaped, and I was all ears.

"Maybe we could—" he continued.

My phone rang, and I nearly groaned.

I fumbled with my phone. "Hello?"

"Abby? Are you okay?" It was Ingo, and he sounded worried.

Pippa echoed him in the background, and she sounded downright frantic.

"Yes, we're fine," I assured them. Then I glanced at Cooper, who nodded grimly. "But we need to talk. Now."

Chapter Twenty-Four

COOPER

As crappy as the start of my Saturday had been, the day ended very...er, pleasurably.

But that was only after hours of conferring with Ingo on what had transpired at Devil's Bridge. He was in the process of calling in more ADMSA agents to Sedona and insisted we leave the rest of the investigating to him.

Fine with me. I was a firefighter and part-time blacksmith's assistant. I also had a night off, and so did my boss — Abby.

Of course, Abby was Abby, and she'd insisted on squeezing in a few more hours of work that Saturday afternoon. We'd put off repeating our candlelight dinner, and even managed to refrain from the *sex on the workbench* part. The minute we got back to my place, however—

We stripped and, *Zing!* I pulled the shower curtain shut behind us. It was a tight squeeze, with both of us crowded in together, but I didn't mind.

Not in the least, my bear hummed as I rubbed soap over her curves.

So, not the most efficient shower, but a damn memorable one. My back had never been cleaner. My dirty mind, on the other hand, was already fast-forwarding to what might come next.

Eventually, the water ran cold, and we moved to the bed.

"I call the top," Abby murmured, pushing my back into the mattress.

"So bossy." I shook my head in mock dismay, while my hands snuck around her waist.

"I know, I know. Nothing but suffering for you today. And I'm about to be even bossier. Condom, please."

I wiggled my hands. "Can't you see I'm trapped here?"

Her eyes twinkled. "Oh, poor you. So helpless. You want help?"

Boy, did I, even if her definition of help was more like torture. Deliciously slow, teasing torture. But somehow, I endured.

"Now, if you don't mind..." she murmured, straddling me.

I had a good comeback. I really did. But it vaporized the moment Abby sank down, taking me deep.

So, no. I didn't mind. Not in the least.

As far as conversation went, things deteriorated from there. But we reached new highs in every other sense.

"Oh... Yes..." Abby rocked over me once we'd fallen into a rhythm.

Her eyes slid shut, and her hair swayed.

I might have uttered a few exclamations myself. A few feral sounds too. Not that Abby seemed to mind.

She likes me! my bear cheered again and again.

She did. But did she love me?

The question kept flitting through my mind, but I pushed it away every time. Love might be on one side of a Venn diagram and sex on the other, but figuring out where they overlapped was not something you accomplished in bed.

"Oh..." Abby groaned, tipping her head back.

Her hair was still wet from the shower, and a drop landed on my chest. I half expected it to sizzle from the heat we generated.

"More..." Abby murmured, close to coming.

My hands were tight on her hips, but if I really stretched...

My thumb found the nub at her core, and she cried out. Again and again, until she rocked into an orgasm. I drove up to meet her with one last, hard push, barely holding back the roar that thundered through my mind.

Mine! My mate! my grizzly declared.

My human side was ready to echo that. How could she be anything but?

My eyes slid open a little before Abby's, and what a sight. Her chin was up, her face a mask of concentration. Her hair was a mess, with a few strands caught on the corner of her lip.

Gorgeous, in other words. Just gorgeous.

Mine. My mate... I nearly whispered out loud.

What would she say if I did? Would she bolt, or would she echo the words?

I strained for her answer, though I knew she couldn't have heard.

Or maybe she had, because when she opened her eyes, they were aglow, like a shifter's, and pulsing. *Mine. My mate.*

I prayed it wasn't wishful thinking. Did witches even know about mates? Was half-dragon heritage enough for her to understand the depth of that kind of bond?

I swallowed hard, hoping.

"You are so beautiful," I whispered in awe.

She hunched, then slowly relaxed, lying down over me. "Wow. Sex so good, you're delirious. I'm a mess."

"A beautiful mess," I insisted.

Incredible, my bear agreed. *Will you be mine? Please?*

She grazed a kiss over my lips, then settled down with a happy sigh.

I held her close, only to grumble and roll away to dispose of the condom. Then I snuggled up again.

Someday, I vowed, we would be doing this skin-to-skin.

Someday, I would convince her she was the beauty I knew her to be.

Someday, I would work up the courage to love her out loud, and she would echo my words back to me. *I love you, my mate.*

But for now...

I kissed her, closed my eyes, and let myself dream.

∞∞∞∞

We had a candlelight dinner on the porch at sunset. Pasta.

We made love afterward. In bed, missionary-style, though we made enough noise to make a missionary blush.

That was followed by another shower, with just a dribble of warm water running over my back while Abby dropped to her knees and brought me to heaven.

And what we got up to next... Well, that would have made a missionary frantically flip through his Bible.

But, hey. We were making up for very long dry spells — both of us. Plus, I was a bear shifter, and I'd found my destined mate. It was my job to love her, and love her well. Or, as Abby put it...

"Harder... Faster..."

Only Abby could order a man around while belly-down in bed. In fact, when I'd paused to check that she was on board with where things were headed...

"Have I ever made it anything but abundantly clear when I *don't* want something?" she'd chided.

I chuckled. Definitely not.

"So let's operate on that principle, shall we?" she'd continued. "Because I will die if you don't screw me right now."

So, really, I was just doing as I was told. And doing it to her (very) deep satisfaction, judging by the happy sounds she made.

Cowgirl was great, and missionary always worked. But nothing beat the sheer power of this position. And since Abby liked it too — no surprise, since blacksmiths were all about hard banging...

I closed my eyes and gave it everything I had. Abby had lit a bunch of candles, and although they had burned low by then, they all started flaring again. I just hoped she didn't inadvertently burn the place down.

Then again, I was a firefighter.

The first time I'd noticed the candles, I'd been thrown for a loop. She was a witch, right?

Now, I decided I preferred *woman with unique abilities*. A woman who made me feel complete.

After all, I was a bear shifter, but I was a regular guy too. And hopefully, I made *her* feel complete.

In any case, the special effects were a sign of her approval — and kind of a turn-on. What guy wouldn't love knowing he was responsible for creating a few fireworks?

Every time I thrust, she squeaked, and the candles pulsed. Every time I pulled back, the candles hesitated, in the same way that Abby held her breath. Then when I slammed in again, the fireworks exploded. Over and over until—

Abby let out a sharp cry, and fire blazed through my veins. Real fire, it felt like. I gritted my teeth, extending the sensation as long as I could. Then I went limp over Abby, and the candles dimmed to tiny, glowing dots.

Abby recovered before I did, patting my thigh softly while I panted over her shoulder. Eventually, I got myself together long enough to clean up, then spoon together. I held Abby close, nuzzling her shoulder. Marking her as mine, even though I wasn't aware of it at first.

"Okay, I have a new favorite," Abby murmured.

My mind was still a little hazy. "Favorite what?"

"New favorite position, dummy. What's that called anyway?"

I raised an eyebrow. "You plan on discussing this with someone else?"

She snorted. "Yes. My sisters, their fathers, and all the secret lovers I've been keeping you in the dark about."

I chuckled and fessed up to my limited sex vocabulary. "Lazy dog? Jockey, maybe?"

She stuck a finger at my chest. "Aha. Someone *has* been discussing it."

My cheeks heated. "Just overhearing. You know, locker-room talk — a co-ed locker room," I added quickly. "Female firefighters can be worse than guys sometimes."

"We are not!"

I grinned. Spoken like a true firefighter — you could leave the job, but the job didn't leave you.

"You absolutely are," I insisted.

"Are not, and I'll prove it."

I waited.

"What starts with the letter F and ends with *uck*?" Her eyes danced.

I laughed, sliding a hand over her hip. "Not obvious?"

"It's *fire truck*."

I rolled my eyes.

"See? You have a dirty mind," she concluded.

"If I do, it's because you're rubbing off on me." Which might have been my own fault, what with all that nuzzling.

Abby nuzzled back — enough for me to work up the courage for a question.

"So, these tattoos..." I murmured, touching her arm.

She looked down, then sighed. "I was going through a stage, I guess." She touched her own skin, then whispered. "I like them, though."

I grinned. "I like them too."

She went still, then kissed my arm in about the same place. Sometime after that, I drifted into deep, blissful sleep. So deep, I didn't wake until seven in the morning, and even then, I snoozed for a while.

It was eight before I gave the day any thought at all. Sunday. A day off. One I ought to make the most of, because as soon as the first real fire of the season came around, the rest would follow hot on its heels.

Ha. Hot on its heels. I chuckled at my own pun.

"Hmm?" Abby turned slightly.

She was still spooned against me, gently stroking my arm.

I grinned. "Laughing at a bad joke. So bad, you don't want to hear it." Then I stretched. "More importantly, I was thinking about the best way to use my day off."

If my hand grazed her breast, it was an accident, not a hint. I swear.

Abby grinned. "Let's see. Sunday... A whole day to do whatever we want."

We. I liked that part best.

I nodded. "Even if it isn't much. No work, no rushing around." I glanced at the clock. "What time do you have to pick up Claire?"

Even if it was early, that would be all right. Claire was a great kid, and it would be nice to do something with her and Abby outside the metal shop. If Abby was ready for that, of course.

But Abby went stock-still.

I nudged her gently. "What?"

"Claire..." Looking aghast, Abby jumped out of bed — worse, out of my arms — and started rushing around the cabin.

Whoa. Was she late to pick up Claire? It was only eight a.m.

I sat up. "What's wrong?"

Abby fumbled with her bra, then pulled on her shirt — and cursed, because it was inside out. She yanked it off and tried again, muttering the whole time.

"I have to go. Shit. I have to go."

"Right now? What time do you have to pick her up?"

"Lana is bringing her to Sedona after lunch."

"So why—"

She whirled and glared like a woman possessed. "Because I forgot about her." She pointed at the bed, like that was Exhibit A. "I didn't think of her once, all night. I only thought about myself."

I patted the air, trying to calm her down. "Abby, it's okay to—"

"It's not okay!" Her blazing eyes practically pinned me to the headboard. "It is *not* okay to forget your own child!"

I got it, but wasn't she kind of overreacting?

"Every parent deserves a little time to themselves," I said. "One night off while your kid is at a sleepover doesn't make you a bad mother."

"But I forgot her. Totally. How could I forget my own daughter? Oh God..."

"You didn't forget her. You knew she was okay, so you let yourself relax for a while."

"Sure. Relax." She kicked her legs into her jeans, then rummaged around for her socks and boots. "So much, I let my brain turn off." She stopped long enough to bury with her face in her hands. "God, how could I be so irresponsible?"

That was when it dawned on me that this wasn't about her and Claire.

"Abby, you're not irresponsible. And you are not your father."

"You bet your ass, I'm not!" She jumped to her feet. "But instead of putting my daughter first, I've been messing around with a guy..."

My gut dropped, and I growled. "This wasn't messing around. This was more than that, and you know it."

My heart hammered. Surely I wasn't the only one who felt that way?

But Abby was not to be reasoned with. She went back to fumbling with her boots, muttering the whole time. "Do I? How can I be sure?"

Now, that hurt. Still, I did my best to keep my cool.

"Because I'm not Jay."

That stopped her cold, and she shot me a long, mournful look. "I know you're not. But I'm me, and I make mistakes."

"This wasn't a mistake."

"What if it was?"

"I swear, it isn't." My heart and soul went into those words, and hope caught in my throat.

Abby looked at me a moment longer. Then a bird whistled outside, and she gave herself a shake. "I have to go."

I wanted to scream. Go — now?

Her eyes were huge. Sad. Regretful.

"You don't have to," I insisted, willing her back into my arms.

She could stay. We could talk. She would get herself together and see this didn't have to be a big deal.

But I was just a bear shifter, not a magician.

Abby turned and headed out the door, whispering, "I have to."

Do something! my bear yelled.

"Please, Abby. Don't g—"

The door slammed.

My legs burned to run after her. To stop her before it was too late.

But Abby was a mustang with one scar too many. Forcing her would only make things worse.

Outside, her car roared to life, then died. She cursed, then started it a second time. Seconds later, gravel scattered.

Paralyzed with shock, I listened to her speed down the drive and out of earshot. Even then, I strained for some hint of her swinging into a U-turn and rushing back.

Seconds ticked by. A minute. Two. Every tick of the clock chipped another piece off my heart.

I listened for a long, long time, but the only sound outside was the mournful wail of the wind.

Chapter Twenty-Five

ABBY

I drove down the road, wiping my eyes. Cursing Jay. Liselle. Even Cooper. But most of all, cursing myself.

The road was scalloped from overuse, but I raced down it anyway, then flew out onto the main road. An oncoming car hit its brakes, beeping wildly.

I cursed them too.

A police car passed in the opposite direction, and I wiped my eyes again. Was driving while blinded by tears a punishable offense?

I drove without thinking, and for some reason, instinct took me to Heavy Metal Sedona. I pulled up by the rear doors, then slumped. I'd never felt more broken or pathetic.

It was Sunday. A day off. The sun was shining. The sky was a postcard-worthy blue. Claire was safe and happily entertained. I'd spent two incredible nights with a sweet, sensitive man.

But I'd walked out on him.

I winced when my own subconscious attacked me. *Just like Mom.*

And, ouch. That cut. Deeply.

My mother had a long *love 'em and leave 'em* history, dumping an entire series of men, as well as her own daughters.

My father had walked out on me countless times too. Even when I'd reasoned and pleaded with him, as Cooper had done.

God. I was just like them.

Don't ruin this, I'd told myself that first night with Cooper. But that's what I'd just done.

I stuck my face in my hands and shuddered with sobs that refused to come. They just dammed in my throat, choking me.

Neither of my parents had real relationships. Neither had real friends. And here I was, alone on a Sunday. At work, for lack of a better option.

Actually, it was even worse — I did have better options.

Option one: rushing back to Cooper and begging for forgiveness.

Option two: driving home and commiserating with my sisters.

Option three: cooling off for an hour, then rushing back to Cooper and begging for forgiveness.

I just couldn't bring myself to do any of those things.

I wrapped my fingers around the steering wheel and leaned my head against it. Pa-fucking-thetic. That was me.

On the other hand, forgetting my daughter was totally unforgivable, especially when I was facing a custody suit. That was what made me march out Cooper's door, despite my soul screaming to stay with him. I couldn't afford to look like a woman who slept around. Jay — and his lawyers — would pounce on that and use it to steal Claire from me. Not only for joint custody, but maybe full custody.

I knew what Erin would say. She was always the reasonable one.

One night with a great guy is hardly sleeping around.

Two nights, Pippa would point out with a waggle of her eyebrows.

I grimaced, glad I hadn't gone home.

But nothing they might say changed the fact that I couldn't let Claire down. I couldn't risk losing her. I was a mother, and that would always be my priority.

I had Claire. I had Roscoe. I didn't need a man. No matter how much I wanted him.

I sat in the parking lot for a long, long time, listening to cars zoom by on the main road. Not many, though, because it was Sunday, and most folks were sleeping in...enjoying the company of their loved ones...relaxing...

I shoved the car door open, punched in the metal shop's key code, and stomped inside to fire up the forge. I had a couple of hours before picking up Claire. Enough to start on the next ax head.

Eighteen down, two to go.

Bang! I slammed the metal with all my might, making sparks fly.

I waited instinctively for Cooper's echoing hit. *Wham!*

But, duh. It never came.

I grimaced and went at the metal with a sullen *bang! Bang! Bang!* No rhythm. No joy. No teamwork.

Two hours later, I sat back, staring at the result. That wasn't an ax head. It was a battered lump of steel.

I threw it into the scrap pile and started a new one. Walt would be furious at the waste, but that wasn't my problem right now.

At lunchtime, I stopped for a grocery run. Not because I was hungry, but in order to stock up for Claire's sake. I got all our usual staples, plus brownie mix. Claire loved making brownies. We could make them together. Everything would be fine.

I threw in two more boxes of mix, then three rolls of chocolate chip cookie dough. Then the edible stuff you used to write on cakes, plus a few edible flowers, plus—

I caught myself there, knowing full well what I wanted couldn't be found on a shelf in the supermarket.

But that didn't matter, I decided, briskly pushing my shopping cart to checkout. As long as Claire was happy, I was happy. I had her, my sisters, and their fathers. I had Roscoe and the ranch. I had everything I needed, and everything would be fine.

∞∞∞∞

Everything was not fine. Starting with the news I got from Ingo, once we met back on the ranch.

That had indeed been Jay in the pickup Cooper and I had spotted on our way to Devil's Bridge.

"Security cameras at one of the resorts along Dry Creek Road caught him passing early that morning — twice," Ingo said, looking grim. "Once on the way in at four in the morning and again on the way out, closer to dawn."

"What about Liselle?"

"The camera didn't get a good enough view to ID his passenger."

"Well, Cooper can ID her. He caught her scent at Devil's Bridge."

Ingo shook his head. "Unfortunately, his word isn't enough without corroborating evidence. I got a team up there as quickly as I could, but the storm destroyed any evidence we could have used. Still, we're working on it. I promise you, we're working on it."

Unfortunately, working on it didn't involve hustling over to Liselle's place and arresting, or even questioning, her.

"We can't do that without firm evidence linking her to Jay, the storm, or the vortex disturbance," Ingo said.

I know he was doing his best, but that was a bitter pill to swallow. Who knew what Liselle was plotting next — and what role Jay played in her nefarious plans?

On the other hand, something didn't add up. Liselle wasn't that powerful a witch. I was sure of it. How could she have stirred up a storm that big alone?

I was starting to think my third theory — the one where Liselle was involved with a stronger witch or warlock — was most likely. If so, why the hell were they after me?

So, things were not at all fine, and even a batch of double fudge brownies couldn't change that.

Still, I did my best to pretend things were normal.

I got Claire to school as usual on Monday morning, then headed to work, stiff as a steel rod until I realized Cooper wasn't there yet. Good.

"Morning, Abby," Bob called.

"Morning," I muttered.

Walt echoed him, and I hung my head in shame. Later on, I vowed, I would dig through the scrap pile, retrieve that lump of steel I'd wasted, and rework it.

"You and Cooper made incredible progress on the axes." Walt patted me on the back. "Good job."

Bob looked over and whistled. "Wow. Did you take any time for yourself on the weekend?"

I puffed air up over my cheeks. Yes, in fact. I'd spent two sizzling nights screwing Cooper, and my girl parts were still tingling. Maybe a good thing, since that was the last action they would see for a long, long time.

But *action* was one thing. Even worse was the damage to my poor, mangled heart. I had no one to blame but myself, though.

The door opened again, and my heart stopped, then clunked back into action.

"Morning," Matt mumbled groggily.

Pablo followed, all cheery, as usual. "Good morning."

No, it wasn't. And it was about to get worse. Because I could sense another person behind him.

The door swung open a third time, and there was Cooper, blocking the view of the massive mesa in the distance behind him.

My heart lunged, trying to reach him. In my imagination, I yanked it back and wrestled it into place, kicking and screaming.

"Morning, Cooper," Bob called.

Cooper nodded, then looked at me from all the way across the shop floor. His features were stiff, his eyes cold and hard.

His voice matched both. "Morning."

"I was just telling Abby what great progress you two have made." Walt gave him an extra-large version of a pat on the shoulder. "If you want a job in the off-season, you come to me, son."

My heart stopped. God, I hoped not.

"Thanks, but I think I'll be in Wyoming," Cooper said.

My heart crumbled at the prospect of him so far away. Worse, the prospect of him together with Greta. But, heck. Cooper deserved happiness.

Still, another corner of my heart broke off and clattered against the floor. One more piece of wreckage for the scrap pile.

"Well, you're ahead of schedule, and that's great," Walt concluded.

Cooper stuck his hands in his pockets and looked at the floor. "About that... Today will have to be my last day. I really have to get back to the fire crew."

My stomach folded in on itself, and my soul screamed, *No! No! No!*

But that was the way things had to be, right?

"Now, that's a real shame." Walt frowned. "But we appreciate what you've done. Right, Abby?"

I nodded, finding Cooper's eyes. "I do. I appreciate everything."

Just a whisper, but it was from the heart. That was the least I owed him.

"I figured I'd work on the last couple of handles today," he said — to Walt, not to me.

Ouch.

"Well, let's get started," Walt announced, and everyone got to work.

Cooper stuck to the woodworking corner of the shop, and the few times we interacted, his demeanor was cold and disinterested. My weak attempts at questions or comments got stinging, single-syllable answers.

All in all, the same treatment I'd given him his first few days in the shop. I deserved it. But damn, did it hurt.

The next time I stopped to heat the metal in the forge, I rubbed my forehead against my sleeve to dry off the sweat.

A full minute later, I was still there, because the tears kept coming.

I had ruined the best thing that had ever happened to me — well, second-best, after Claire. I would be alone forever. I was a terrible person, and I could barely wield magic. Nothing useful anyway. And when it came to dream weaving...

Well, if I could do that, I would dream up a world where all my mistakes were erased. Where it was just me, Claire, and my sisters. A small, simple world without pain, heartache, or outside interference. Especially the kind with warm brown eyes that came wrapped in soft flannel.

But life didn't work that way, did it?

"You okay, Abby?" Bob asked softly.

I snapped my head up, wiping the last tears in the process. "Fine. Thank you."

The sound of my hammer drowned out the words, but so be it.

Chapter Twenty-Six

COOPER

I thought my first few days in the metal shop had been the worst, but that one took the cake. At least it was my last day.

I'd spent all of Sunday desperately looking for solutions before finally giving in. Abby had made it perfectly clear that she was done with me.

Fight for her! Talk to her! my bear insisted.

I wanted to, but *no* meant no, and I had to respect that... even if it killed me.

I loved her, and deep down, I was sure she loved me back. But Abby was just too scarred for a relationship. A healthy one, at least. The kind I'd taken for granted my whole life.

So, lucky me. That didn't make my soul weep any less, though. For me, and for Abby.

My mother liked to say that love was infinite — a party that always had space for one more. When someone left the party, they left an empty chair, like Peter had, but the love was still there.

But maybe not everyone was up for that kind of party. Maybe all Abby could manage was tea for three or four. The same three or four, with no tolerance for party crashers like me.

Plus, there was Claire, and I got that Abby needed to put her first. I just wished *first* didn't mean *only*.

I took a deep breath. Ultimately, all that mattered was that Claire was happy. But, damn. I would really have liked to contribute to that, even in a small way.

I glanced at the drawings decorating my locker. I would be taking those with me, for sure.

Heaving a sad sigh, I got back to sanding the edges of my latest ax handle. If only regrets could be smoothed out as easily.

About an hour into that torturous day, a motorcycle revved outside, and everyone turned.

"Well, look who's back in town," Bob said fondly.

The other guys were all grins.

Outside the open rear bays of the shop, a man gave his custom Harley a few last revs before cutting the engine. He dismounted in one easy motion and made a beeline for Abby.

A growl built in my throat, but Abby lit up. "Mike!"

I frowned.

"Her stepfather," Matt whispered. "Or something like that anyway."

Mr. Hells Angel was tall, solid, and supremely confident. He moved with the grace of a panther, though not as quietly, due to the way his leather chaps and jacket creaked. His hair and horseshoe mustache might have been gray, but the guy was incredibly fit. He wrapped his arms around Abby and rocked from side to side protectively.

My inner bear growled. Jealousy was a bitch.

"Sorry, sweetheart. I came as fast as I could," he murmured.

She'd practically disappeared in his embrace — all but her hands, patting his back. I barely heard her muffled reply.

"Thanks for coming."

"I already stopped by the school," he told her.

Aha. So, stepdad was here to protect Claire.

I told myself not to be jealous. That the more people Claire and Abby had covering their backs, the better.

But, damn. It hurt not to be one of them.

"Thanks. I'm sure it will be okay," Abby told him.

"It will be," he growled while thunder rolled in the distance.

I glanced at the perfectly blue sky, then froze in realization. Slowly, I peeked back at the biker. And, yes, there it was — the slight shimmer of air around his shoulders.

Warlock. A powerful one, judging by the angry crackle in the air.

When he turned to glare at me, clouds blotted out the sun, and another drum roll of thunder rumbled over the landscape.

Bob peered out the open rear doors. "Are we getting a storm? It looked so clear a minute ago..."

Abby stuck an elbow in the warlock's ribs, then waved to me. "That's Cooper. You know Pablo and Bob..."

She skipped from me to the others, like I was just another colleague.

I let out a long, wounded breath, then went back to work. I had three last ax handles to finish.

An hour passed, then another. The stepfather — Mike — leaned against his bike out back, coolly contemplating life, the universe, and the mechanics of cam chain tensioners. I half expected him to whip out a copy of *Zen and the Art of Motorcycle Maintenance* and start reciting.

But behind that calm, casual demeanor lay the restless soul of a predator. His eyes roved the area continuously, and every time a car approached the shop, he held his hands at his sides like a gunslinger prepared to spray an entire town with bullets for his cause.

Abby. Claire. They were his causes.

They could have been mine, too.

I hacked and sanded the hickory handle.

At eleven thirty, Hells Angel mounted his Harley, revved as loud and long as an Indy500 car on the starting line, then peeled away. An hour later, he returned, revving several more times before killing the engine.

I made a face. Okay, okay. He was a rough, tough motorcycle guy. We got the message.

Rough, tough, but with a heart for the people he loved. I could tell by the way he prowled over to Abby.

"She's fine."

She, I gathered, was Claire, and judging by the time, she'd just had recess. I had the impression Mike would have preferred to stake out the school parking lot all day, but that kick-ass principal had probably chased him away until the end of the school day.

Mike didn't add, *No sign of Jay,* but I figured that was who he'd been watching for.

Abby nodded and went back to hammering the last ax head. The very last one. One we ought to have sweated — and triumphed — over together. But all I heard was a solitary *bang. . . bang. . . bang.*

The tension between us must have been palpable, because Matt came over to whisper, "Damn. What did you do to piss her off?"

I glared him away.

Even Bob wandered over to whisper his own two cents. "Just give her time, son."

I'd come to the same conclusion. Sadly, that probably exceeded my life-span.

Destiny had either made a huge mistake, or it was out to punish me.

Abby worked through lunch, as I'd intended to. I had to finish those handles — but I needed something from the supermarket too. So I made a quick run there, forcing down a sandwich on my way back.

The moment I turned the corner to the back lot of the metal shop, Mike stepped out, casting a dark shadow.

"Not so fast, kid."

I stopped, meeting his glare. If a lightning bolt flashed out of the sky to fry me, so be it.

My inner grizzly growled, and for once, I didn't try to muffle the sound.

His eyes glowed, and he leaned in. "Let me make a few things clear to you. If you hurt Abby, I will hurt you twice as bad. I will draw it out slowly, and you will be screaming for your mother before I'm done."

I heard him out, because I'd been raised to respect my elders. Even elders who wanted to crush my bones.

"You got that?" he finished.

A cloud passed over the sun, casting a bigger, even more menacing shadow over the entire area.

"Yes, sir."

He frowned. "You think I'm messing with you, kid? Because I swear, I'm not."

Thunder rolled, emphasizing his point.

I shook my head, "No, sir."

His nod said, *Damn right, I'm not.*

"I would never hurt her," I said, because now it was his turn to hear me out.

I love her, my bear declared, though I managed to suppress that part.

"I would never hurt her. Not Abby, not Claire. Never," I swore so fiercely, my voice cracked. "There's just one thing I can't figure out."

He crossed his arms. "And what's that?"

"How to keep her from hurting herself."

The corner of his eye twitched, and he didn't say a word. But I could tell I'd struck a chord.

Unfortunately, I'd struck one in myself too, and the words kept coming.

"Whatever hurt she has comes from a long time ago, not from me," I growled, keeping my voice low. "Hurt she keeps wrapped around her like armor. And I get it. I get the pain, the need to put up walls. But it's those walls standing between her and happiness, not me."

Mike pursed his lips, and the wind that had been swirling around my ankles faded slightly.

"The rescue train could stop right in front of her, and she could have a free ticket, but she would still refuse to get aboard," I continued.

He cocked his head, confused.

I shook my head, exasperated. "I want her to be happy. I want to *make* her happy. But she won't let me. And that kills me." My voice cracked again, but I went on croaking. "It kills me." All the steam went out of me, and I shoved my hands deep into my pockets, muttering, "Maybe she's right. Maybe this is all she needs."

Mike's eyes dropped to the ground, telling me he disagreed.

Well, so did I. But what could I do?

I kicked the ground. I really had to get back to work. I couldn't leave without one last word, though. "I'm glad she has you."

It hurt to admit, but it was true. Abby loved her sisters, and she adored her stepfathers. A damn good thing, because if she didn't have them, she would have nobody. Plus, having Mike around to protect her made it that much easier for me to walk away.

Not that any part of this was easy.

I stepped away without waiting for Mike's reaction. Back in the shop, I used the last scrap of momentum I had to walk over to where Abby banged away.

She straightened, giving me a sharp look, but I kept my eyes on the bench behind her.

"That's for Claire." I put down a pint-sized juice, then walked away.

Funny how a carton of juice could make your throat go dry.

The damn thing stayed with me for a while, though. I suspected it would for a long, long time.

At 2:45, I dusted off the last ax handle, checked it again, then added it to the neat row of nineteen — now twenty — leaning against the wall. Then I put away my tools and swept up.

At three, Abby's watch alarm rang, and she and Mike left to pick up Claire.

I carefully peeled back the tape holding Claire's drawings to my locker and rolled them the way museums did with masterpieces. Then I grabbed a crayon and drew my own picture, along with a few words. *Dear Claire...*

I stopped, momentarily stuck. Then I went on.

Sorry to leave on short notice, but it's time for me to go fight fires. Thanks for teaching me about horses and other things. Take good care of yourself and your mom for me.

Love, Cooper.

I looked it over, then stuck it under the juice and did an about-face. It was 3:10, and I had to get moving.

I shook Walt's hand, took one last look around the shop, and walked out forever.

Chapter Twenty-Seven

ABBY

"Closing time, Abby," Walt called quietly.

I didn't so much as glance at the clock. I just kept hammering away.

Normally, my boss communicated in a firm boom. Now, his voice was soft and gentle, like I might break.

And, hell. I was close.

"Now, Abby..." Walt murmured, coming over to me.

Even Louie, his floppy-eared mutt, looked at me with pity.

I stopped hammering but kept my eyes on the anvil.

Drip... Drip. Beads of sweat fell from my chin to my project — the very last ax head.

Walt reached out to touch my shoulder, then stopped and sighed when I shuffled away.

"Listen, you've had a long day..." he started.

Ha. That was one way to put it. First, Cooper, then Claire. She'd been delighted to see Mike after school, but when we'd arrived at the metal shop and discovered Cooper gone, she'd been crushed.

Me too.

But... But... Like a dog looking for its owner, Claire had run around the metal shop, checking my workspace, Cooper's locker, the parking lot...

Her hands had formed tiny fists, and she'd faced me, furious.

How could you let him leave? How could you?

The same question I asked myself, over and over.

I thought my heart was already crushed, but Claire's tears proved there was a bit left to torture. Even worse was the fact that she only shed one or two tears, then turned away to hide them.

Like mother, like daughter. She was that tough.

I hung my head in shame.

In the end, Claire refused to talk to me, and Mike had taken her home. I remained at work, banging away.

"Time to take a break, don't you think?" Walt finished.

I shook my head sullenly. No, I didn't. I couldn't. I couldn't face Claire or home or my family. I couldn't face anything. I just wanted to curl up in the forge and hide for a while.

Louie leaned in, meekly thumping his tail against my legs.

"I'll close up." My voice was dry and raspy.

Walt stood there another minute, then walked off with Louie, shaking his head. He stopped briefly at the door to call back, "Goodnight."

"Goodnight," I murmured into the flames. Then I took a deep breath and went back to hammering.

How long I worked, I wasn't sure. Traffic on the main road peaked, then fell. I finished shaping the last ax head, then got to work on etching the blade. The sun set, giving way to a cloudy night. My phone rang, then pinged with a text.

Are you coming for dinner? Erin asked.

Go ahead without me, I typed back and shut off the device. Then I went back to work.

I was still working when the front door creaked open an hour later.

"We're closed," I called without looking up.

"Sure look open to me," a man drawled.

My head jerked up as Jay sauntered in from the darkness. I reached for my hammer, tempted to throw it at him.

Shadows shifted behind Jay, and Liselle followed him in. Her dress had a metallic sheen and was gaily lined in vertical, rainbow stripes — perfectly appropriate for a socialite lunch.

If only it were noon and we were at a trendy restaurant.

But we weren't. We were alone in a strip of businesses that had all shut down for the night.

Two men filed in after Liselle, and she nodded to a third outside. I heard footsteps crunch as he took up a lookout position.

My nostrils twitched. Were those three men the cougars Cooper and I had confronted at Devil's Bridge?

I twirled my hammer. "We're closed. Come back tomorrow at nine."

"We're not here for business," Jay shot back, looking dangerously cocky.

I glanced toward my phone, wishing I hadn't turned it off and tucked it away in my bag.

"Now, now. I'm sure you can spare a few minutes," Liselle cooed. "You and that lovely daughter of yours."

My blood turned to ice, and I thanked my lucky stars Claire was safe at home.

"If she's even here," Jay grumbled. He stalked around, looking behind tables and yanking lockers open as if Claire might be hiding there.

"She's not," I growled. "Now, get out."

"The hell I will!" Jay stomped forward but halted like a dog when Liselle snapped her fingers.

Wow. She really had him under her spell. Then I frowned. Literally?

"Step outside, Jay," she said in a perfectly even tone.

He turned to her with glassy eyes.

"Step outside," she repeated in a monotone.

Her mind-bending wasn't aimed at me, but I could feel the air tingle.

"Sure thing, babe," Jay murmured, strutting for the door like he was in charge, not her. "You call me if you need anything."

I had the sinking feeling he was nearing the end of his shelf life when it came to being useful to Liselle. What then?

The thought sickened me, but that was his own doing. I had to think of myself and Claire.

I piqued my senses so as not to fall for Liselle's mind-bending again. I'd been distracted when I'd visited her home, but I sure as hell was on guard now.

"What do you want?" I demanded.

"Not much. Just that brazier I ordered."

"Well, I hate to disappoint you, but it's not done." And it never would be. Not by me, at least.

"I need you to make it. Now."

I laughed, indicating the clock, then the darkness outside. "Now?"

She nodded sweetly. "Now would be perfect, thank you."

Such a bitch, yet so polite.

"Well, we're closed, as I said."

"Oh, I'm sure you can manage."

"I'm sure I can't."

She smirked. "You haven't asked me what I'm offering in exchange."

Right. Like she was here to close a fair deal.

I tossed my hammer from one hand to the other. "I'm not interested in anything you have to offer."

"Oh, I think you are. Just consider, what is your daughter worth to you? What if I could make that custody case go away?"

The custody case she'd bankrolled. I was sure of it now.

"Like any judge would award Jay custody," I scoffed, sounding more confident than I felt.

She slid a manicured finger across Bob's workbench. "Maybe. Maybe not. But custody battles cost money. Lots of it."

Money she had, and I didn't.

"And the process can be so confusing, even harmful to an innocent child..." she went on.

I swallowed hard. She had a point there.

"But I can make all that go away," she cooed.

The itch at the back of my mind became a burn.

"No need to do things the hard way," she said, friendly as can be. "All I need is that brazier, and that custody case will go away, along with Jay."

Tempting, but no way.

"You mean, scraping at vortexes with the ax you stole isn't getting the results you wanted?" I said, laying out my suspicions.

Her eyes flickered. Obviously, her efforts had failed so far. The question was, what result was she after?

"That's my business, not yours," she snipped. "Just make me that brazier."

"I'd rather face that custody suit, thank you." I made a show of cleaning up my workspace. I did keep hold of my hammer, though.

"You think I don't have other forms of collateral?" Liselle arched an eyebrow. "Say, this town."

I frowned. What did she mean?

"Let's say misfortune rained down on beautiful Sedona." Liselle circled me, predator that she was. "Just think — if a wildfire were to strike here at the peak of the dry season, and the winds were to kick in..."

A bush swayed, scraping my car in the back lot. But that was hardly the tempest Cooper and I had survived at Devil's Bridge.

Magic was a cloak that shimmered around the shoulders of powerful witches and warlocks. But Liselle only had the barest glint, and most of that came from the dazzling effect of her dress.

Then again, it didn't take a tempest to whip a tiny fire into an inferno. A small, steady breeze at the right time and place could be just as dangerous.

"Just imagine — all that property damaged, all those lives at stake." Liselle sighed sadly, like she was watching a documentary and not actively plotting arson. "All those firefighters, risking their lives..."

I tensed. Was she that ruthless?

The sparkle in her eyes said yes. Very.

My mind jumped to Cooper, Rich, and the other members of the Yavapai crew. To those killed in action, like Kevin and Peter...

Then I froze, recalling what Cooper had said.

I met her during a job in Nevada. The Clark Canyon fire.

And not just that, but something about her making a scene after his brother turned her down.

My mind spun. The brother who'd been killed in a fire.

I stared at Liselle. Had she. . . ? Would she. . . ?

My knuckles tightened around my hammer.

"Such heroes, those firefighters. . ." she lamented. "And with so many other fires to fight. Wouldn't you like to spare them one more?"

"Wouldn't you?" I snarled.

"Of course. And it's all perfectly avoidable — if you help me." She leaned in. "I ask so little of you, really. Yet you stand to gain so much."

"*You* stand to gain, you mean."

But what exactly was that?

Power, the back of my mind hummed. *Unfettered power.*

Liselle had been trying to siphon the energy of the vortexes with the stolen ax. Maybe she'd even succeeded but needed a more effective tool, like the brazier she'd shown me.

Those slots along the top edge are especially important, she'd said. *I love how they make the smoke swirl.*

Part of a recipe for magic?

"Let me spell things out," she chirped. "You get nothing for doing nothing. But if you help me, I'll make your custody problem disappear."

And replace it with an inferno? No, thank you.

"You know, I don't get it," I admitted. "First, you try to kill me. . ."

Her eyes glowed. "Oh, that little storm at Devil's Bridge was just a warning."

No. It had been a goddamn tempest, but I doubted she'd been the one controlling it. Who, then?

"A warning?"

She nodded. "Not to mess with me. Just make me that brazier, and there won't be trouble."

I didn't buy that for a minute, but I indulged her, just to gain time to think.

"And you want it done. . . when?" I asked.

"Tonight."

My eyes nearly bugged out of my head.

"You can skip the runes," she added. "Those were just for show."

"Oh, well. In that case..." I muttered.

"Get to work," one of the men muttered, drawing a gun.

All the blood drained from my face.

"Picture that gun aimed at your daughter." Liselle smiled.

With my phone out of reach, I tried screaming to my sisters in my mind, but my cries seemed to bounce back from a brick wall.

Liselle's lips curled, and the lipstick that matched the peach stripe in her dress glinted.

Shit. I could resist her mind-bending tricks, but I was blocked from reaching out to my sisters. I couldn't reach Mike or Greg either.

"Come now. It's just a little brazier," Liselle cooed. "That's all you have to do."

My mind spun, trying to formulate some plan. But all I could come up with was to stall for time.

So stall, I would. All night if necessary.

Chapter Twenty-Eight

ABBY

Liselle rolled up her sleeves, rubbed her hands together, and waved everyone back.

I rolled my eyes. Drama queen.

We were in the back lot of the shop, where she'd insisted on a test run of the brazier.

I'd slaved away for the last two hours, stalling at first, then speeding along when I realized help wasn't coming and I needed another plan. An all-or-nothing, risky-as-hell plan, as it turned out. But it was the best I could come up with.

Liselle wanted a brazier that would help her tap into the energy of the vortexes? I would give her one. More energy than she'd bargained for.

"Get the wood, Doug," she snipped to one of her men.

I made a mental note. Doug. Five-foot-ten, 160 pounds, dark hair, dark eyes. Tiny scar on his chin. If I ever had a chance to pick him out from a police lineup, I would be prepared. Not that I was all too optimistic of that ever happening.

Doug hustled over to his vehicle and returned with a couple of artificial logs — the kind city folk used in the fireplaces of fancy apartments because they didn't want to chop wood or fuss with kindling.

"You're kidding," I muttered.

Even Jay wrinkled his nose to indicate, *Real men chop wood.*

Yeah, and real witches used real wood.

So, at least Jay and I saw eye-to-eye on something.

"I can't believe you let that witch con you into this," I hissed at him.

He shrugged. "Gotta make ends meet."

I scoffed. "Ever consider a real job?"

He shook his head. "Not cut out for that."

I cursed my twenty-year-old self. What had I ever seen in him?

"Is she even good in bed?" I snipped, keeping my voice low.

He looked at me, over to Liselle, then back to me, a little stuck.

I couldn't help gloating a little. Then I caught myself. What the hell did I care what a lowlife like Jay thought?

Doug lit a match, and within seconds, a fire was crackling inside the brazier.

It was a smaller, rougher version of the one at Liselle's home. The body of the brazier wasn't much — just four legs, a bowl, and a lip made of sheet metal. The slots in the lip had been the tricky part, and Liselle had leaned over my shoulder the whole time as I let sparks fly with my plasma torch.

Yes, the plasma torch. I missed my hammer and anvil already.

And Cooper. Boy, did I miss Cooper. And not just because a big, burly bear would come in handy at a time like this.

I missed rubbing shoulders with him while we took turns delivering blows. I missed glancing up and losing myself in those warm brown eyes. I missed his smile and his soft touch.

I swallowed hard, wishing for a second chance.

Liselle stirred the air with her hands and moved her lips. Was she uttering a spell?

Everyone looked on, rapt. I fantasized about this turning into an Indiana Jones-style scene, where the bad guys melted alive while the good guys survived.

But Liselle and her magic weren't exactly Arc of the Covenant level, so I doubted it.

The fire crackled, and smoke wafted out the open top of the brazier as well as the slots in the sides. Liselle leaned over, grasping at the streams of smoke.

Good luck, I nearly snorted.

But, yikes. The smoke thickened and followed her movements. She drew on the strands, hand over hand, like a magician pulling out an endless handkerchief.

The glow at the heart of the fire intensified, and sparks crackled into the night. And, whoa. Was the space around Liselle beginning to glow too?

I shuffled from foot to foot, sensing the earth groan.

"Is there a vortex here she can draw from?" one of Liselle's men whispered to another.

No, but magic flowed deep in the ground throughout Sedona. Vortexes were simply where that gushing, subterranean river pushed closest to the surface. But you could mine just about anywhere and eventually strike a vein of magic.

I sensed a restless force stir, like a chained tiger.

Liselle wouldn't be able to siphon much energy from Walt's back lot, but this was just a test run. If she summoned all her power and positioned the brazier directly over a vortex, energy would gush like oil from an unchecked well.

At least, it should. But I'd woven a little of my own magic into the brazier, and if it worked...

You need to be real careful using magic if you don't know exactly what it's capable of, Cooper had said.

I puffed out my cheeks. Did *fairly certain* count?

Liselle kept pulling, and the earth kept groaning.

Then an engine sounded, and headlights illuminated the driveway.

"Dammit..." Liselle dropped her hands, and the fire dropped too, leaving only a few crackling embers.

Her men fanned out, raising their hands to shield their eyes from the headlights.

I turned toward the car, praying the driver had the good sense to make a quick U-turn and disappear.

But he — or she — didn't. They drove all the way into the back lot and stopped with their lights trained on Liselle. The door creaked open, and a man stepped out.

"What's going on here?" he asked — and not in a nice way.

My heart leaped. Cooper?

"Private function," one of the men grunted. "Move along, please."

Cooper considered the man, then Liselle. He took in the brazier, then looked at me.

My lips quivered. I'd assumed he would have left town by now. Had he seen the flare of the fire and stopped to investigate? To come to my rescue, even?

The man was too good to be true. I just prayed that wouldn't get him killed.

"Everything okay?" His voice matched the rumble I'd heard in the earth — low and dangerous.

"Just fine, thank you," Liselle chirped. "We're just testing my new—"

"I didn't ask you. I asked her," Cooper grunted, demonstrating that he could, in fact, be less than polite sometimes. A first, at least from what I'd witnessed.

It made for a pretty badass impression. My knees shook, for sure.

"Liselle decided her order couldn't wait. So, she and her three friends stopped by." I pointed each out in the dark. No one was going to ambush Cooper on my watch. "Oh, and Jay," I added sourly. "Remember him?"

"Oh, I remember, all right," Cooper snarled.

Jay's sneer said he remembered too.

"So, you'll be moving along, then." Cooper's tone made it clear that was an order.

"Yes, you will." Liselle motioned to his pickup. "Thanks for dropping by."

I ground my teeth. She was trying to mind-spell him, wasn't she?

When he hesitated, she continued in the same chummy tone. "I know, I know. This woman is pure trouble, and you've had enough of her using you."

I fumed. Me, using Cooper?

"She's been bewitching you," Liselle went on, planting a whole conspiracy in his mind. "And all this time, you've yearned to be free..."

"Cooper..." I warned.

He looked at me, then Liselle, then scratched his head. "Not sure I would put it that way."

"Of course you do," Liselle chuckled.

He shook his head. "No, I was yearning for something else." His eyes slid to me as if to say, *someone.*

Liselle cackled. "Her? You want her? Honey, you can do so much better than that."

That stung, but it was true.

Cooper huffed. "Who? Like you?"

I nearly stomped. Was he actually having this conversation?

Her eyes drifted up and down Cooper's big, toned body. Then she ran a hand over her hip and purred, "Satisfaction guaranteed, honey."

Ha. I was tempted to refer him to Jay. But that would be petty, right?

Cooper flashed a tight smile. "Not interested, sorry."

So, whew. Apparently, mind-spelling didn't work on bears.

"Not interested?" Liselle hooted. "I don't believe that for a second."

Cooper went silent — very silent — and Liselle's cheeks burned with fury.

Still, I was tempted to yell at him. Why was he even wasting time with this? Why provoke her?

Then it hit me. Cooper needed answers, and as long as Liselle was talking...

She snorted. "Think before you speak, honey. You wouldn't want to set off trouble you'd regret."

"Trouble? Like you starting a fire, maybe?"

She laughed. "Oh no. I don't start fires."

"No, she'll just make sure the wind kicks in," I muttered.

"Like the Clark Canyon fire, maybe?" Cooper advanced on her. "A couple years ago in Nevada? The one that killed that firefighter..."

Her eyes darkened. "You never know. Maybe the guy got what he deserved."

If I were two steps closer, I would have smacked her into the next county.

Cooper's fingernails extended into claws as he stalked toward her.

One of Liselle's men stepped in his way. "Hold it right there."

Jay tugged on Liselle's sleeve. "Aren't we done here?" Clearly, he was ready to move on before more trouble appeared.

The guy was smarter than I thought. Not exactly a genius, though.

"No, we're not done," Cooper murmured.

I'd never seen him look so menacing. Especially when Liselle's hired hand grabbed his arm.

"Oh, I think we are." Liselle signaled to the others.

She was wrong, because all hell broke loose just then.

Cooper twisted out of the man's grip and shoved him toward Jay. A second man rushed Cooper, while the one nearest me drew a gun.

"Get down!" I yelled, lunging for the man's arm.

Bang! The blast deafened me, and the man shoved me down. But the gun fell too, and I managed to kick it away in a move Messi or Ronaldo would be proud of. Then I skidded painfully across the ground.

"Dammit..." The man hurried toward his weapon.

I rolled to my feet and—

"Take cover!" Cooper yelled, running toward me.

We dove behind a workbench in the metal shop as another bullet rang out.

Cooper ducked, then muttered. "Shit."

Yes, I was thinking the same thing.

"Stop shooting!" Liselle yelled to her men. "I need her alive if this thing doesn't work."

"You just tested it," Jay grumbled. "Let's get out of here."

At least there was that. My ex might be an egotistical, no-good sellout, but he wasn't a cold-blooded killer.

The other three guys, on the other hand...

I glimpsed one motioning to the others. They spread out and disappeared into the darkness.

Cooper hunched beside me, and we both listened for footsteps. Half the shop lights were on, the other half off, so everything was thrown into competing shadows.

"How did you know to come?" I whispered.

His eyes took on a warm glow. "I was driving by, and something didn't feel right."

Something, huh?

He didn't elaborate, but a word whispered through my mind.

Destiny. . .

My heart thumped in a whole new way. I'd heard the stories, of course — of two souls meeting and knowing they were meant to be. As if they hadn't met by chance but had been steered together by destiny. Shifters were especially big on the concept of fated mates. Bears, most of all.

I gulped as the glow in Cooper's eyes intensified.

Other supernaturals were less sold on the notion. Weak supernaturals, like me.

But, hell. Maybe I wasn't all that weak. Just an untrained, late bloomer. Maybe if it could happen to my sisters, it could happen to me.

And suddenly, I believed.

Something clanged in the darkness, and we both whirled. Destiny would have to wait.

"Come on, already," Jay urged Liselle.

"Not before I'm sure," she snipped.

The air wobbled, and flames lit the back lot once more. Liselle had rekindled the fire in the brazier for a second test run.

Second and last, I hoped.

I grabbed Cooper's arm, whispering, "Watch out. I rigged it to—"

A shadow moved behind him, and I yelled, "Move!"

Wham! We rolled as one of Liselle's men slammed a metal bar down between us. Cooper grabbed it, and they wrestled for control. I backed away, then whirled at another sound.

A second man grabbed a hammer from Bob's station and threw it. It flew end over end, coming straight at me. For a split second, I stared. Then I ducked and threw up my hand.

The hammer spun aside and crashed into a shelf. *Bam!*

I did a double take, because it hadn't actually touched me.

The guy grabbed another hammer and threw it at Cooper, who was still tussling with the first man.

And damn, could that guy aim. It went flying right at Cooper's head.

I stuck out a hand, yelling for Cooper to duck. He didn't, and I was nowhere near the hammer. But it arced off to the side, smashing into the wall instead.

The second man frowned. I ducked down and stared at my hand.

Metal lay all around me, reflecting the light of Liselle's fire. The tongs at Matt's workstation flickered. The ingots stacked by the wall reflected the flames. The scrap metal in one corner took on a fiery glow...

Liselle murmured, coaxing the fire in her brazier along.

The earth rumbled, and all around me, metal glowed. More than that. It hummed.

For years, I'd worked with metal and fire. And every once in a while, I'd sensed a similar thing — but rarely more than a barely there hint, and only when I was really in the zone. I'd always dismissed the faint sound as the echo of my own hammer.

But now, the sound wasn't quiet at all.

The more magic Liselle stirred up outside, the louder the sound became, going from a whisper to a roar.

The air vibrated all around me, and iron and steel shone.

"Yes..." Liselle coaxed more smoke out of the brazier — and more power out of the earth. Power that flowed into her and into me, too.

I faced the man who'd thrown the hammers, daring him to try again.

He did, flinging a chisel this time. It sliced through the air, smooth as an arrow. But when I swatted upward, it detoured and pinged off the ceiling.

All around me, metal hummed.

Me, me! clamps, tongs, and files begged. Even the bolts of my anvil jiggled.

"Oh!" Liselle's tone changed to one of alarm as the flames in the brazier rose higher.

"Not so big," Jay warned. "Someone will see."

Ha. If he only knew.

A pair of feline eyes glittered nearby — one of Liselle's men had changed into cougar form. The man who'd targeted Cooper followed suit, and both advanced on Cooper, who roared.

Yes, roared. He'd shifted too, and the flames of the fire added the outline of a huge grizzly to the two cougars shadowed on the wall.

I picked up a sledgehammer and advanced, then retreated from the blur of fur and fangs.

"Liselle..." Jay warned, skittering away from the fire.

"I've got it," she cried.

No, she didn't. The brazier shot flames as high as the roof. They swirled and spiraled outward, covering a wider and wider area.

Liselle's lips were peeled back, her eyes wild. "I've got it..."

The earth rumbled, angrier than ever. A powerful witch or warlock might have been able to control that power, but Liselle was out of her league — and in serious trouble.

Flames swirled, reaching over, around, and behind her. She made a patting motion, trying to douse them. But the flames closed in, igniting her sleeve.

"Help! Help!" she yelled, swatting at the fabric.

I looked away. Helping Cooper was my priority, not a witch who'd dug her own grave — or lit her own funeral pyre.

Screams pierced my ears, and Jay shouted, but none of that mattered. Not with two cougars fighting Cooper.

Wait. Two cougars... Where had the third guy gone?

I dove aside as an ax sliced past my shoulder. It clanged against the cement floor, but the man raised it again. Flat on my back, I looked up at the wide, gleaming blade.

The man swung, and I screamed, throwing up a hand.

I cringed, expecting a crushing blow. But nothing happened.

I blinked as the man strained at the ax. It hovered inches over my face, near the end of its deadly swing.

"Dammit," he grunted, pulling this way and that.

Sweat broke out on my brow, and I kept my hand up, pushing at air thick with magic. The hum of metal became a roar, and I gritted my teeth.

"Fucking witch," the man snarled.

The ax inched back, away from me. Then, with a mental shove, I sent it flying backward. The man toppled back, releasing it, and it clanged to the floor.

Liselle screamed. Jay yelled. Cooper roared. Ax man grimaced, pulled out a gun, and aimed it at me.

I scuttled backward, but there was nowhere to go.

Bang! He shot. Once. Twice.

I threw out my hands, terrified. But bullets didn't pierce my body, and no blood flowed.

Ping! Ping! Ping!

The gunman ducked as bullets ricocheted off the cement floors. One of the cougars fell away from Cooper with a yelp. A dark stain spread across the floor. Blood?

A moment later, Cooper heaved the second cougar across the room. It struck an anvil and crumpled to the floor.

Outside, the fire diminished, along with Liselle's anguished cries. Inside, the roar of metal calmed to a hum. The magic was ebbing away, seeping back into the earth.

But the gunman facing me didn't need to know that. I walked toward him, looking as menacing as I could.

"Drop the gun and get out of here before I put a chisel through your heart," I snarled.

It was a bluff, of course. I might be able to deflect metal with a magical force field pulsing all around me, but I sure wasn't going to try to maneuver pieces through the air like a ghost.

"I said, drop it!"

The gun clattered to the floor, and the guy ran for the door.

I hurried over to grab the gun, but I wasn't the only one. I lunged, grabbing the weapon first, then whirled around.

"Don't shoot!" Jay raised his arms in surrender.

My hands shook. If Jay had gotten the gun before me, would he have pulled the trigger?

Yes, I decided. If not at me, then at Cooper.

A car roared away from the street side of the shop, and I bid the hammer-thrower goodbye. Then I narrowed an eye over the gun barrel, aiming at Jay.

He backed up, hands up, eyes wide.

"Don't shoot," Jay begged. "And don't — er, bite."

Cooper lumbered up beside me with a long, low snarl.

I pointed Jay to the cougar stirring weakly on the floor — the one who'd been hit by the stray bullet.

"Get him, and get out of here."

Jay frowned. Clearly, the second part of my order was fine with him. But why bother with the first part?

"I said, get him."

Jay dragged the cougar outside by one paw. At a roar from Cooper, the remaining cougar dragged himself groggily in the same direction. Together, they stepped past the brazier, where a small fire burned.

"Flip it over." I motioned with the gun. "Put out the fire."

"Hell no. I'm not touching that!" Jay grunted.

I braced my feet and steadied the gun with both hands.

"Okay, okay!" Jay reached for the brazier, cringing.

"Put out the fire," I ordered.

He hooked one of the brazier supports with his boot and flipped it sideways. The embers rolled onto the scorched lump that had been Liselle. They flared, then died down to a dim glow.

My stomach turned, but hey. I wasn't the one who'd tried to tap into the earth's hidden power.

By then, both cougars had dragged themselves toward the road, where Jay's truck stood.

I motioned to Jay. "Get them and go."

"You are one crazy bitch, you know that?"

Cooper snarled while I retorted, "Says the guy who sold his soul to the devil. A guy prepared to sell out his own daughter."

Shame passed over Jay's features, but only momentarily. Then he went back to thinking of his number-one man — himself.

"Just don't...don't..." he stammered, backing toward his vehicle.

I fired over his left shoulder, making him duck.

"Get out of here, Jay. I never want to see you again. Ever. But if I do — and if I ever hear another word about custody — I swear I will kill you."

My Dirty Harry side scared him, all right. It scared me too, because I meant every word.

Jay stumbled to his truck, shoved the cougars into the back, and started the engine with a roar. Then he peeled away — out of sight and out of my life.

Good riddance.

Cooper let out a long, continuous growl until the sound of Jay's engine faded.

I glanced at Cooper. What would he say? What would he do?

Of course, as a bear, he wouldn't say much. But what was going through his mind?

I took a few deep breaths. As long as Claire was all right, nothing else mattered.

Then I froze. "Claire..."

I ran into the metal shop and grabbed my phone. But Erin didn't pick up, and neither did Pippa. When I reached out with my mind, that barrier was still there.

When I glanced up at the sky, my gut lurched. Dark clouds swirled overhead, blotting out the stars. Really dark clouds, especially over to the west. The direction of home.

Home. Claire. My family.

"No. Please..." I murmured, running to Cooper's truck.

He followed, flicking his ears up.

I hesitated. I had no right to ask him for anything more. But I sure wouldn't mind his help on one last matter.

"Something's wrong," I explained. "Something at home."

His fur bristled, and his eyes flared.

Two minutes later, he was in human form, behind the wheel of his pickup, and roaring down the road, speeding me homeward.

Chapter Twenty-Nine

COOPER

Abby's hands were in a knot as I sped through the night. Clouds swirled over us, and lightning cracked ahead.

"Where's the ranch?" I asked.

Abby pointed to the lightning. "Right there."

I sucked in a deep breath. Claire was stuck in *that?*

According to Abby. Mike, the stepfather, was there too, along with the rest of the family. But that wasn't much comfort.

"I think you were right about option three — the one about Liselle not working alone."

Abby nodded. "The question is, who else is it?"

Or *what*, I wondered. What kind of supernatural could kick up a storm like the one raging ahead?

Thunder cracked and lightning sizzled, illuminating the same spot again and again.

Abby tried her phone, then cursed and went back to fidgeting.

I rolled down the window, sniffing the wind. Then I rolled it up again, wishing for my bear pelt instead of bare human skin. I'd been packed to leave town, so I'd pulled on a spare pair of jeans before leaving the metal shop, but I hadn't had time to button the shirt I'd grabbed.

"There. Turn right." Abby pointed once we were a few miles down the road.

My pickup creaked over the dirt road, but I still drove at breakneck speed. The sooner we got to Claire, the better.

"That brazier..." Abby started haltingly. "I only made it because Liselle threatened to burn the whole town down."

I grimaced, thinking of Peter and the Clark Canyon fire.

Maybe the guy got what he deserved, Lisa — Liselle? — had had the nerve to say.

I grimaced. If that witch weren't already dead, I would have turned around to kill her.

"I did have a backup plan," Abby went on nervously.

I looked at her. Did she think she was to blame?

"You did the right thing," I said. "And it worked, right? I mean, having it backfire on her the second time."

Backfire — literally, my bear grumbled bitterly.

Abby nodded but remained hunched. I yearned to reassure her, but with the vehicle jerking around in fierce gusts of wind, I had to focus on steering.

And, damn. If the storm was this severe here, how bad was it at the ranch?

The wind howled, flattening trees and kicking up dust — so much, I could barely see a few car lengths ahead. But that didn't account for the total absence of a road in the spot Abby indicated for me to turn into.

"Here?" I checked, seeing only bushes and dirt.

"Trust me. Turn here."

I did, slowing to a crawl. To my surprise, the tires rolled smoothly — or as smoothly as they would on dirt — and a road gradually appeared out of the haze.

"The entrance is spelled," Abby explained, fidgeting even more.

My skin crawled a little. Bears and magic...not a natural mix.

But then I thought of magic protecting Claire, and that sat much more comfortably with me.

"If it's spelled, how did someone sneak in?" I asked.

"I don't know. It's only happened once before." She trailed off, then froze.

"Who? When?" I demanded.

"Harlon Greene. Almost a year ago."

She'd mentioned the name before. A warlock, from what I remembered.

"Just one more mile..." Abby murmured nervously.

It felt more like a hundred as the storm raged all around us. The road rose in an incline, with visibility so poor, I couldn't tell what came next. Another turn, or the edge of a cliff?

Thunder boomed, and lightning illuminated thick, swirling clouds. The hood of my truck pointed up, then down as we crested a hill.

Boom! Lightning scorched the ground directly in front of us.

I hit the brakes. The sky blazed with enough lightning to electrify the entire state. And not just sky-to-ground lightning. Bolts speared forward and backward too, zipping parallel to the ground.

The hair on the back of my neck stood. This wasn't a lightning storm. It was a lightning *fight*.

Abby braced herself against the dashboard, whispering desperately. "Claire..."

I moved my foot back to the gas. If Claire was in that storm, so were we.

Over the next few seconds, the storm roared to a crescendo, like the grand finale at Fourth of July fireworks. After one last ear-cracking *Boom!* it petered out gradually.

I drove onward, glancing around warily. Now what?

Thunder rumbled in the distance, no longer over our heads. One last, feeble bolt of lightning blinked behind the clouds. The wind died, and everything went still.

I peered forward, letting the headlights slice through the darkness.

The dust settled, and the clouds slowly parted, allowing a slice of moonlight through. Enough to reveal several small buildings, a corral, and a barn. Abby's ranch.

"Wait! Stop," Abby said.

I hit the brakes as a man emerged from the dust by the main house. He held his hands like a gunslinger ready to crack off another few rounds.

"Mike," Abby breathed.

The stepfather. That was a good sign, right?

Then I spotted another man, closer to us with his back turned. That had to be the other gunslinger — er, lightning slinger? — that Mike had faced off with.

"Harlon," Abby hissed.

Whoever he was, he looked hunched and defeated.

Other figures appeared from in and around the house, and a burst of fire revealed a dragon over to the right.

I did a double take.

"That's Nash, over by Erin's vortex," Abby explained. "She must be over there, helping fight Harlon."

Another vortex? Right here on the ranch? I gritted my teeth.

And, yikes. A dragon shifter. At least he was an ally, judging by Abby's tone.

Ingo appeared next, running past Mike to tackle Harlon. Harlon raised his hands, but Ingo threw him to the ground and whipped out a pair of handcuffs that shimmered with magic.

I exhaled a little. Whatever had just happened, it was under control now.

Two more people emerged from the house — Pippa, and a shorter figure in pink pajamas that matched the stuffed rabbit she held by one ear.

"Claire!" Abby cried.

I floored it, following the shortest route to the house. Mike looked up in alarm, then waved to let us pass.

Abby hit the ground running before my car came to a full stop. When she reached Claire, she fell to her knees and hugged her daughter tightly.

I sagged a little. Safe. They were both safe.

I pushed open the car door, ready to run over and join them. Then I stopped. Abby and I had already said our goodbyes. Well, sort of. And anyway, the message had been pretty clear. She didn't have space for me in her life.

She can make space, my bear insisted. *Just ask her. Beg if you need to.*

But bears and witches didn't mix. They couldn't.

Says who? my bear rumbled. *A bunch of old-timers who've never seen, let alone gotten to know, a witch?*

My mind ran through all Abby's interactions with Claire. With me, too. The bossy, bitter part was just her outer layer. Beneath that, she was all heart.

A lot like a bear, my inner grizzly said.

I pictured Abby laughing. Touching. Opening up to me, then shutting down completely.

I gulped. Life with Abby truly was a roller coaster.

A pretty thrilling one, my bear whispered.

"Cooper?" Pippa broke away from Abby and Claire to motion me over.

But Ingo yelled at the same time, and I turned that way, because subduing Harlon was the priority. As I ran toward them, a woman appeared, sprinting for the main house. The sister, Erin, I gathered, hurrying to check on everyone there.

Further proof that Abby didn't need me. I continued toward Ingo.

Then a horse whinnied, and things went downhill fast.

"Domino!" Claire called from the porch. I glanced back, seeing her run to check on the horse.

Alarms sounded in the back of my mind. Claire...the horse...the corral, with its aluminum fence...

Something about it felt off, but I couldn't understand why.

Then it hit me, and I whirled to cut her off.

"Claire! Stop!" I yelled.

She kept running, too focused to register my words.

"Stop! Stop!" I yelled.

I could see it now — Claire jumping to the corral fence, then climbing to perch on the top rail. But she wouldn't make it that far. Not if my hunch was right.

By then, she was only a few steps away from the fence. I was a little farther but speeding in quickly from her left.

"Claire!" I yelled again. "Stop!"

"Domino!" she called, and the horse nickered back.

She was three steps from the fence...two...one...

I dove, hating myself for what I was about to do. But I had no choice.

"Hey!" Abby protested from behind me.

Everything went by in a blur. Tackling Claire out of the air... Twisting as we fell so I wouldn't crush her... Crashing to one shoulder, then scraping along the gravel.

I winced, more from Claire's cry than the cuts in my skin.

Claire whimpered, confused, but I kept her cradled against my chest as I lay in the dirt. My heart pounded so hard, I thought it would burst. But I wasn't letting her go anytime soon.

Everyone ran up, kicking dust into my eyes. I coughed as Claire whimpered.

"Mommy..."

"Are you nuts?" someone barked.

I gestured with one hand. "Stay away from the fence! Nobody touch it!"

Pippa helped us up, and Mike snatched Claire away from me.

"What the hell?" he growled, only refraining from a roar because of Claire in his arms.

Abby stood at his side, staring at me, then the fence.

"Cooper?" Claire's eyes were fearful and confused, and that hurt.

"The fence—" Abby pulled Mike back.

"What about the goddamn fence?" he snarled at me.

"It's electrified," Abby finished, and everyone jumped back.

For a few seconds, we all stared in stunned silence. Then Pippa picked up a rake and tossed it against the fence.

Sparks flew, and the air crackled.

"Whoa." Pippa leaped away, along with everyone else.

"All that lightning...the metal fence," I panted.

Mike studied the fence, then shook his head. "No ordinary lightning." He thrust Claire into Abby's arms and stormed past me. "Fucking Harlon..."

Over by the bluff, Harlon struggled, but Ingo held him tightly. The dragon circled overhead, spitting fire.

I picked Hopper out of the dirt, dusted him off, and handed him to Claire.

"I'm real sorry. I couldn't think of another way of stopping you. Are you hurt?"

She sniffled, craning her neck at a scratch on her elbow. "Yes."

But, whew. That was a small price to pay, like the gravel embedded in my shoulder.

"You would have been hurt even worse if you'd touched the fence," Abby chided her gently, then squeezed her and Hopper close. "That's why Cooper had to stop you. But you're okay. You're okay..."

Her sisters pressed in, cooing in comforting tones, and I backed away. Blood seeped through my shirt sleeve, but the ache in my heart was worse. I was back in the same inevitable place. Abby had everything she needed — her daughter, her family, and the ranch.

I shuffled back toward my car, not part of that equation. I was done here. Done in Sedona, too.

I looked at the moon, high and bright in the rapidly clearing sky. I ran my eyes over the dramatic rock formations, silent sentinels in the night. Then I steeled myself and looked at Abby, memorizing every detail, from her auburn hair to her green eyes to her lithe figure.

With a deep breath, I closed my eyes, silently wishing her well. Then I turned to my truck.

A steely hand clamped over mine, and a man growled right in my ear.

"Not so fast, kid."

I sighed. This again?

"I said, I'm sorry," I told Mike. "I couldn't think of a better way to stop Claire without—"

He cut me off. "You did good." His throat bobbed. "You did good."

A rare compliment, but I was too dazed to care.

"If you'll excuse me..." I pushed toward my car.

His thick arm chopped into the space before me, blocking the way.

"I said, not so fast."

I kicked the ground. Now what?

"You wait right here, kid." He pointed at me, giving me the evil eye. "Don't move a hair, you got that?"

What he was up to, I had no idea. But whatever. When he was finished haranguing me — as I was sure he planned to — I would leave. I would head straight to Wyoming and never look back.

My bear mourned.

"I said, you got that?" Mike growled.

Never in my life had I been more tempted to disrespect one of my elders. But bears had those rules ingrained in them young, and I just didn't have it in me.

I sighed and looked at my shoes. "Yes, sir."

Mike stomped over to the others, still huddled by the corral.

One last tumbleweed rolled by. In the darkness, a bird chirped cautiously from a thicket, the first to peek out after the storm. The scent of pine and juniper filled my nose, and I savored that special Sedona scent. Pine, juniper, and something else. Huckleberry. Dandelions...

Two sets of steps sounded behind me, one heavy, one light.

"All right, now. You two talk," Mike ordered gruffly.

I looked up, finding Abby there. Behind her, Erin and Pippa walked Claire to the main house.

"Go on, now." Mike nudged Abby gently. "Talk." Then he pinned me with a dark look. "And you listen."

"Yes, sir," I mumbled.

Mike nudged Abby, then walked away.

Abby looked at her feet for a while, then whispered, "Thank you. Thank you so much."

"Nothing to thank me for. I'm just glad Claire is okay."

"She is. But I do have to thank you. And I need to apologize too."

"No need. Really."

She snorted. "Big need. I'm sorry. For everything."

"It's okay, really."

"No, it isn't, because I owe you. Big-time."

I didn't want her to owe me. I wanted her to trust me — and her heart.

"And, actually, you owe me too," Abby went on.

Huh?

"I owe you?" I thrust my hands deep into my pockets and formed tight fists.

She nodded. "Yep. All that blacksmithing I taught you. . ."

Her voice wavered, and my initial burst of anger faded away. This wasn't Abby being demanding. This was Abby trying to lay something bare. Something hidden for so long under so many layers of protection, it would take a while to wrestle out into the open.

But, hell. Patience was a virtue, and I was all ears. Big, African-elephant-sized ears.

"So, I figure it's time you taught me a few things in return," she went on, barely above a whisper.

My heart pounded in hope. "Like what?"

"Like, how to be nice. How to be patient. How to be as good a person as you."

I shook my head. "I'm not—"

She cut me off in a whisper. "How to see the best in people. And how to trust." Her eyes were wide and pleading, her lips tight. "I really want to. But I don't know how."

I clasped her hand in both of mine. "It's not as hard as you think."

"Maybe not, but it scares me. Really scares me." Abby's eyes glistened, and I ached at seeing her so lost. But, hell. I was here to find her, right?

"I would never hurt you," I vowed quietly.

"I know. But what if I hurt *you*?"

I thought it over, because she had. But we all made mistakes, didn't we? And anyway, what kind of bear would I be if I didn't have a thick hide?

I shrugged. "I'm a bear. We bounce back."

Her cheeks flushed. "You shouldn't have to." Then she sniffled. "I bet Greta wouldn't hurt you."

I waved, dismissing that. "She wouldn't, but I don't love her. I love you."

Abby's eyes jerked up to mine, and I held perfectly still. There I was again, with that butterfly on my nose. A moment of truth.

"I love you too." Her eyes shone. "Desperately. But I'm afraid I'm not good at it. At loving, I mean."

I gestured toward the house. "One look at you with Claire proves you wrong. You're *very* good at it."

"You're not Claire."

I grinned. No, I wasn't. And I was hoping for a different kind of love. But, still. It was like my mother liked to say. Love was a party, and there was always room for one more.

"No, I'm not Claire. But maybe I like to live dangerously. I'm a firefighter, right?"

She didn't look convinced. "Greg always says, firefighters don't live dangerously. They live with calculated risks, and they calculate those really, really well."

"Well, then. Consider the risks calculated."

She stood there, gazing up into my eyes. Her lips wobbled with words that never came, so I covered them gently and said, "I'll make you a deal."

She tilted her head.

"I'll teach you if you keep teaching me," I proposed.

The moon glinted off her hair when she shook her head. "What could I possibly teach you?"

"Teach me about you. About blacksmithing. Maybe even ranching. And you let yourself trust."

"Kind of a lopsided deal, don't you think?"

I shook my head. "I think we both stand to win big."

Her eyes sparkled, so I went on.

"Of course, I'm not a very good blacksmith, and with fire season coming up... Well, I'll be gone a lot."

She gulped, then wrapped her arms around me like I was about to ship out.

"That will be hard." Her voice was muffled. "But as long as you come back..."

I held her tightly. "I will always come back." Then I glanced over her shoulder and chuckled. "Mike might kill me if I don't."

Abby's laugh was music to my ears. "He means well." Then she touched my shoulder and froze. "Oh God. You're bleeding..."

I shrugged. "Nothing serious."

"But your shirt—" Her eyes welled as she fingered the fabric. "Peter's shirt..."

I looked at the torn sleeve, then took her hand. "I think he would find it a worthwhile sacrifice."

"But... But..."

I shook my head. "No buts. I'm sure he would approve."

She looked up at me, still unsure. "You think so?"

I leaned in to kiss her. A kiss of comfort, hope, and relief. One I broke only long enough to whisper, "He would definitely approve."

Chapter Thirty

ABBY

Cooper was a champion kisser, and I never wanted that moment to end. It wasn't every day a girl got a second — or third — chance at her dream man. But car engines sounded, and headlights cut through the night. Cooper and I whirled. With the dark clouds breaking up, the moon bathed the landscape in enough light to make out a convoy of four cars.

Cooper and I hurried toward the main house, intercepting the others there — everyone but Ingo and Mike, who kept watch over Harlon.

Two of the vehicles screeched to a halt by them, and a troop of armed men piled out. Armed to the teeth, in fact, just like the men who flooded out of the remaining two cars when they pulled up to the house.

Every dog on the ranch broke into frenzied barks. I stood beside my sisters and Claire on the porch, along with a snarling Roscoe.

"Great. Now what?" Pippa griped.

"This is the ADMSA. Everyone freeze!" one of the men ordered.

"This again?" I sighed.

"Again?" Cooper muttered.

Oops. Someday, I would have a lot of explaining to do.

"I said, hands up!" another agent boomed.

"Captain Edwards. What a pleasure," Erin said without a hint of enthusiasm.

"Miss Sattler. Miss Martin. Miss Carson," he grumbled.

You knew life had taken a wrong turn when the leader of a top-secret law enforcement agency knew your name by heart.

"Hello, Todd," Pippa quipped, borrowing a page from our mother's playbook.

"Captain Edwards. Captain *Tom* Edwards," he grumbled, not at all pleased.

Pippa made a gesture that mimicked our mother's — the one that said, *Whatever.*

Ingo and Mike jogged over, leaving Harlon in the custody of Captain Edwards's troops.

"Oh, Captain Edwards. You came personally," Ingo said, not at all pleased.

"You bet I did. How is it that this family always manages to attract trouble?"

"How is it that you always arrive a little too late to be of any real help?" Erin shot back.

Edwards glared, but he didn't answer the question.

Hmpf. Didn't think so, Erin muttered in my mind.

Several tension-packed moments ticked by, before Ted — er, Tom — spoke.

"What exactly happened here?" he demanded.

I looked at my sisters, wondering the same thing.

"Ask Harlon," Mike growled, pointing.

Edwards's eyebrows jumped up. "Harlon Greene?"

Pippa nodded. "Yes, Harlon. The warlock you put away after his last attack." After pausing for effect, she added, "Or did you?"

The captain's face went dark with fury. "He was under a restraining spell cast by a panel of class-one warlocks."

Mike crossed his thick arms. "Not any more, apparently."

"But...but...how?" Edwards fumed at his men, who looked at their feet.

The bravest pulled out a phone. "Shall I call in to ask, sir?"

"Yes, goddammit!"

"I beg your pardon!" I bristled, covering Claire's ears.

In truth, she'd heard far worse from us. But the sooner we got a leg up on the blustery captain, the better.

Amen, Erin mumbled into my mind.

Ha. If only we had Mom here, Pippa joked. *She knows how to get a leg up on him — and a lot of other things.*

Ugh. I tried to block out images of Mom and Captain Edwards getting down and dirty, but it was too late.

Erin looked around uneasily. *Don't jinx us—*

Another set of headlights came over the hill. We three sisters groaned, and Claire cheered.

"Grandma!"

I winced. Mike went on guard. My sisters gritted their teeth.

Captain Edwards's eyes went all shiny, and his voice cracked. "Virginia..."

A sleek Lexus SUV whisked up — the kind you saw parked in front of country clubs and five-star restaurants. When Mom traveled, she traveled in style.

The car stopped, but she didn't emerge. Seconds ticked by as she waited for someone to open the door for her.

"Oh, for goodness' sake," Mike muttered while we sisters rolled our eyes.

Captain Edwards and his men practically fell over one another to reach the door first.

Edwards won — no surprise there. In one smooth move, he managed to straighten his jacket and hair as well as open the car door. He kept his eyes down, the way the queen's footmen did.

One toned leg appeared, along with a very high, stylish heel. Mom paused there, letting the men get a good, long look. Then she stuck out a hand, which Edwards took gallantly.

I could hear his heart pounding from ten yards away. And that was before Mom had even exited the vehicle.

Finally, she slid out with a wiggle calculated to make every sequin on her dress glitter.

Yep. Mom sure knew how to make an entrance. Captain Edwards and his men practically drooled.

Cooper cocked an eyebrow and whispered, "That's your mom?"

"Yep," I sighed. "The apple fell pretty far from the tree, huh?"

Pippa chuckled dryly. "All three of us apples."

"Wow. She looks like a movie star," Cooper said, not all too impressed.

She did, especially in that glittery 1930s-style dress. On me, it would look like a moldy potato sack. But Mom could have graced the cover of *Vogue* magazine in it.

"Mom," Erin said flatly. Then she cleared her throat and attempted — but failed at — a peppier tone. "I mean, Hi, Mom. Good to see you."

"Grandma!" Claire ran over and hugged her legs.

Mom looked down, patting Claire's head awkwardly, then pivoted away. "Watch the dress, darling."

"It's beautiful!" Claire breathed, missing the snub.

Captain Edwards's eyes shone in a way that said *ten out of ten.*

And, hey. Mom *was* beautiful. Even spellbinding.

I froze. Was Mom more than just a dragon shifter?

Pippa must have picked up on the thought, because she muttered into my mind, *I shudder to think she might be one-quarter witch or something.*

Erin shuddered. *If she is, I don't want to know.*

Yikes. I decided I agreed.

"Oh. Hello, Dom," Mom said as if she'd only just noticed him.

"Tom," Captain Edwards breathed.

Mom gestured in a way that said, *Whatever.*

"Well hello, Mike," she purred at Erin's father.

"Virginia," he said gruffly. He didn't seem ready to fall at her feet, though.

My mother frowned. If *mojo* came in a spray can, she would be shaking hers and trying again.

But no such luck. Her charm worked on most of the men there, but not Mike, Cooper, or Ingo. Nash was still circling the sky overhead, but I knew he wouldn't fall for her either.

My mother shot Mike a sour look and glanced around, then sighed dramatically. "So, we find ourselves here again."

Our cue to feel guilty, because we'd inconvenienced her one more time.

"Yes, we do." Captain Edwards shot me an accusing look.

Thank goodness for Erin stepping in.

"Harlon showed up about two hours ago, kicking up a storm," she said. "All we did was defend ourselves."

Cooper glanced at me, and I whispered a nervous joke. "Doesn't every family wield lightning, thunder, and hurricane-force winds?"

He shook his head, a little awed. "Here I was thinking everyone used claws and fangs."

Well, then. We'd both broadened our perspectives.

I squeezed his hand, and he squeezed back.

"And that incident reported back in town..." Edwards consulted a notebook. "At...Heavy Metal Sedona?"

Cooper raised a hand. "That was us."

I elbowed him in the ribs. Drat good, honest men raised never to fib.

"He means, that was us defending ourselves against Liselle Steinmeier," I corrected quickly.

Edwards consulted his notebook again. "That's an alias. Her legal name is Lisa Greene."

All eyes slid over to Harlon, and Erin blurted, "They're related?"

Edwards nodded. "She's his daughter. Or should I say, she was?" He eyed me closely.

I gripped Cooper's hand extra tightly in case his principles made him say something like, *Yes. In fact, she died because of the way Abby spelled the brazier. We only acted in self-defense, but please feel free to lock us up for all eternity.*

I cleared my throat to cover Cooper's pained squeak and answered, "I'm not sure what happened. I was too busy taking cover from her armed accomplices."

Or too busy deflecting bullets with magic, but Edwards didn't need to know that. Also, I decided to withhold the name *Jay Wilson* for now. Claire didn't need to hear that.

"Lisa... Harlon... The disturbances in the vortexes..." Erin mused out loud.

Pippa figured it out faster than I did. "Could Lisa — Liselle? — have used the vortexes to break the restraining spell on her father?"

"That's what we're here to find out." Edwards puffed out his chest.

"So, go find out." My mother huffed and pointed him to Harlon. "That would allow you to stop harassing my daughters."

"Harassing?" Edwards protested.

My mother crossed her arms. "Yes, harassing. Not to mention that it's past this poor child's bedtime." She patted Claire about as warmly as she tended to pet Roscoe — stiffly and from a distance.

Since when does Mom know about bedtimes? Pippa muttered in my mind.

Shh. She's on a roll. Don't mess this up, Erin warned both of us.

"Much past her bedtime, not to mention the trauma of having armed vigilantes appear on her doorstep," my mother went on, incensed.

"It's okay—" Claire started cheerily.

I led her briskly inside. "I know it's scary, sweetie. Let's go to bed."

"Yeah," Pippa announced, standing guard at the door. "We can decide about suing for harassment in the morning."

"Suing?" Edwards's eyes bulged.

Ingo touched his boss's sleeve and pointed to Harlon. "She does have a point about starting there, sir."

Having bribed Claire with brownies in the kitchen, I peeked out from behind a curtain and listened in.

Edwards glared at Ingo, then Mike, and finally, his men.

"What the hell are you waiting for?" he hollered at them. "Get over there and secure the suspect for questioning." Then he backed away from the house. "We'll need you to come in for a full report tomorrow, but that's enough for now." Looking at my mother, he added, "Thank you for your time."

My mother rewarded him with a bored smile. His men piled back into their vehicles, leaving Edwards and my mother at ground level, with my sisters, Ingo, and Cooper looking on from the porch.

My mother looked between Edwards and Mike, waiting, no doubt, for one to challenge the other to a duel over her. Edwards would probably have jumped at the chance, but Mike turned away with a firm wave.

"Goodnight, Virginia. Take care."

My mother watched him go, eyes flaring. She'd always been the *want what you can't have* type. On the other hand, *heartbreaker* came a close second, and she had a willing Edwards to indulge her.

Her eyes slid over to him, and I could see her calculating.

"I don't suppose someone can recommend a decent hotel in town?" she asked.

Decent, unlike the ranch, her tone suggested.

Edwards jumped on the opportunity. "As a matter of fact, I know one."

"You don't say," Mom cooed softly.

I caught Mike rolling his eyes. Had he once fallen for a similar line?

It was easy to picture him thirty years younger, an irresistible, handsome devil on a motorcycle, revving away at the alluring mystery woman who'd caught his eye. Hell, he still was an irresistible, handsome devil with a motorcycle. Just a little grayer around the temples — and a lot wiser.

For once, I was fully supportive of Mom putting her moves on Edwards. The sooner we were rid of our unwelcome visitors, the better.

Fifteen minutes later, red taillights shone, marking the ADMSA's exit. My mother drove in the middle, which gave every impression of a presidential limo flanked by its escort.

By then, I'd rejoined the others on the porch. We watched the convoy drive off, then breathed a collective sigh of relief. Quiet stretched — the good kind — for the next minute or so. Then a slight breeze made the weather vane on top of the barn squeak.

I'd made that wind vane — a dragon spitting fire — without really knowing why I'd chosen that particular design. Now, with so many trials and tribulations behind me, I wondered if I'd unconsciously imbued it with a little special something.

Like magic.

I thought of the lucky ax that had kept the fire crew safe all these years. Had the wind vane done the same for us? Would it do so in the future?

"Ah, Mom. She sure has timing," Pippa sighed.

"Does she even care about us?" I couldn't help asking.

"She cares," Mike assured us. "In her own way, but she cares."

"I'm starting to think so too," Erin mused, rubbing her chin.

I seriously doubted it, but I indulged her. "How?"

"Three times now, we've been in trouble. And Mom has shown up every time."

We all stared toward the road. Could it really be?

Finally, Pippa sighed. "Maybe. Or maybe she just enjoys torturing Captain Edwards."

I laughed, but the way Mom moved from man to man tipped the scales in favor of *she cares*. Which was kind of mind-blowing.

Pippa hooked her elbow through Ingo's and headed toward their converted barn. "Well, it's been a long night. See you tomorrow, everyone."

We waved, and Erin signaled to Nash, who flew toward her cabin and landed there. Two points of light marked his alert dragon eyes, then faded as he shifted to human form. Erin waved to him, then looked at Mike, Cooper, and me.

"You're welcome to sleep at my place tonight, Dad," she offered.

His eyes blazed as he looked protectively between Erin and me. He was still on the long, rocky road to accepting that "his little girls" — a category I was touched to be included in — were all grown up with men in their lives. Plus, Erin's cabin was pretty small, and having a warlock in close quarters with his dragon shifter son-in-law was a potentially combustible combination — literally.

Usually, Mike stayed in the ground-floor guest room in the main house, below where Claire and I lived. But with Cooper here...

"I could, uh..." Cooper started.

I clutched his hand tighter. He was not going anywhere.

"I'll take the couch," Mike said gruffly.

Ha. I could see right through his logic — strategically positioning himself between Cooper, in the guest room, and the stairs leading to me. No hanky-panky with a warlock in residence, no siree.

But it wasn't a night for hanky-panky. It was a night to...to... Well, a night to put an end to one day and hope for a fresh start tomorrow.

And boy, was I hoping for a fresh start.

Cooper, too, judging by the way his eyes glowed.

I hugged Mike. "Goodnight, and thanks for being the best grandfather ever."

"Co-best grandfather," he said softly.

That was a joke he and Pippa's father had come up with over the years. And boy, did we welcome the total lack of drama as far as those two were concerned. It helped compensate for my mother... A little anyway.

"Goodnight," I whispered again. Then I took Cooper's hand and whisked him upstairs before Mike could protest. "Feel free to use the guest room, Mike. Cooper can have my bed. I'll be with Claire," I said, loud and clear.

No sense in getting a warlock worked up, right?

I didn't specify how long I planned to stay with Claire, but I hoped an hour or so would do it. She'd survived a terrifying storm and nearly been electrocuted. Amazingly, she didn't seem too traumatized, but it was hard to judge.

As for me, I was definitely traumatized, because my daughter had witnessed a terrifying fight and nearly been electrocuted. All that after fighting my own battle.

Fresh start, I told myself over and over. *Tomorrow.*

You could hear a pin drop — or a warlock eavesdropping — when Cooper and I hugged at the top of the stairs.

"Thank you," I said. "For everything. See you in the morning?"

He cupped my cheeks and kissed me softly. "See you soon."

Chapter Thirty-One

COOPER

Most nights, I slept like a log. But that night, as I lay in Abby's big queen bed, I could only stare at the ceiling, listening. Wishing. Yearning.

Abby whispered to Claire, and their sheets rustled. Roscoe paced back and forth in the hallway, unsure of the strange new sleeping arrangements. Finally, he turned in place three times and lay down outside Claire's open doorway. No sound came from downstairs, just Mike's vigilant silence — until, a long time later, heavy breathing signaled he'd finally fallen asleep.

The atmosphere on the ranch was similar — tense, then quiet as everyone succumbed to exhaustion. But even then, I couldn't sleep.

Finally, I caught the soft pad of Abby's bare feet. A floorboard squeaked, followed by more silence when she hesitated. Then the footsteps resumed, coming closer.

Without a word, I lifted the sheet and blanket. She slid in, nestling along my body. When I wove an arm over the notch of her waist, she grasped my hand and held it at her heart.

I inhaled her floral scent — once. . .twice. . .

Then I slept, not just like a log, but a whole forest of them.

∞∞∞∞

I really, really wanted to take things slow for a few days. Weeks, even. But first, we had to rush around and deal with the aftermath of all that had transpired.

Step one: driving to the metal shop the next morning to explain the damage of the previous night. On Ingo's advice, Abby and I kept our story simple. Jay had come — alone — to threaten Abby, pushing around equipment and firing a few rounds from his gun. A few harmless rounds, thank goodness.

Walt was furious — at Jay, not Abby. In fact, at great risk to his own health and safety, he caught her in a huge hug of relief.

"Just glad you're okay, kiddo. You, Claire, and Cooper."

Abby, Claire, and Cooper. It had a ring to it, I decided.

Destiny, my bear reminded me in an *I told you so* grumble.

Destiny, indeed.

Abby stood stiffly, enduring Walt's hug. Maybe even patting his back a little. When he eventually released her, he insisted that Abby take a few days off.

She accepted, but only after disassembling the brazier, banging the pieces into lumps, and throwing them into separate scrap bins.

If Walt and the others wondered why, they didn't ask, and I didn't tell. It was better that way.

Step two was a trip to the fire crew I'd quit the previous evening. Luckily, Rich welcomed me back with a level, "We all make mistakes, son."

True, but I hoped that would be my last big one.

Step three was reporting to Captain Edwards for grilling — er, questioning. Luckily, enough incriminating evidence had emerged on Harlon, Lisa, and their recently acquired Edelweiss Corporation that the ADMSA was less interested in us than them.

"Fucking Harlon. It was him all along," Abby muttered.

"Well, you won't need to worry about him again," Captain Edwards growled.

Apparently, tapping into magic that wasn't your own was risky business. During the fight at the ranch, Harlon had dug so deep into the magic he'd "borrowed" from Sedona's vortexes that he'd burned himself out permanently. No more casting spells of any kind for him, ever.

"You mean, kind of like being castrated, but with magic?" Abby asked.

Captain Edwards winced and shifted in his seat. "That's one way to put it."

So, whew. Lisa was dead, and Harlon no longer posed any danger. That left Jay as the only loose end, but the way he'd fled the metal shop said he would never mess with Abby again.

And if he does, we'll be here, my bear growled.

So, whew. As soon as we were finished with Captain Edwards, we headed back to the ranch and straight to bed. Claire was at school, with Mike on guard in the parking lot — even with Jay gone, he'd insisted — so we had the house to ourselves.

And boy, did we make good use of it.

We took our time, though, teasing through every discarded layer of clothing and relishing every kiss. Even when we were skin-to-skin, I went slowly, exploring every inch of Abby's body and working her up to the first of many orgasms.

Very, very many, I vowed to myself as she lay panting afterward.

Abby being Abby, recovery didn't take long. In no time, she had her legs wrapped around me and her arms braced against the headboard, ready to push back when I pushed in.

With a groan, I slid home to heaven. No condom this time, and no hesitation, because this was forever.

Forever. . . My bear hummed.

I pushed deeper, then remained anchored, sucking in a long, sharp breath. I withdrew slowly, aching the whole way, then thrust back in, faster and harder.

And wow, did that bring us to the razor's edge of ecstasy. We wobbled there, on the brink of exploding, before backing away, catching a breath, and zooming right back again. Because something that good oughtn't be rushed. It ought to be treasured.

But at some point, even the most well-intentioned bear lost self-control, and the whole operation peaked in a flurry of cries, groans, and throaty exclamations.

"Oh!" Abby cried, clenching down around me.

I flew off the edge, and she flew right after me.

A whole, happy future danced through my mind, blurry but so real, I knew it would someday be our reality. My jaw ached, and my bear couldn't stop chanting like a husky cheerleader. *Mating bite. Mating bite!*

Someday, I promised. Today was just day one on our journey to *forever*. No need to rush things.

We lay panting for a long time afterward. Even when we caught our breath, we lay close for a long time, gazing into each other's eyes.

Abby's expression became one of intense focus, and she tapped her fingers thoughtfully.

"What?" I whispered.

"Just wondering if there's a way to count luck."

I grinned, holding her flush against my body. "Not in numbers."

"Definitely not," she murmured, running her hand over my arm. "I guess my conclusion is, I have a lot."

I pressed her hand against my heart, and we slowly drifted off to sleep, making up for the all-too-short previous night.

I'd only slept one brief night on that mattress and under those covers, but they already felt like home. Well, the mattress and covers were pretty interchangeable. The *home* part was Abby.

Abby took three days off work, and each passed with the same basic schedule. We woke, ate breakfast, drove Claire to school, then returned to the ranch for a couple of blissful hours in bed. We would rouse ourselves in time for Mike to bring Claire home, eventually have dinner, and the cycle would slowly tick over again.

But then the inevitable happened — a forest fire, in Oregon. The first real blaze of what turned out to be a very busy season. I struggled to focus at first, but it wasn't long before tunnel vision kicked in, and days one and two turned into twenty, thirty, and forty. We wildland firefighters worked in cycles of two weeks on, forty-eight hours off, with *on* often hundreds of miles from home.

My first two weeks away were a killer. The second fortnight, after a blissful weekend at home on the ranch, was even harder. But old habits kicked in, and I learned to flip a switch, speeding time up at work and slowing it down for days off.

And days off had never been so good, with lazy mornings and delicious pancake breakfasts. Long, ambling walks, horseback rides, or bear rambles. We ate out on my first evening back each time — pizza, in the very same place as our first dinner together — followed by dinner with the entire family the next day, and an early dinner with just the three of us on my last day home.

Off times also meant reading Claire bedtime stories, then waiting in bed for Abby to finish her turn. After that came studiously quiet sex, what with Claire just down the hall. Then I would head off to work again, changing gears back to that high-speed time warp of firefighting.

The Yavapai Hotshots fought fires all over the West, earning a reputation as the "on fire" crew of the season — pun totally intended. A lucky crew armed with axes that sang in our hands and roared right back at blazing fires, or so some of the crew claimed.

I kept my mouth shut on that one. But when it came to toasting their creator, I was all in.

The original ax had been recovered from Lisa's house and returned to cheers from the entire crew. Needless to say, it went everywhere with us.

But as far as I was concerned, the luckiest ax was mine — the very last one Abby had forged. She'd etched a roaring bear face into the blade, and anytime a fire raged too close for comfort... Well, let's just say the fire rapidly retreated.

We crossed paths with the Pine Ridge crew several times, so I still got to work with my siblings, cousins, and other family members. At the same time, I'd gained two new families — the Yavapai crew and Abby's wonderfully eccentric family. I loved going home to them. And if the three sisters were a tight sorority, we three guys — Ingo, Nash, and I — quickly grew close too.

So, yes. Home and family. Days were full, and nights passed in deep, peaceful sleep.

I still had dreams about leaving Peter behind. But I had other dreams too, like catching Claire just in the nick of time at that electrified fence. That didn't make up for my brother, but it provided a little perspective, in a way. A little more peace.

Peter, I figured, wouldn't mind me thinking such things. And I was sure he would have approved when fire season finally tapered to an end and I got to go home and stay there. Home, in Sedona.

"You think you'll even remember how to relax after a season as hard as that?" Nash asked my first week back.

Relaxing hadn't been my concern. Magic was. But I quickly concluded that living on a ranch surrounded by vortexes was pretty okay. Idyllic, even.

I laughed. "I'm a bear shifter. Downtime is our specialty."

Still, I found myself plenty busy, between work on the ranch, helping Abby in the metal shop from time to time, and my own projects — especially the one I'd mapped out in my head during the long fire season. Nash helped me with it some afternoons, and even Claire had pitched in at times. When it was done, we had a big unveiling — Pippa's idea.

"Any excuse for a party," she joked.

She set up balloons and a long red ribbon that Claire cut for the grand opening.

Mike whistled. "Now that's what I call a playground."

"Sure is," my father murmured, giving me a proud wink.

Yes, my parents had come down from Wyoming to visit me in my new home. It wasn't Thanksgiving yet, but it felt like it. They hadn't been all too sure about the witch thing, but Claire — and Abby's firefighting background — had won them over in no time.

We all stood back, admiring the new playground — everyone but Claire, who raced off to test the monkey bars, slide, rope bridge, and jump stumps.

"Oh my gosh. It's great!" Pippa gushed.

Her father, Greg, nudged her. "Space for lots more kids, you know."

"Dad." She stretched the word to four syllables and rolled her eyes.

He stuck up his hands. "Just saying."

"The man has a point," Mike chimed in. "You don't want Claire growing up all spoiled. She has to learn to share."

Yes, those two had a clear agenda when it came to the next steps in their daughters' lives.

Abby wasn't half as vocal as the others, but I could tell by the way her eyes shone that she loved the playground. Doubly so since she'd never had anything like it as a kid.

I hugged her, because that had been part of my goal, too — letting Abby catch up on some of the things she'd missed out on herself.

My sister, who'd also come to visit, pointed at us and laughed. "You two look cute in those shirts."

My mom had followed a long family tradition by bringing us early Christmas gifts — matching flannel shirts, one for every member of the family, even Claire.

So, cute? I grimaced. Maybe.

Abby patted my chest and shot me a sly wink. "Adorable."

"Exactly the look I was going for," I sighed.

Then Claire called out. "Come on, Mommy! I'll show you how it works!"

I let Abby go with another kiss and watched them play, grinning so hard, my cheeks hurt.

My mom wore a similar expression, as she so often did. It had always confused me, because standing around watching kids play hadn't seemed super special to me. But now, I got it.

Boy, did I get it.

"Come on, Cooper! You too!" Claire called.

"Yeah, come on, Coop. Let's see you try that tunnel," Ingo joked.

I joined Claire, but not in the narrow tunnel or on the rope bridge, which Pippa raced toward.

"The ultimate test," Ingo laughed as I headed for the monkey bars.

Oh, they were plenty sturdy. I knew, because I'd personally reinforced them.

That was the special bonus in all this. All summer, I fought fires — preventing destruction but not actually creating anything. Now, I got to make things and watch others enjoy the outcome. Especially Claire. And, hey. If Abby and I ever had more kids, they could play here too.

My bear was all over that one. *Cubs! Soon!*

Well, we would have to see about that. But I hoped so.

The blueprints for Claire's playground had come from the business my sister ran with her husband and our cousin. I'd laughed off jokes about me opening a new branch of the company in Sedona, but now that I was done with Claire's set... Well, maybe that wasn't so crazy after all.

All in all, breaking in the playground was a highlight of my first month on the ranch full time. The next highlight came a little later, when, after months of waiting...

Claire was at another weekend sleepover at her friend Tana's. Pippa and Ingo were out dancing, while Erin and Nash were already in bed due to their *early-to-bed, early-to-rise* ballooning schedule. So, the ranch was quiet, and Abby and I had the house to ourselves.

"So, I was thinking..." Abby said as we watched the stars from the porch.

My mind had been wandering, so I assumed she was going to follow with something like, *I was thinking it's time for dessert.*

Not exactly what she'd meant, as it turned out.

"...now that you're home for a while..." Her hand dropped to my leg.

Foolish bear that I was, I remained focused on the stars.

Now that you're home for a while, we can start renovating the spare room, was what I absently expected to come next.

She stroked up and down a little, and boy, was that nice.

"...it would be a good time to... You know, to..."

She trailed off, blushing. I wasn't looking, but I could sense her cheeks heat. We were that tuned in to each other.

Or maybe not as tuned in as I thought, because her hand slid toward my groin next.

Which was when it finally dawned on me that renovations were not what she had in mind.

Less than a minute later, we were panting, naked, and in bed.

Well, almost naked.

"Let me..." I broke off a kiss long enough to unclasp her bra. Maybe not the best idea, because I got a little distracted, kneading, kissing, and nipping her soft flesh.

Best distraction ever, it could be argued, but a distraction, nonetheless.

A good thing one of us was goal-oriented.

"Here," Abby panted minutes later, guiding my hand to her core. "I need you here. And I need that mating bite. Now."

She wasn't kidding, and I was totally on board with that plan. Still, I did my best to throw on the brakes a little.

"A mating bite is a little like blacksmithing," I mumbled, rolling away her panties.

"How?" she growled, kicking them off her ankles and feet.

"You need to lay the groundwork first."

"*Lay* is the only part of that sentence I like—" she started, then broke into a cry of delight as I touched down.

I circled my hand around, then...um...heated up the forge.

Abby arched as I probed and rotated, letting out another cry and another...

A damn good thing we had the house to ourselves.

While I worked her, she worked me, gripping my shaft and stroking up and down.

She moaned, tapping my back the same way she gave the anvil a few warm-up taps at work. A cue, of sorts. At work, that meant I should ready my sledgehammer and prepare to pound.

In bed, it meant... Well, pretty much the same thing.

She wrapped her legs around me, drawing me in deep. We settled into a steady rhythm, with her inner clenches timed to meet my powerful thrusts. The decibel level was a lot like work, too, except with heavy groans and sharp cries instead of metallic blows.

"Wait..." Abby panted.

I stopped so fast, it hurt. "Not good?"

"Very good," she assured me. "But this would be even better..."

She pushed me back and rolled to her stomach, taking up... whatever we'd decided that position was called. The one with her on her belly with her rear raised and me on all fours behind her. Lazy dog?

My bear scoffed. *I'll show you lazy...*

"Oh..." she breathed as I slid back home.

We picked up right where we left off, moving at a steady, perfectly matched pace.

But the longer we went, the more my control crumbled. My canines extended, and I scraped them along the side of her throat.

"Yes..." Abby bucked under me.

Instinct led me to the right spot, and I bit down — hard — and exploded inside her.

Abby let out a long, low moan. Or maybe a loud one. Hard to tell, because my bear drowned her out with a roar.

Mine! Mine! Mine!

The words echoed in a higher, feminine note in my mind. Because as surely as I was claiming Abby, she was claiming me.

Shocks of ecstasy racked my body. I held on, anchored deep in both places — teeth and core — while our essences mingled, forging an eternal bond.

My vision went blank, and sound and light blurred. I heard rustling trees and a rushing river. I smelled an alpine meadow flooded with flowers. I felt my thick pelt rub against something soft and sleek. Something that moved, rumbled, and hummed in delight — another bear, slight and trim, with a reddish tint to its brown fur.

My mate, the she-bear sighed as she wound her neck around mine, marking me with her scent.

All that played out in my mind as we flew through our high. My teeth remained deep, my body wrapped around Abby's. Then, as the high gave way to waves of softer pleasure, my teeth retracted, and I pressed my tongue against her skin. Then I slowly let go, kissing the tiny wounds to make them heal instantly.

Abby gradually relaxed her grip on the sheets, letting me wind my fingers through hers. I lay over her, limp, panting, and thrilled.

After months of pining for this moment, we were here.

"Holy shit, was that good," Abby murmured in her usual poetic style.

I chuckled into her shoulder blades. Yes. Yes, it was.

"Are we... Did you..." she mumbled.

I nuzzled her shoulder. "I did. We did." We were mated now. Forever. "No second thoughts, I hope?"

She snorted and wiggled her rear. "The only thought I have is for seconds. Can we do that again?"

I laughed. "Anytime we want."

Dangerous words, knowing Abby was the impatient type. Happily, she relaxed into my arms and let me hold her for a while.

"So, I get to be a bear now, huh?" she murmured once we'd eventually cleaned up and rearranged ourselves, spooning together in her — er, our — bed.

I stroked the patterns on her arms. "Yes. Well, pretty soon."

"How soon?" she demanded.

I laughed. Abby had always assured me she loved the idea of being able to shift, but it was good to know she hadn't changed her mind.

"It's different for everyone," I said. "But knowing you—" I felt around her ears, then snuck a hand along her hip "—that could be any time now. No sign of fur yet, though."

Her laugh rippled through her body, and I tugged her closer, trapping her in my arms.

"Soon," I murmured, tucking my chin over her shoulder and closing my eyes. "Very soon. I'm sure of it."

Chapter Thirty-Two

ABBY

Four weeks later...

"Go home, Roscoe." I shooed the dog gently away. "Go home."

He whined and paced in place.

"I'll be back soon. Go home." I pointed sternly.

He returned to the porch, watching me go with a weak wag of his tail.

I walked a few steps, glancing at the striking sunset colors, then back at the house, where colored lights flashed, framing the windows and door. Christmas wasn't far off, and we'd gone all out.

Correction — *Cooper* had gone all out. He blamed it on Ingo and Nash, who'd set a standard by decorating their homes. I blamed it on Pippa, who'd kicked off the whole arms race in the first place. The ranch looked like a strip mall with all those blinking lights.

I grinned. It was pretty nice, actually. *Really* nice. My Christmas cheer had never extended to decorating anything but the actual tree. But this year...

Well, there was a lot to be cheerful about.

Like the sound of Claire's laughter, coming from the living room. Cooper was reading her a story — something about mermaids, from the sound of it — and I closed my eyes, listening to the low rumble of his voice.

In a few months, he would be off fighting fires, and that would be hard, but we would figure it out. We had to, because firefighting was important to him — not to mention to the crew and the communities depending on them. Besides, Cooper didn't hold me back. In fact, he set me free. So, I would do the same for him.

Set me free. . . a voice whispered eagerly in my mind.

"Just a second," I whispered, walking toward the mesa.

There was a boulder there where I'd first shifted into bear form, three weeks earlier, and I'd been going there to shift each time since. I was still a novice, and anything that helped me make the transition was a plus.

In the distance, a door creaked then slammed shut. Pippa had offered to stay with Claire while Cooper and I went out, so she was on her way over to my house, while Cooper had given me a head start.

"See you soon," Pippa called to Ingo, then strode toward the main house. Spotting me, she waved. "I'm on my way over to Claire now."

"Thanks a lot." I waved back.

One day, I hoped to pay her back if — no, when — she and Ingo had kids. And the way those two carried on, kids couldn't be too far off in the future.

I walked on toward that special rock. The one directly below "my" vortex, farther upslope.

My vortex, like Erin's and Pippa's, had been strangely quiet for a while. We'd worried that Liselle might have inflicted permanent damage on Sedona's hidden hot spots, but the ADMSA had sent a committee of experienced witches to investigate around town, and Ingo had shown us their report.

Tests conducted at all known vortexes demonstrated normal energy levels. The outlets that are currently dormant represent fluctuations in a natural cycle and do not reflect any impact caused by human or supernatural interference.

So, whew. The next part of the report had been more startling, though.

Our data supports that of the 1972 Watkins study, which suggests that Sedona's vortexes are not discrete entities, but rather, one interconnected system originating at a single source. The hunt for that source, however, must continue.

One source... like the ranch? Pippa had asked when we'd first read the report.

We weren't sure, and we didn't want to find out. More importantly, we didn't want *anyone* to find out, especially if that single source turned out to be beneath our ranch.

So far, we'd managed to keep our vortexes — and our magical abilities — out of the ADMSA's official reports. We hoped it would stay that way, too. Happily, Ingo agreed.

And as for magic... Well, I was finally embracing who and what I was — a hephaestid, named for the blacksmith to the Greek gods. My ability to control metal came from my father, and my affinity for fire came from my dragon shifter mother.

But I was me, not them, and I could be damn proud of that.

I'd finally agreed to lessons from Mike and Greg to better control my abilities — just in case. I didn't want to inadvertently make another lucky ax — or a lucky *anything*, for that matter — that could be used for ill means.

As for my own father... I hadn't heard from Ed since he'd visited the shop that day, so hopefully he'd gotten the message. I had to give him one thing, though — he'd been right about the Edelweiss Corporation, though neither of us could have predicted how personal that danger had been.

Nobody would have predicted the news we'd recently received either.

Entrepreneur Harlon Greene found dead at his residence while released on bail pending trial for racketeering, fraud, and embezzlement, the headlines had said. Authorities suspected foul play, but so far, the perpetrator hadn't been found.

It was Erin who'd come up with the most plausible explanation. *If he managed to make enemies of us, he must have made lots of other enemies. Really dangerous ones, like mafia guys...*

Vampires... Pippa added grimly.

Shifters... I threw in.

Or other warlocks, Erin finished.

Well, whoever did it, we all agreed that Harlon had it coming — and that we would never have to look over our shoulders again as far as he was concerned.

So, whew. That was all behind us now, and I was living my best life. A new life with a wonderful, loving partner.

I glanced back, eager for Cooper to join me. But story time came first, so he would be a few minutes yet.

When I reached my special boulder, it was still warm from the sunny day that had just faded to an end. I took a deep breath to concentrate on shifting. I shook out my hand, picturing paws instead. I rolled my neck, knowing it would soon grow thick. Layer by layer, I peeled off my clothes and tossed them onto the boulder. The chilly evening air made my skin prickle.

Warm. Help me stay warm, I asked my second self.

Coming, a cheery voice rumbled. My bear side.

I hunched and sank to my knees. I barely registered the bite of gravel, because the shift was already underway.

Set me free... my inner bear mumbled.

"Doing my best," I grumbled. Really grumbled, which meant—

Opening my eyes, I spotted fur. Paws. Claws.

Yippee! my grizzly cheered, dancing in place.

It — er, I — gave myself a hearty shake, settling my fur in place. Then I looked down my long, dark nose and sniffed the air.

A barrage of scents flooded my nose, making me sneeze. I'd never considered the ranch a place particularly rich in odors — except maybe the manure pile out beyond the corral — but my sensitive bear nose amplified every scent, from acrid manure to sharp pine and the dry, sweet odor of prickly pear cacti.

I shook myself again, startled, as always, by the heavy mantle of my fur and the flop of my ears. Then I set off toward the creek, where Cooper and I had agreed to meet. Taking advantage of my time alone, I tried out my paces, going from walk to trot to sprint, because coordinating four feet still didn't come naturally.

Just leave it to me, my grizzly reminded me cheerily.

My bear side, as it turned out, was more like Claire than me — all upbeat and happy. Or maybe it was a better version of myself, without the emotional baggage. Either way, I liked the new me. A lot.

But thinking made me stumble, so I went back to concentrating on my feet.

Just switch off and leave this to me, my bear said.

I made it to the creek without further incident, even running at an exhilarating clip for a while. Then I hastily hit the brakes before I slammed into a tree and covered up by roaring, as if the tree were at fault.

Very impressive, Cooper said, appearing behind me.

Actually, he growled, because he was also in grizzly form. But I was fluent in bear-talk now and pretty damn good at reading my lover's mind — a handy side effect of the mating bite.

I whirled, rearing to my back legs to look ferocious, because ferocious was always good.

Cooper's eyes sparkled. *Even more impressive.*

I waved my front paws for good measure, but oops. That threw off my balance, and I toppled backward.

I rolled in the dirt, a little chagrined. Not so impressive after all.

Cooper hurried over to snuffle me. *Are you all right?*

I assured him I was, but his sniffs of concern tickled, and I laughed.

Hey, I'm trying to be ferocious here, all right?

You don't have to try to be ferocious, he assured me. *You just are.*

My insides went all warm. For years, I'd thought I would be single forever. Now, I had the world's sweetest mate. How had I gotten so lucky?

Destiny, Cooper reminded me, nudging me to my feet.

As soon as I was on all fours, he nuzzled me, long and hard. Enough to make me topple again.

I cursed, falling over.

Cooper lunged forward, catching me with his body, then gently nosing me to my feet. The fur of his muzzle was baby-soft, like his human beard when stroked in the right direction. The thick layer of fur around his neck was coarser, but equally good for nuzzling.

So much for ferocious, I sighed.

You'll get it. You've already learned so much, so fast, he said.

I had — and not just about being a bear. I'd learned how deeply Cooper slept in the off-season. How gentle his touch was. He much he loved me, and how much love I was capable of too.

And then there was the icing on the cake: the dream weaving part. I'd finally figured it out.

For years, I'd dreamed of living a normal life with loving parents who were there for me and cared. Well, I had that now — in Mike and Greg, if not my mother or Ed.

I'd dreamed of happy days in a stable home and being part of a family.

I inhaled, savoring every sweet, familiar scent of the ranch. Home. Happiness. Family.

Check, check, check.

I'd given up on dreams of ever finding true love, but then Cooper had come along and rekindled them.

My eyes misted as I added another check to my list.

All those dreams had come true — and more.

So, had I learned to weave dreams? Yes and no.

I could. I had. But not with magic, and not overnight. That wasn't how it worked, I'd come to realize.

Now, I knew how. Bit by bit, over many years, I'd been slowly weaving my dreams. All those hard hours, earning respect in the metal shop. All those endless nights with baby Claire, who had turned out to be a great kid. All the mistakes I'd learned from — and the few smart decisions I'd made. . . they all wove together into what I had now.

My dreams had come true. I was living my very own happy ending.

And that wasn't a magic power only certain special people had. It was something anyone could do with persistence, drive, and determination. A sprinkle of luck didn't hurt, but the foundation of my dreams was mostly hope and hard work.

Nothing magical about that.

Cooper bumped his shoulder against mine. *Are you okay?*

I nuzzled him, hiding my misty eyes, and rumbled my reply. *Doing great,* my love.

Sneak Peek: Desert Moon

The scent of destiny... The danger in desire.

Lana Dixon knows well enough to steer clear of alpha males, but Ty Hawthorne is as impossible to avoid as the sizzling Arizona sun. Her inner wolf just won't give up on the alpha who's tall, dark, and more than a little dangerous. One midnight romp under the full moon is enough for Lana to know she'll risk her life for him — but what about her pride?

Ty puts duty above everything — even the overwhelming instinct that says Lana's the one. She's the Juliet to his Romeo: forbidden. And with a pack of poaching rogues closing in, it's hardly the time to yield to his desires. Or is love just what this lonely alpha needs to set his spirit free?

RAVEN AWARD FINALIST - FAVORITE PARA-NORMAL ROMANCE

Books by Anna Lowe

Spellbound in Sedona

Wind Whisperer (Book 1)

Fire Dancer (Book 2)

Dream Weaver (Book 3)

Sherwood Forest Shifters

Tempting the Sheriff (Book 1)

Tempting the Outlaw (Book 2)

Tempting the Maiden (Book 3)

Lure of the Dragon (Book 1)

Lure of the Wolf (Book 2)

Lure of the Bear (Book 3)

Lure of the Tiger (Book 4)

Love of the Dragon (Book 5)

Lure of the Fox (Book 6)

Aloha Shifters - Pearls of Desire

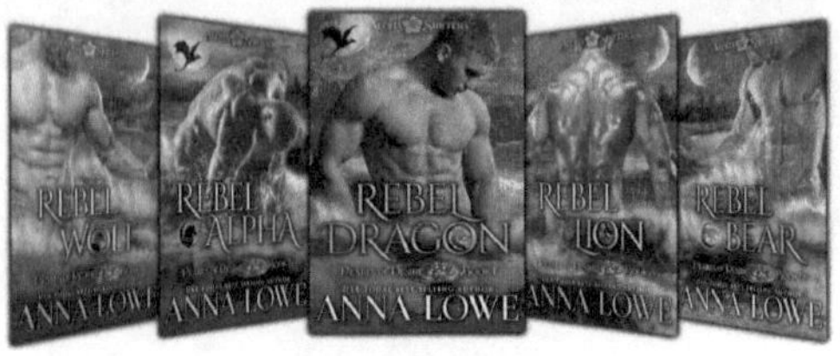

Rebel Dragon (Book 1)

Rebel Bear (Book 2)

Rebel Lion (Book 3)

Rebel Wolf (Book 4)

Rebel Heart (A prequel to Book 5)

Rebel Alpha (Book 5)

Fire Maidens - Billionaires & Bodyguards

Fire Maidens: Paris (Book 1)

Fire Maidens: London (Book 2)

Fire Maidens: Rome (Book 3)

Fire Maidens: Portugal (Book 4)

Fire Maidens: Ireland (Book 5)

Fire Maidens: Scotland (Book 6)

Fire Maidens: Venice (Book 7)

Fire Maidens: Greece (Book 8)

Fire Maidens: Switzerland (Book 9)

The Wolves of Twin Moon Ranch

Desert Hunt (the Prequel)

Desert Moon (Book 1)

Desert Blood (Book 2)

Desert Fate (Book 3)

Desert Heart (Book 4)

Desert Rose (Book 5)

Desert Roots (Book 6)

Desert Destiny (Book 7)

Sasquatch Surprise (Book 8)

Desert Yule (a short story)

Desert Wolf: Complete Collection (Four short stories)

Blue Moon Saloon

Perfection (a short story prequel)

Damnation (Book 1)

Temptation (Book 2)

Redemption (Book 3)

Salvation (Book 4)

Deception (Book 5)

Celebration (a holiday treat)

Shifters in Vegas

Paranormal romance with a zany twist

Gambling on Trouble

Gambling on Her Dragon

Gambling on Her Bear

Gambling on Her Panther

Serendipity Adventure Romance

Off the Charts

Uncharted

Entangled

Windswept

Adrift

Travel Romance

Veiled Fantasies

Island Fantasies

www.annalowebooks.com

About the Author

USA Today and Amazon bestselling author Anna Lowe loves putting the "hero" back into heroine and letting location ignite a passionate romance. She likes a heroine who is independent, intelligent, and imperfect – a woman who is doing just fine on her own. But give the heroine a good man – not to mention a chance to overcome her own inhibitions – and she'll never turn down the chance for adventure, nor shy away from danger.

Anna loves dogs, sports, and travel – and letting those inspire her fiction. On any given weekend, you might find her hiking in the mountains or hunched over her laptop, working on her latest story. Either way, the day will end with a chunk of dark chocolate and a good read.

Visit AnnaLoweBooks.com